D0498485

TEAM

Also by Karla Manternach

Meena Meets Her Match
Never Fear, Meena's Here!
Meena Lost and Found

The Meena Zee Books

TEAM

meena

By Karla Manternach
Illustrated by Mina Price

Simon & Schuster Books for Young Readers
New York   London   Toronto   Sydney   New Delhi

In loving memory of
Eleanor and Leroy

SIMON & SCHUSTER BOOKS FOR YOUNG READERS
An imprint of Simon & Schuster Children's Publishing Division
1230 Avenue of the Americas, New York, New York 10020
Text © 2023 by Karla Manternach
Illustration © 2023 by Mina Price
Jacket design by Tom Daly © 2023 by Simon & Schuster, Inc.
For information about special discounts for bulk purchases, please contact Simon & Schuster
Special Sales at 1-866-506-1949 or business@simonandschuster.com.
The Simon & Schuster Speakers Bureau can bring authors to your live event. For more
information or to book an event, contact the Simon & Schuster Speakers Bureau at
1-866-248-3049 or visit our website at www.simonspeakers.com.
Interior design by Tom Daly
The text for this book was set in Excelsior LT.
The illustrations for this book were rendered digitally.
Manufactured in the United States of America
1222 FFG
First Edition
2 4 6 8 10 9 7 5 3 1
Library of Congress Cataloging-in-Publication Data
Names: Manternach, Karla, author.
Title: Team Meena / Karla Manternach.
Description: First edition. | New York : Simon & Schuster Books for Young Readers, [2023] |
Series: Meena Zee vol. 4 | Audience: Ages 8–12. | Audience: Grades 4–6. | Summary: Meena
learns that it is possible to have a long-distance friendship with Sofía
while still making new friends.
Identifiers: LCCN 2022008169 (print) | LCCN 2022008170 (ebook) |
ISBN 9781665903929 (hardcover) | ISBN 9781665903943 (ebook)
Subjects: CYAC: Friendship—Fiction. | Schools—Fiction. | LCGFT: Novels.
Classification: LCC PZ7.1.M368 (print) | LCC PZ7.1.M368 (ebook) | DDC [Fic]—dc23
LC record available at https://lccn.loc.gov/2022008169
LC ebook record available at https://lccn.loc.gov/2022008170

The brush makes a scratchy sound as I paint the brown paper bag on my desk.

Next to me, my cousin Eli is drawing a rabbit on his bag. On my other side, Pedro is covering his with clippings from sports magazines.

I set down the brush and use my fingers to blend the rainbow stripes. The bag looks like my tie-dyed hoodie now—the one I gave Sofía right before she moved away. A lot of things make me think of her, like her cleaned-out cubby or the empty seat next to mine at lunch. It's like there's a hole everywhere I look, the exact size and shape of Sofía.

I glance at her empty spot across our pod of desks. I wonder what she'd be making if she were here. I bet she'd paint a portrait of her cat. Or maybe she'd draw a picture of the two of us, smiling together under a rainbow, the words *Best Friends Forever* printed underneath. That makes me smile. It makes my chest ache, too. I feel happy-sad—a mix of both, like yellow and blue turning green.

Then Lin plops down in Sofía's place.

"Can I use those?" she asks, pointing at Pedro's magazines. "Mine just have pictures of golf." She grabs one without waiting for an answer and starts flipping through it.

I sit up straighter. "That's Sofía's desk."

She looks up. "So?"

"So you can't sit there. It still has her name tag on it."

Lin frowns. Then she rips the tag off Sofía's desk and tosses it onto mine. "Not anymore."

I suck in a breath and wave my hand in the air. "Mrs. D! Lin is trying to take Sofía's place!"

Our teacher stops shuffling papers in the corner. "It's okay, Meena. I don't think Sofía would mind."

When Mrs. D turns away, Lin sticks out her tongue at me.

I grit my teeth and go back to blending, but the paint doesn't seem as bright and cheery as before. Out of the corner of my eye, I see Lin tear a page out of the magazine, paste it onto her bag, and push it away.

"That's all you're doing?" I ask.

She shrugs. "It's not graded."

I scowl at the sloppy bag. She might be at Sofía's desk, but Lin is nothing like her. Sofía is nice, for starters. And she actually cares about art.

It seems like all Lin cares about is sports. She wears a different team jersey almost every day. Her creative writing stories are all about winning some championship. She always wants to play kickball at recess, too. She's bouncing her knees right now, watching the clock, waiting for the bell so we can get back to our game. The clip starts to fall out of her short, black hair. She unfastens it and pins her swoop of bangs to the side again.

"If your bags are finished," Mrs. D says to the class, "you can come and get the rest of your art to take home. I thought we'd get a head start on our end-of-the-year cleaning."

Lin springs up, heads over, and stuffs her art

into her bag. Then she walks straight across the room and dumps the whole thing in the trash!

Mrs. D gasps. "Lin!"

"What? I don't want it."

"I'm sure your family would like to see it. Please take it home."

Lin groans and pulls it back out of the wastebasket.

I smirk. I wouldn't want that stuff either if I were her. None of Lin's art is any good. Her president portrait was nothing but a stick figure. When we did panda bear paintings, hers looked more like a hippo. And she didn't even try to make a nice take-home bag!

The recess bell rings. "Walk," Mrs. D calls as we all rush for the door.

We hurry down the hall and tumble onto the playground. The grass is bright green, and the sky is my favorite shade of blue. I'm itching to get back to the kickball field. My team fell behind at morning recess, but after lunch, we tied it up five to five. I bet this recess—

I stop short.

Eli pauses beside me. "Are you coming?" he asks.

I finger the friendship bracelet around my wrist and look across the playground at the orange tube slide.

Eli follows my gaze. His shoulders sag a little.

Then he gives me a nod and heads to the field without me.

I scuffle across the blacktop, checking the ground for cool trash to add to my collection. I spot a silver gum wrapper and a pink paper clip that's bent out of shape. I pick them up and stuff them into my pocket.

When I get to the bottom of the slide, I look back. Lin is heading to the pitcher's mound. Aiden stays behind to catch. The rest of our team scatters onto the field while Pedro steps up to the plate. I feel a twinge of jealousy, but I take a big breath and climb into the slide.

It's roomy in here by myself—another Sofía-size hole. Before she moved away, we always spent at least one recess together. We played four square or looked for interesting trash or just sat in the slide and talked. Every day, I still spend one recess in here for her.

At least I'll see her tomorrow. We do a video chat every Saturday for our Finders Keepers Club. I've been saving things to tell her all week! I can feel them piled inside of me, like colorful trash filling up a bin. Talking to her last Saturday felt like dumping everything out to show her. Afterward, I felt light and clean as a whistle.

But right after our call, I saw a blue jay swoop into one of our bird feeders, and there it was: the next thing I wanted to tell her. I could almost feel it landing—*thump*—at the bottom of me. Right away, I started filling up again—with the SOLD sign I spotted in our neighbor's yard and the new haircut I gave my stuffed zebra. I've saved so many things to tell her since then that it feels like they're piled right up to my throat.

I lie back in the slide and try not to think of anything new. I stare at the inside of the tube and remember old things instead, like the way Sofía moved her jaw back and forth when she was thinking and how her laugh reminded me of bubbles rising into the air. I press my hands against the smooth plastic of the tube, like I'm giving it a hug from the inside.

"Meena!"

I sit up and see Lin poking her head into the foot of the slide.

"Why aren't you playing?" she asks. "We need a catcher."

"I thought Aiden was catching."

"He went in for an ice pack."

"Well, I'm busy."

She raises her eyebrows at me. "You aren't doing anything. Come on, please? Pedro's gonna score!"

I lace my hands behind my head and lie back down.

Lin lets out a huffy breath. "Fine. But if we lose, it'll be your fault."

When she's gone, I scoot forward and watch her stomp back to the pitcher's mound.

I could go with her. I kind of want to. It's not like Sofía would know if I missed a recess.

But here's the thing I'm not saving up to tell her—that I don't even want to admit.

Sometimes I forget she's gone.

Sometimes, for a few minutes, I get busy and stop missing her. It happened when Lin started the kickball game this morning. I ran off to play, even though I always spend first recess in the slide. I told myself I'd make up for it at lunch, but I forgot. And just now, I almost forgot *again*.

I give myself a little shake. No. I can't play. Not this recess.

Nora is up to kick now. Pedro is leading off of third base, but there's no one to cover home. When Lin pitches, Nora kicks it right back and takes off for first. Pedro tears toward the plate. The infielders shout as Lin scoops up the ball and throws, but at the last second, Pedro pulls up short and lets it whip right by!

His team lines up to give him high fives. Lin lets out an angry howl and kicks the ground. Then she turns around and glares right at me. I shrink back into the slide, feeling a new mix of emotions.

I'm glad I stayed put.

But I'm a little bit sorry, too.

When I head out with Eli after school, I don't get the same burst of excitement as usual. Sofía and I always had playdates on Friday afternoons, but now the week sort of ends with a dud.

Maybe I can hang out with Eli. A cousin your age is kind of like a built-in friend. "You wanna come over?" I ask, swinging my rainbow bag of art.

"I can't," he says. "Mom's taking me to pick up my new rabbit."

"Can I come?"

He looks at me, surprised. "You hate the animal shelter."

"Only because it smells bad." I shrug. "But I don't have anything else to do."

He doesn't look too sure. "How about you just meet him at club tomorrow? I'll see you then." He waves and turns down the sidewalk to his house.

I stand for a minute, watching him go. What am I supposed to do now? I wish the walkie-talkie in my backpack reached all the way to California. Maybe it would still feel like a Friday playdate if I could at least *talk* to Sofía.

Hang on. Why can't I?

I run all the way home and bang through the kitchen door. "Mom!"

She flinches at her laptop. "Jeepers, Meena! You startled me."

"Sorry." I shove Rosie's plastic ponies to the side and slam my rainbow bag on the table. "Can I call Sofía? It's Friday, so maybe we can play a game or work on a project or—"

"She's still in school, honey," Mom says.

My shoulders slump. I keep forgetting it's a different time in California. "It's not fair," I say. "When I get up, Sofía's sleeping. When I get home, she's still in school. And by the time she's done with dinner, I'm in bed!"

"You want to send her a message?" Mom asks.

"It's not the same," I mutter.

She tucks my hair behind my ear. "How about you invite another friend over? Someone from your class, maybe?"

I scowl. "They're play-at-recess friends, not come-over friends."

Just then, my little sister comes in from the backyard holding her pink plastic pony by the mane. She only has kindergarten in the morning, so she always beats me home.

"Gosh." Mom rubs her chin. "There must be *someone* here who'd like to play."

Rosie brightens. "Me! I'd like to play!"

"I don't know, squirt," I say. If Sofía were here, we'd make projects or put on a play or climb a tree. I like Rosie and all, but she can't cut straight. She doesn't remember her lines. She can't even get onto the first branch without a boost.

She's also obsessed with her ponies.

"Let's play Ponytown in the sand tire," Rosie says.

See what I mean?

"Nuh-uh," I say. "No ponies. It's boring."

Her face falls. "But I want them to have a picnic on the beach."

That gives me an idea. "They can go to the beach," I say, "but let's pretend they're trapped on a desert island. Or they have to flee from a giant tidal wave. Ooo! Or how about they get attacked by a mutant sand lizard?"

Rosie doesn't answer right away.

I grab a purple pony and dangle it by the tail. "Take it or leave it."

She sighs. "I'll take it."

We scoop up the rest of the ponies and head outside. It's not as good as a playdate with Sofía, but it's better than nothing.

★ ★ ★

"Anybody home?"

When I peek into Eli's room on Saturday morning, he's lying on his stomach in front of one of his cages. His *All About Rabbits* book is open next to him.

He grins at me. "Come meet Stanley."

The smell of hay and wood shavings gets stronger as I step into the room. It's chock full of tanks and pens and habitats. Sofía knows all Eli's pets by name, but there are so many that I just remember things like "the green one" and "the snake."

Hang on. Does he even have a snake? I better not give him any ideas.

At least I can tell the rabbits apart. Vernon is snowy white with pink ears. The new bunny is in a cage next to him. He's white too, but with brown splotches that look like someone dribbled chocolate milk on him.

"Why aren't they in the big hutch?" I ask.

"I have to bond them before I put them in a new space together," Eli says.

"Bond them? Like with glue?"

He laughs. "It means they need to get to know each other. Some rabbits like each other right away, but usually they need a little time."

I plop down on the floor. "How are they supposed to bond if you keep them apart?"

"It's better if they have their own space. That

way they know they're safe, but they can still check each other out. Tonight, I'll have them swap cages so they start getting used to the smell of another rabbit."

I crinkle my nose at that. "How long before they can be in the same place?"

"A week maybe. But it'll just be for a few minutes at first."

I peek at Vernon. He's been on his own for a while now, so you'd think he'd be overjoyed to see another bunny, but he's facing the other way like he couldn't care less. "I don't think it's going so great," I say. "They're just ignoring each other."

"Actually, that's a good sign. It means they aren't scared." Eli's face lights up. "And this morning I put their food bowls pretty close together, and they ate at the same time!"

I can tell I'm supposed to be impressed, so I say, "Wow," just to be nice.

"You wanna hold him?" Eli asks.

Before I can think of a way to say no, he dumps Stanley into my arms. I give him a few pats. Fur sticks to my fingers, but I try not to make a face. When I stop petting him, Stanley nudges my hand with his head, like he wants me to keep going.

"Whoa." Eli sits back on his heels. "I guess he likes you."

He reaches out his hand, but Stanley turns his face away. Eli frowns. Then he lifts Stanley out of my arms and settles him back into the cage. For a while, we watch Vernon and Stanley eat lettuce leaves and twitch.

It's about as exciting as it sounds.

When it's finally time for our meeting, we get Aunt Kathy's tablet and head outside. I feel a pinch of sadness as we walk by the new rabbit hutch on the back porch. It's across from the chicken coop, right where our milk jug igloo used to be. Since we don't have a clubhouse anymore, we throw a blanket over the clothesline instead. We're settling down in the grass underneath it when we hear an electronic ringing sound. Eli taps the screen and Sofía appears!

I squeal. She's wearing my rainbow hoodie.

The sight of my best friend in my favorite shirt floods me with happiness.

"Hey, you two!" Sofía is waving both hands. For a minute we all sit there, laughing and waving, then someone starts making faces, and pretty soon we're all doing it, and the next thing I know, Eli is doing sound effects with his mouth, and Sofía is giggling, and I'm bouncing on my knees like I'm jumping for joy.

When we start to settle down, I grab a bucket from the back porch and prop the tablet on top so Sofía is the same height as us. I make a hugging motion. She makes one back, and even though it's my own arms around me, it feels like we're hugging for real.

I take a closer look at her then. Her hair is in low pigtails, and she isn't wearing a flower headband like usual. "Hey, I like your hair," I say.

"Thanks! My cousin Elena did it for me."

"Where are you?" Eli asks. "All I see is a railing behind you."

"On the balcony of our apartment. Wanna see?" She picks up her phone and turns in a circle to show us the tiny patio. I get another jolt of happiness when I spot the milk jug bird feeder I made, hanging from the ceiling. There's a tumble of movement on the screen while she plops back down.

"It's your turn to be president," Eli tells her.

"Okay." She must hit something against the railing then, because I hear a clanging as she calls out, "Order, order! The Finders Keepers Club is now in session! Did you bring snacks?"

I dig out my baggie of Rainbow Pop cereal. Eli holds up a packet of gummy worms. Sofía shows us a blurry handful of the rainbow candies she used to share with me at lunch.

"Who's treasurer this week?" she asks as we all shovel in a handful.

Eli checks the milk jug we use for a bank. "We're down to eight cents, because I threw one of our pennies into a fountain."

"What for?" Sofía asks.

"You said you lost your stuffed animals when you moved. I made a wish that you'd find them."

"I did! The box got mixed in with the kitchen stuff." She smiles. "That was so nice of you."

The tips of his ears turn pink. "Collections next?"

I sit up straighter. This is when we show off the cool things we found during the week. It's the best part of our club!

"Let's each show one thing," Sofía says, "then we'll go around again if there's time."

I blink. If there's time?

"Meena, you go first."

Yes! I reach for the front pocket of my hoodie before I remember that Sofía is the one wearing it.

I dig into my back pocket then and hold up a circle of foil, red on one side and silver on the other. "They served these little yogurts at lunch the other day, and I went around collecting the lids. This one was strawberry, but I got a whole *bunch* of colors!"

"What are you gonna make with them?" Sofía asks.

"I don't know. I'm still waiting for Inspiration."

"What'd you bring, Eli?" she asks.

He grins. "Only the coolest thing ever."

We take the tablet to his room so he can show off Stanley. Eli usually brings nature stuff to club, like leaves or walnuts, but I guess rabbits are a part of nature too. Sofía gasps and coos and pretends to pet him through the screen.

"How about you?" I ask when we settle under the blanket again. "Did you spot any new birds this week?" That's usually Sofía's thing.

"Yeah," she says, "but I want to show you something I learned instead."

"Oh!" Technically, that's against the rules, since she didn't find or collect it, but I guess I don't mind, as long as we're together. "Okay, what?"

Sofía backs away from the phone. She's a little crooked now, but I see her set down a soccer ball and put one foot on top of it. "These are called toe taps," she says. She does a little jump and switches feet. She jumps and switches a few more times, tapping the ball with one foot, then the other—left, right, left.

"Nice," Eli says when she sits back down.

She smiles. "It's harder than it looks. You have to move your feet the whole time but keep the ball still."

"Did you learn it in gym class?" I ask.

"No, Elena is teaching me. I missed part of the soccer season here, but if I catch up a little, they might still let me play on her team."

"I thought you hated sports," I say.

Sofía blinks at me. "I haven't tried out for any. That doesn't mean I hate them."

"Oh." I scratch the front of my neck. "I guess not."

Just then, someone calls to her in Spanish. She answers and looks back at the phone.

"You want to see my second thing?" I ask, reaching into my pocket again.

"Actually, I have to go. We're leaving for Elena's game."

My eyes widen. "But it's club day."

"I know. I'm sorry. It's game day, too." She gets up. "I'll see you next week, okay? Tell Rosie hi, and give Stanley another pet for me. Bye!"

"Bye," Eli says. They smile and wave, but I'm too stunned to join in. Then the screen goes dark, and the call timer in the corner stops.

Twelve minutes, it says.

That's all I got to spend with Sofía this week.

3

I push my bike all the way home. I can't ride it. I'm too heavy with all the things I didn't get to tell Sofía.

How am I supposed to hold onto everything until next week? How can I save up anything new when it's so crowded inside me already?

You know what happens when you try to cram too much cool trash into a wagon? Some of it falls out!

What if I start forgetting things? What if I keep forgetting her?

Dad is trimming bushes in front of the house when I dump my bike in the grass. "You're back early," he says.

I slump onto the front step. "Sofía was busy with her cousin."

"Oh, good for her."

"What's good about it?"

He wipes the back of his hand across his

forehead. "Moving is hard. I'm glad she has some-one to hang out with."

Someone? Sofía has a whole *bunch* of cousins in California. I think about this Elena person, doing her hair and teaching her soccer. Does Sofía even miss me, or is somebody else filling her Meena-size hole?

I scuff my sneaker against the sidewalk. "What's the point of a weekend if I don't get to see my best friend?" I ask. "And what about this summer? If Sofía isn't here, I might as well stay in school!"

Dad starts working the clippers again. "You still have Eli."

I grunt at that. Eli is always distracted when he gets a new pet. That's one of the reasons I've never been a big fan of his animals. He did have a hermit crab I liked once. It started out in this swirly green shell, but then it switched to a plain white one and I couldn't get excited about it anymore.

Yeah, I know: It was the same crab on the inside, and blah, blah, blah.

"You still have your sister, too," Dad says. "She's out back if you're interested."

I hug my knees. "Probably playing with ponies."

"Nope." His eyes twinkle. "She's spying on the new neighbors."

I gasp and look at the house next door. The

SOLD sign is gone, and there's a minivan parked in the driveway. "They're here?"

"See for yourself."

I race to the backyard. I don't see Rosie at first, but it's hard to see anything with all the milk jug bird feeders I made before Sofía left. I can hardly get around without running into one that's hanging from a branch, staked into the ground, or spinning from a clothesline pole.

I move a jug out of my way. "Rosie?"

"Over here," I hear her whisper.

She's in the middle of our lilac bush. "What are you doing in there?"

"Shhh!" She waves me over.

The lilacs are blooming, and their purple buds make the air smell like perfume—but don't let that fool you, because if you try to squeeze into the middle, the branches will scrape up your arms. "Ouch!"

"Shhh," Rosie says again.

"Shush yourself! They're poking me!" I hold my breath to make myself skinny and slide the rest of the way in. "Did you see anybody?" I ask, peering through the leaves.

"Sort of."

"Any kids?"

"I couldn't tell." She scrunches her eyes shut. "Oh, I hope, I hope, I hope!"

"Why are you hiding?"

She looks at me with big eyes. "In case they don't like me."

"Why wouldn't they like you?"

"I didn't like cheese the first time I tried it."

"You don't like cheese at least once a week."

"So, what if I'm like cheese to them? Or what if I'm like turkey?"

"Since when don't you like turkey?"

She looks a little sick. "Since I found out it's made from turkeys."

A curtain flutters at an upstairs window. That's right across from my workshop! If I knew a kid in that room, we could rig up one of those phones you make out of cups and string. Or we could breathe on the glass and write each other messages!

A movie starts to play in my head. I imagine a girl pulling back the curtain. She looks friendly, but nervous, too—like maybe she moved away from her best friend, and she's worried that she'll never be able to fill the empty space it left.

And I don't know how, but in my daydream I can tell that the new girl likes Rainbow Pop cereal and Flaming Crunchers and apple juice out of a can. She climbs trees and wears flower headbands and lines up her markers in a row. And I just know that if you get her laughing hard enough, she might snort strawberry milk right out of her nose.

She's like Sofía.

But all of a sudden, a guilty feeling mixes into my excitement, like red and blue making purple. I don't need another Sofía. I already have one!

A voice whispers inside me, *But she isn't here.*

I gaze up at the window. What if there's a new friend for me, right next door? What if every morning, I look out and see someone looking back at me?

The neighbor's back door bangs open. We jump.

I push a branch out of the way and peer across the yard. Above the fence, I see a man and a woman with dark brown skin. The guy is muscly and completely bald, but it looks like the kind of bald you do on purpose, not the kind you're stuck with. The lady's hair is short and comes to neat points by her ears.

Something else is behind the fence. I see it moving through the cracks, but I can't tell if it's kids or dogs or trolls.

I hope it's kids!

Although trolls would be pretty cool too.

"Come on," I say to Rosie. We pry ourselves out of the bush, dive for the grass, and crawl toward the fence on our elbows.

Please let it be kids! And let them have the kind of parents who let them get a trampoline instead of listing emergency room facts every time they bring it up.

By the time we reach the fence, we're panting. I find the place where the old neighbor's dog chewed a board loose. I swivel it open, peek through, and see—

Kids!

I knew it! And they don't have flower headbands or lonely looks on their faces, but they're real, live kids—right next door! My insides feel like they're singing. Rosie starts pumping her fists.

Then I take a closer look.

The kids both have soft brown curls. One of them is little. Really little. She's toddling around the yard making babbling sounds, like she doesn't even say words yet. I get a sinking feeling in my stomach as my eyes zoom in on the other kid. He's bigger than the girl, but still smaller than me. He looks like he's Rosie's age.

The daydream girl starts to fade from my mind, like breath on a window.

I clench my hands into fists. Well, so what? I don't need a new friend anyway. Nobody can take Sofía's place!

But Rosie is staring through the fence like she's in a trance, her eyes shining.

Oh, no.

She starts to get up.

I pull her back down. "What are you doing?"

"I'm gonna ask him to play."

"You can't!"

She blinks at me. "I want to be friends."

But Rosie is all I have left! I glance at her necklace, the one I made her, thinking fast. "You don't make friends just like that." I try to snap my fingers, but they make a sort of thump instead.

"Why not?"

I lean my back against the fence. "It's like with Eli's rabbits. You have to stay in your own space and watch each other for a while."

"For how long?"

"At least a week."

She groans. "I want to meet him now."

I let out a huffy breath. "I don't make the rules, Rosie. Next week, you could probably wave across the yard or something. The week after that, maybe you could talk through the fence."

The light goes out of Rosie's eyes. I put my arm around her. "It's okay, squirt. You can invite him over in a month or two."

Something moves against my back.

I scramble away as the wood slat swivels open behind us. The boy is looking right through the gap! Then the slat drops and his head appears above the fence for a second and disappears. He must be jumping, because his head starts popping up again and again.

Jump. "I'm Roger," he says. Jump. "What's your name?"

I try to grab my sister's arm, but she bounces out of reach. "I'm Rosie!"

Roger grabs the top of the fence, pulls himself up, and hangs there. "You want to be friends?" he asks.

"Yeah!" She runs along the fence and opens the gate.

"Rosie, wait," I call. But she doesn't hear me. Or maybe, for once, she doesn't listen.

Roger bursts into our yard, and they run off across the grass together, just like that.

Rosie and Roger play together while the grown-ups chat across the fence. They chase each other around the yard all afternoon, their heads skimming beneath the bird feeders.

They don't invite me, but who said I want to play, anyway?

On Sunday, while Rosie and Roger have a pony picnic in the sand tire, I black out the teeth in a princess coloring book. I hug my rainbow-striped zebra and watch my monster truck show. I make piles of my yogurt lids, one color at a time, then mix them together again.

By Monday, I'm sick of being by myself. I spend first recess alone in the tube slide for Sofía, but the whole time I keep wondering if she's with Elena, talking and giggling in some slide of their own. Just imagining it makes my stomach hurt.

So after lunch, I step outside and look around the playground. There must be someone around here I can play with. Eli is shooting baskets with Pedro, but that's kind of their thing. Lin is hitting a tennis ball against the building, but she's scowling and smacking it like she's mad about something. I spot the Taylor twins on the swings, but they're only second graders. I head over anyway. They're swinging in rhythm, taking turns calling out words.

"Strawberry!"

"Blueberry!"

"Blackberry!"

"Grape!"

I nod along and try to think of something to add.

"Cranberry!"

"Raspberry!"

"Gooseberry!"

"Tomato," I cry.

The twins skid to a stop and look at me. "That's not a fruit," says one.

"Is too," I say. "Look it up."

"It's not a fruit if you don't eat it for breakfast," says the other.

"You could," I say.

"But you don't," they say together.

"Fine." I plop down on a swing. "Then let's do vegetables."

"We did vegetables already," says one.

"Let's do hockey teams," says the other.

"I don't know any of those," I answer.

They shrug and start swinging again.

"Flyers!"

"Rangers!"

"Penguins!"

"Knights!"

I roll my eyes and wander off to look around again. I see a girl leaning against the building. She's lanky and tan with long black hair, and she's scrolling on her phone, which she's not supposed to have on the playground. I think she's a fifth grader. Am I allowed to be friends with someone older? It seems like everybody sticks with their own grade, but there's no rule about it, is there?

I walk up to her. "Hi." When she doesn't answer, I say it again, louder. "Hi."

She looks up. "Are you talking to me?"

"Yeah. What's your name?"

"Brooklyn." She doesn't ask my name. She just lowers her phone and says, "Aren't you the kid who had a seizure at lunch a while ago?"

I stiffen. "I take medicine now. Didn't you used to have a cast?"

"So?"

"So what happened?"

"I broke my arm on a trampoline."

"That stinks," I say. "I hope the trampoline was okay."

She narrows her eyes at me. "Do you want something?"

"Um, yeah." I rock back on my heels. "Wanna play?"

She scrunches her nose like she smells something bad. "Play?"

"Sure. We could run races or have a jump-rope contest or look for funny-looking wood chips."

"What for?"

I blink at that. "For fun."

"What are you, in second grade?"

I stand up straighter. "Third."

She rolls her eyes. "I'm good." She waves to someone over my shoulder. "Avery!"

The girl who walks up to us is pale and freckly. "Who's that?" she asks.

"Nobody," Brooklyn says, and they turn their backs to me.

I scuff my feet across the blacktop. I don't get it. Rosie and Roger made friends just like that. Why does it feel like I'm selling cookies, and all I have left is maple nut?

Then I think about Eli's rabbits again. They didn't act like they wanted to be friends. They ignored each other. Is that what I'm supposed to do?

I spot Maddy and Nora on a bench. This time, instead of barging up to them, I creep closer and turn away. They keep playing with their horse figurines behind me, but I pretend to watch a game of tag across the grass.

They don't seem to notice me, so I move closer.

I shuffle my feet.

I clear my throat.

"Meena?" Maddy finally says.

"Oh!" I turn and make a surprised face. "I didn't see you there."

"Do you want something?"

"Who, me? Nope." I scratch the back of my neck. "Unless you want me to play with you or something."

Nora's eyebrows shoot up. "You want to play horses?"

"I mean, I guess I could."

They trade looks. Maddy shrugs. "You can be him if you want." She points to a brown horse on the ground.

Yes! I grab him and pull a bit of grass out of his tail. "I'm gonna call him Frederick."

"His name is Brownie," Nora says.

Well, that's not very original. "What does he do for a living?" I ask.

She gives me a funny look. "He's a horse."

"Oh. Right."

"And he's on his way over to ask one of our horses to the ball," Maddy says.

I tilt my head at her. "He doesn't have a job, but he's going to a dance?"

"A ball," Maddy says.

"A horse ball," Nora adds.

"Can't they all go together?"

"Then it wouldn't be a date." Maddy puts a hand on her hip. "People don't go to a ball as friends."

"Do horses?"

She reaches for Frederick. "Just forget it."

I pull him away. "Geez, I'm just asking." I smooth back his mane. "Wouldn't they rather go to a monster truck rally?"

Maddy crosses her arms. "Do you want to play or not?"

I sigh. "Yeah, okay." I make Frederick gallop along the bench. Maddy and Nora's white horses prance in place and flick back their yellow manes. Their eyes are painted open, but Maddy and Nora flutter their eyelashes and say in a singsong, "Hi, Brownie."

I make Frederick talk in a low voice. "Hello, girls."

Maddy and Nora blink faster.

Their horses look exactly the same. I don't know how I'm supposed to pick, so I just turn Frederick to Nora's horse and ask, "Would you like to go to the ball?"

Maddy jumps up. "Why'd you pick her?"

"I don't know, I just—"

She stomps off. Nora beams and nuzzles her horse's face against Frederick's. They spend the rest of recess swaying back and forth to music nobody can hear.

It's worse than doing nothing by myself.

After that, I start spending almost every recess in the tube slide.

Once in a while, I climb the monkey bars with Eli instead, but then he goes right back to shooting baskets or watching Pedro play battle cards with Aiden. Whatever. I'm fine on my own. I don't even want anyone else.

Although sometimes, when I'm sitting alone in the slide, I look down at the scuffs on my sneakers and the marker stains on my fingernails and wonder . . . why doesn't anyone want *me*? Sofía used to. Now she barely even has time for our club.

Then on Thursday, while I watch from the slide, my class starts a new kickball game during morning recess. After lunch, I walk right up to Pedro in the kicking line. "Can I play?"

He nods toward the field. "They need someone."

Lin is on the pitcher's mound again. I square my shoulders and turn to her. "Where do you want me?"

She dribbles the big rubber ball without looking at me. "Why should I let you play now?" she asks. "You wouldn't the other day."

I cross my arms and wait. She has to let me. It's the rule, and she knows it.

But here's the other thing: I'm actually kind of great at kickball, and Lin knows that, too.

For a few seconds, we face off without speaking. Then she jerks her head behind her and says, "Outfield."

I jog to center field. The other kids spread out to make room for me as Eli steps up to the plate.

"One out," Lin calls. "Force at first, but watch the runner!"

Nora is leading off of second base. I bend my knees and wait, my body loose and ready. When Lin pitches, the ball sweeps across the grass so fast it barely touches the ground. Eli makes a running kick and whiffs it.

Nora goes back to second. Lin pitches again before Eli is ready. He kicks sharp to the left, foul. When Lin gets the ball again, Eli tucks his chin and balls up his fists, his body as tense as a rubber band pulled tight.

I know that look. Once in a while, Eli sends the ball sailing way over our heads, but when he tries too hard, he kicks high and shallow.

The other outfielders go deep, but I come in closer. Lin checks over her shoulder, like she's about to tell me what to do, but when she sees me, she nods and turns back to the plate.

She pitches. The ball whips across the grass, and Eli wallops it. His team cheers as he takes off running, the ball spiking high.

"I got it, I got it!" I wave my arms and run forward. "It's mine!"

The ball seems to hang in the air above me. Then all at once, it starts to drop—down, down—until it lands in my arms with a hollow thump.

"Go back, go back," someone shouts.

Nora has stopped halfway to third. She didn't tag up! She looks at me with big eyes and breaks for second. My arms are still stinging, but I take three running steps toward her and throw.

Bam! She's out! Double play!

Lin whoops. My team cheers. I scoop up the ball again and drop it on the pitcher's mound as we all hurry in to kick.

Lin waves me over to stand next to her. "Nice play," she says.

"Thanks." I try not to look too proud of myself.

"You'll play at next recess, too, right?" Lin asks.

I already spent morning recess in the slide, so I say, "Sure."

"Get us started, Aiden," Lin cries as he steps up to the plate.

I clap along with the rest of our team. This is so much better than horse dancing! "Same teams tomorrow?" I ask.

"Not if Pedro and Aiden bring their battle cards again. Nobody wants to play kickball when they do." Lin brightens. "But are you going out for softball?"

"I don't know," I say. "Mom tried to get me to sign up for T-ball last year, but I'd rather go swimming with—"

I suck in a breath and look down at my bracelet.

Sofía won't go swimming with me this summer, I realize. We won't ride our bikes to the pool or make wet body prints on the hot cement or see whose mouth turns bluest from the snow cones.

"Well, if you want to do softball," Lin says, "the evaluation is after school tomorrow."

"What's that?"

"It's like tryouts, but everyone gets to be on a team."

I shift on my feet. "I don't know."

For a few seconds, Lin looks annoyed. Then she turns back to the field. "It's not like you have anything else to do now that Sofía is gone."

I suck in a breath. That was mean.

But then Aiden grounds out to first, and Lin groans. "You could at least try it," she says, her shoulders slumping a little. "We need good players, or it won't be any fun."

"Maybe," I say, hiding a smile. Because I'm not gonna lie. It's nice that she thinks I'm good.

And it's nice that somebody wants to play with me, even if it's only Lin.

Dad takes me to the city gym on Friday afternoon. A woman behind a table gives him some forms to fill out, then hands me a little square of paper. It says three-seven. "Pin this to the front of your shirt," she says.

"What does it mean?"

"It means you're the seventh third grader to check in. The fifth graders already went, and the fourth graders are finishing up now." She smiles and waves toward the gym door. "Go on in."

"Is it okay if I decide not to be on a team?"

"Of course. Just let us know before you leave. Have fun!"

The gym smells like the one at school—like rubber mats and old varnish. Girls are spread across the floor while parents watch from the bleachers. One girl is batting while a few grown-ups take notes on clipboards.

Clink! The girl hits a ball back to the coach. *Whiff!* She misses the next pitch.

Most of the kids here must be from another school, but I see Maddy and Nora hanging out near the equipment cart. Nora's big sister is huddled in a corner with Brooklyn and that freckly fifth grader, Avery.

"Meena!"

Lin waves to me from the top of the bleachers, smiling really big. I wave back, tramp up the wooden steps, and thump down beside her.

"Number four-seventeen," a coach calls, "you're up."

A girl with about a thousand black braids jogs in and picks up a bat.

"We went to camp together," Lin says. "She's good."

She sure looks like a professional. She has on special pants that are fitted and gray with a yellow racing stripe down each side, and before she picks up her bat, she pulls on a pair of grippy gloves.

The girl steps up to the plastic home plate while the coach collects all the balls in a bucket. "Why do you think softballs are bigger than baseballs?" I ask.

Lin rolls her eyes. "Somebody probably thought girls couldn't hit a smaller ball."

"That's dumb."

"Right?"

"Is that why they're bright yellow, too?" I ask.

She snorts. "Easier for our weakling eyes to see."

I hold my arms out and pretend to feel around in the dark. "I sure hope a boy comes along to hit for me," I say in a squeaky voice. "I can't see anything with my girly eyes!"

Lin laughs and gives me a shove.

I grin. "Have you played before?"

"Just at camp and in my neighborhood."

"Are you nervous?"

"No way. Not for this league."

"Is there another one?"

Lin perks up. "Oh, yeah. This is just the fun league. The club team is way more serious. They travel for tournaments, and they don't take everybody. You have to try out."

"How come you're not playing for them?"

"My mom wouldn't let me. She says I'm too competitive and wants to wait until I'm *more mature.*" She says that last part like the words taste sour.

The batting starts again. *Slam! Smack! Pop!* The girl hits every pitch!

I hope I'm as good as her.

When she's finished, the coach collects all the balls again. "That's it, girls! Someone will be in touch tomorrow to let you know which team you're on. Parents, we could still use one more coach, so

pick up a volunteer form if you can help us out." He
turns to the bleachers. "Third graders, find a partner, and warm up! If you need a glove, grab one
from the equipment cart."

Lin springs to her feet.

"Did you bring a glove?" I ask.

"Nope. Mine's all broken in, and I want them
to think I've never played before."

"Why?"

She hesitates. "Can you keep a secret?"

I feel a prickle on my arms. "Yeah."

She glances around. "The coaches want to
know who the good and bad players are so they can
spread them out and balance the teams." She leans
in closer. "So if I pretend I'm a bad player, my team
might not get stuck with any others."

"Huh. That's pretty smart. Can I try it?"

She looks doubtful. "You can't be obvious
about it."

"I won't be."

She eyes me up and down. "Okay, but I'm gonna
be worse than you."

I cross my arms. "Wanna bet?"

She grins . . . and runs for the cart. I tromp
down the stairs after her and weave in and out of
other players on the gym floor, but Lin slaps the
cart right before me. "I win!"

"You got a head start!"

She grabs a glove. I start rummaging for one too. "Need some help?" a clipboard lady asks me.

"I can't find one for my right hand," I say.

"Are you left-handed?"

"No." I use my most patient voice. "That's why I need the right glove."

She reaches into the cart and pulls one out. "You wear it on your left hand so you can throw with your right."

I slip it on. "Well, what do you know? Thanks!"

When I turn around, Lin is standing there, shaking her head. "Good one," she says.

Balls are zinging back and forth across the gym as we line up next to the other pairs of girls. Lin gives a wimpy little throw that clunks to the floor between us. I giggle and give a limp toss back to her. I've seen Lin dive ten feet for playground balls, but she pretends to flinch away from this one. Then she throws it back so crooked that I almost slam into another girl chasing it.

It's hard not to laugh, especially when people stop to take notes, but I keep my face nice and straight as I throw at the floor, and I don't even crack a smile when Lin throws way over my head.

After that, the coach has us spread out for field-ing practice. Only about half the girls can catch a pop-up, but Lin is the only one who runs the other way!

Then it's my turn. The ball comes toward me in a high, gentle arc, but I cover my head with both arms. *Smack!* It hits the outside of my glove.

"Are you okay?" A clipboard guy is standing over me.

"Sorry," I say.

His face relaxes. "Gotta watch the ball, kiddo."

I glance at Lin. She smirks and looks away.

Finally, it's time to bat. The clipboards really get busy then! Some girls hit almost every ball. Some barely hit any. One girl misses so many times that I cheer when she finally nicks it.

"Next batter," the coach calls. "Number three-six."

Lin steps up to the plate. I hear a burst of laughter from a few fifth graders who are still huddled in a corner. The coach pitches. She misses.

Ha! Of course she does.

She hits a weak dribbler next but frowns like she didn't mean to. She's lifting her bat again when I hear a low voice behind me, "No batter, no batter."

When I turn, Brooklyn is watching Lin with her arms crossed.

"Quiet on the floor," the coach says.

I turn back around. Lin is staring wide-eyed at Brooklyn, her bat hanging limp. For a few seconds, she looks exactly like Rosie does right before she starts to cry.

Then her expression hardens. She steps back up to the plate and thrusts her chin at the coach like she's daring him.

Crack! She hits a line drive right at the coach's head. She smacks the next one against the wall. She blasts the next one into the rafters!

The clipboard pens are still scribbling when the coach calls out again. "Next batter! Number three-seven."

Lin throws down the bat and gives Brooklyn a long glare as she struts away.

"Number three-seven?" the coach calls again.

Oh, that's me!

I jog in, yank off my glove, and pick up the bat. Dad stands up in the bleachers and starts cheering. "Woo-hoo! Go, Big Zee!"

For a few seconds, I feel guilty that I'm about to be bad on purpose. But it's fun! I swing at the first pitch while the coach is still winding up. I wait to bring my bat around until the next ball is already past me.

When I sneak a peek at Lin, she wiggles her eyebrows up and down at me.

Finally, when the evaluation is over, Dad claps a hand on my back. "Don't worry, rookie," he says. "You'll get the hang of it."

Someone hands him a paper then. "Volunteer form?"

"Sure," Dad says.

I gape at him. "You're not gonna coach, are you?"

"Probably not."

"Good, because you don't even win at cards."

He smiles. "I have other gifts."

"Like what?"

He starts ticking them off on his fingers. "I have excellent hearing for my age. I hardly ever cut myself shaving. And I make the best banana bread on the whole school board."

I giggle.

"So what do you think, kiddo?" he asks. "Are you in or out?"

I don't answer right away. Maybe Sofía won't be as busy this summer. Maybe we'll play and do projects together like always, even if it has to be by video.

But what if she doesn't save space for me? What if summer comes and I still never see her?

Suddenly, Lin grabs my arm. "You win," she says into my ear. "You were definitely the worst one here."

I smile and watch her head out with her mom. For a few seconds, my daydream of the girl at the window floats back into my mind.

"So what'll it be?" Dad asks again.

I give myself a shake and nod. "I'll do it."

6

If I'm gonna play softball, I want to look the part. So as soon as we get home from the evaluation, I get right to work.

I dig out a pair of Rosie's stretchy pants and put them on. They're squeezy and come down to my shins, like the special pants I saw that girl wear at the evaluation. I head to my workshop next, get out my bright yellow duct tape, and add a racing stripe to each leg. Then I run to my parents' room and find a pair of Dad's socks. The extra fabric bunches up inside my sneakers, but when I pull them up, they come all the way up to my knees.

Perfect!

I get into my fielder's stance and check myself out in the mirror. I look like a real ball player now. I can't wait to show Lin!

I'm still thinking about the evaluation when I get into bed that night. I remember the gleam in Lin's eyes when she told me her secret, how she tried not to laugh in front of the coaches, and the wide grin she gave me before she left.

But when I wake up on Saturday morning, Sofía is the one I think of first.

It's club day!

I have so much to tell her—about kickball and softball and the new neighbors. I know I've probably lost track of some of the things I was saving up for her, but I have so many more!

I spring out of bed, race to my workshop, and breathe Magic Mist on the window. I trace a picture of a clock in the foggy spot and wish for a nice long meeting today.

I glance at the house next door. Something is moving in the room across from mine. For a few seconds, I picture my girl at the window again. But then I see Roger's mom lift his little sister out of a crib, and when I blink, my daydream is gone.

Before I leave for Eli's, Mom makes me take my seizure medicine, shovel in a bowl of Rainbow Pops, and hook my walkie-talkie to my waistband in case I want to call home. I take big breaths of sunshine as I walk, jingling my treasures in my pocket.

"You're here early," Eli says when Aunt Kathy lets me in. He's sitting on the floor of his room, holding Vernon in his lap.

"I thought you'd want to play," I tell him.

"I was gonna work on bonding my rabbits." He

looks wary. "I guess you can help if you want."

I sigh and reach for Stanley's cage. "Yeah, okay."

"I'll get him," Eli says quickly. "Here."

He shoves Vernon into my arms. He's soft and smells like wood shavings. "Where are we taking them?" I ask, following Eli down the hall.

"To the bathtub."

I stop. "We're giving them a bath?"

"We just need a closed-in space so they can't run away."

"Why not use one of their cages?"

"It's supposed to be a neutral place so they don't get territorial."

He throws back the shower curtain, sets Stanley down at one end of the tub, and has me put Vernon at the other end. He rummages in a cabinet next and slips on a pair of yellow cleaning gloves.

"What are those for?" I ask.

"Sometimes they bite when they get worked up." He gets out a spray bottle, fills it with water, and hands it to me. "Just be ready," he says.

We kneel down by the tub. I point the spray bottle at one bunny, then the other.

The rabbits look at each other. They look away. Their faces twitch. Eli coos at them and gives them banana slices. After a while, Vernon starts nosing his way across the tub. Stanley quivers.

"Is that good?" I ask.

Eli shushes me.

Vernon moves closer and nuzzles into Stanley's neck. Stanley doesn't react at all. He looks bored, actually.

Then for some reason, Eli stiffens. "Vernon," he warns, "be nice."

Vernon's ears go back. He lets out a low growl . . . and bites!

"Squirt him," Eli cries.

I hit him with a cold stream of water as Eli slides him to the other end of the tub. Vernon makes a sharp movement, and Eli yanks his hand away.

"Did he get you?" I ask.

"Just the glove." He points to a little tear in the wrist.

I sit back on my heels. "How did you know he was gonna do that? He was acting so innocent!"

Eli shrugs. "I saw it in his eyes."

I check, but Vernon's eyes are exactly as beady and black as before. This kid sure knows his pets!

The rabbits go back to ignoring each other. At first, I keep the squirt bottle ready. Vernon sniffs at the drain. Stanley trembles behind a bar of soap. After a while, I set the bottle down. "They seem fine now. Can we get ready for club?"

Eli gives me a look. "We can't leave them alone."

"Why not?"

"Because I'm the biggest rabbit."

I laugh. "The what?"

He sticks out his chest. "I'm the boss. They know when I'm here I won't let them hurt each other. It's like how Mrs. D always stays in the room, because as soon as she leaves, Aiden starts doing arm farts."

I nudge him with my elbow. "He's not the only one."

Eli grins. "I guess that's enough for today."

We scoop up the rabbits and head back to his room. "So does this mean they won't be friends?"

"They'll probably bond if we go slow and give them a chance," he says. "Some bunnies are stubborn, though. I can't *make* them get along, but I'll keep trying."

I plunk Vernon back into his cage. Eli sets Stanley on the floor and starts scratching him behind the ears. Then he pulls off the gloves and tosses the ripped one into the wastebasket.

"Hey, I want that," I say, grabbing it and slipping it on. It's floppy and bright yellow and comes up to my elbow, but I stick my finger in the hole and tear carefully all the way around the wrist. When I'm finished, it's short and has plenty of grip: a perfect batting glove.

I stick it in my pocket and check the clock. "Are you ready?"

Eli lets out a breath, still petting Stanley. "I guess."

"What's the matter?"

"I don't know. I just get used to Sofía being gone during the week, but then I see her at club, and . . ." He rubs the back of his neck. "It makes me miss her more."

I feel my chest tighten. "At least you have someone to hang out with the rest of the week." I hold my hand out to Stanley. The rabbit nudges his head against my hand to ask for pets, like he did last week.

Eli stiffens. "You could get a rabbit, too, you know. Then maybe you won't keep hogging mine."

I stare at him. "I'm not hogging your rabbit."

"Then why are you so interested in him all of a sudden?"

"I'm not! I came over to see you."

Eli slumps a little. "But look how much he likes you."

I stop petting Stanley, but he bumps his face against my hand again.

"You're already Sofía's favorite," Eli says. "Rosie's, too. I just want to be *his*."

"Eli . . ." I don't know what to say to that. I don't feel like anybody's favorite these days, and I don't even want to be Stanley's.

Eli settles him back in the cage. I follow him to the kitchen, and we rummage for snacks. Then he grabs Aunt Kathy's tablet, and we head out back.

The ground is wet today, so I get buckets for us to sit on and hang the blanket over the clothesline again. My heels start to bounce with excitement while Eli looks for a funny filter.

"Unicorns or aliens?" he asks.

I smile. "Aliens."

When he holds the screen up, we turn green and sprout antlers. When we wave at the camera, little suction cups form on our fingertips. Then the call comes.

Sofía!

I tap to start the video. The image flickers and shakes, and for a second, I think she's pranking us too, because she looks like she has two heads! But then the screen clears and brightens, and I can see that there really are two heads where she is.

Sofía isn't alone. She brought someone else to our club.

7

I open my mouth, but I can't speak.

The other girl has dark hair in low pigtails. It looks just like Sofía's did last week.

Like Sofía's does now.

I turn off the filter. "Who's that?" I have to choke out the words.

Sofía smiles. "My cousin Elena."

The other girl does a little wave. "Hi."

I don't wave back.

"You looked like two Sofías for a second," Eli says.

Elena laughs. "Everybody always thinks we're twins."

"You don't look that much alike," I mutter. Sure, they're wearing matching shirts, and they have the same black hair and brown skin. But even through the screen, I can see that Elena's eyes are darker, not greenish gold like Sofía's.

Hang on. Where's my hoodie?

Heat spreads up my neck as my eyes zoom in

on their light blue jerseys. "What are you wearing?" I ask.

Sofía's face lights up. She pulls her shirt straight so we can see the soccer-ball design on front. "They let me on the team!"

"Really?" Eli says. "That's awesome!"

"And since I'm joining soccer," Sofía continues, "I told Elena she could join our club."

Wait, what?

"Cool," says Eli.

But it isn't cool! I mean, we used to talk about expanding the club, but that was before this was my only time with Sofía. Her cousin sees her every day!

They trade smiles with each other. "Is it okay if she's president this week?" Sofía asks.

I stare at Elena, feeling like steam is blasting out of my ears.

No. No way. The club is my territory. I'm the big rabbit here.

I grit my teeth. "It's Eli's turn."

"I don't mind," he says.

"We haven't even said she could join yet."

"Fine." He picks up our big metal spoon and clanks it against the clothesline pole. The ringing is so loud that I have to cover my ears. "Order, order," Eli calls. "The Finders Keepers Club is now in session. First up, snacks."

Sofía and Elena have a bowl of grapes. Eli holds up an apple. I show them my banana, then grip it in my hand as they start eating.

"You're treasurer this week," Eli says to me. "Anything to report?"

"I thought I found a nickel next to the curb," I mutter, "but it was a metal washer, and I'm not falling for that again."

"Collections next," Eli says.

I glare at Elena through the screen. "She probably didn't even bring anything."

"She will," Sofía says. "She collects all kinds of stuff."

"Like what?" Eli asks.

Elena starts listing them on her fingers. "Magnets, bouncy balls, funny erasers—"

"You can't bring those," I say, jumping in. "It has to be something you find, not something you buy."

"Then how about rocks?" Elena asks. "Or shells?"

I shake my head. "Eli already finds nature stuff."

Elena's face goes blank for a few seconds, then brightens again. "I could bring sea glass."

"What's that?"

She perks up even more. "It's little bits of broken glass that wash up on the shore. They get tumbled around in the ocean until they're smooth and cloudy. I find them whenever we go to the beach. I have all different colors—green, blue . . ."

"Hang on," I say. "How does it get in the ocean in the first place?"

"From bottles that fall in the water, I guess. Or the ones people throw away."

"Well, we already have someone who finds trash." I jerk a thumb at my chest. "Me."

"But I can't think of anything else," Elena says.

I shrug. "Then I guess you can't join."

Sofía gapes at me. "That's not fair. Eli brought his new rabbit last week, and I showed you soccer moves!"

"Well, it's called the Finders Keepers Club." I sit up straighter. "Maybe it's time to get back on track."

Sofía crosses her arms. "I say we take a vote."

I cross my arms right back. "I say we don't."

"I'm president this week," Eli says, "and I say we do."

I suck in a breath. "But—"

"Who's in favor of letting other people join and show off whatever they want?" Eli asks.

He, Sofía, and Elena all raise their hands.

"She can't vote," I cry. "She's not a member!"

Elena lowers her arm.

"Who's against?" Eli asks.

My hand shoots up in the air.

"Two to one," Eli says. "She's in."

I stomp my foot. "No!"

"You know what?" Sofía says, eyes flashing. "If you don't want her here, then maybe I won't come either."

I look at her and her cousin—two matching girls on the other side of the world. Then I feel something shrivel in my chest. When I try to speak again, I have to squeak out the words. "She can stay."

Eli looks from me to Sofía and back again. He clears his throat. "So . . . collections?"

For the rest of the meeting, I squish the banana in my hand and try to ignore Elena. My mind is screaming, but I press my lips together so the sound doesn't leak out.

Sofía holds up her new book about California waterbirds and points to a few she saw this week. Eli shows us a bit of moss, a shriveled mushroom, and a spongy-looking rock. Finally, I dig into my pockets for the interesting trash I brought: a notebook spiral, a broken hairclip, and the handle of a screwdriver that looks like crystal.

But even while I'm showing off my treasures, all I can think about is the stuff I saved up to tell Sofía—the stuff I'm still holding inside.

I want to tell her how the grass sparkled this morning after the rain and how the dandelions are turning to puffs. I want to describe how I got a double play in kickball and how I was the best-worst kid at softball. Most of all, I want to tell her how empty the slide feels now, and how much I miss the plink of a can tab when she pulls it off her apple juice for me.

But I'm not saying any of that in front of Elena. She's already hogging Sofía. I'm not giving her anything else.

When it's time for soccer, someone in the background calls to them. For a few seconds, everybody waves at the camera. Then the screen goes dark.

"Wow." Eli lets out a long breath. "That was our worst meeting ever."

"I know. I can't believe her."

"Her?" He looks hard at me. "What about you?"

"I'm not the one who brought someone to our club without asking! How could she do that?"

"You know she likes to include people."

I grunt. Of course she does. But at least there used to be a lot more of her to go around.

"Who cares if she brings her cousin, anyway?" Eli says. "You should be happy she still wants to hang out with us."

"What do you know?" I grumble. "All your best friends are rabbits."

For a minute, he just looks at me. Then he says, "You're not the only one who misses her, you know."

My shoulders sag. "I know. I'm sorry."

He gets up and heads for the house.

"Where are you going?" I call after him.

"Back to my rabbits. At least I can tell when they're gonna bite."

8

By the time I get home, I've squeezed my banana into mush inside a brown peel.

I can't stop thinking about Sofía and Elena in their matching jerseys. Maybe she can't wear my rainbow hoodie every day, but where is it now? At the bottom of a closet? In the back of a drawer?

I don't want to think about it. And I definitely don't want to talk about it. Mom and Dad are in the kitchen, but I slam my mushed-up banana into the trash and storm right past them to the living room. They'd just give me another pep talk. *Good for Sofía,* they'd say. *You must be so-o-o happy for her.*

But I'm not happy. I'm mad and sad—black mixed with blue, like a bruise.

Rosie is lying on her stomach in front of the TV with Roger when I slump onto the couch. He's everywhere these days. They're watching

Pink Pony and her friends roller skate around a cartoon rink.

At least Maddy and Nora play with horses that look real. The ones in Ponytown are all different colors: Aqua Pony, Scarlet Pony, Lavender Pony. They're all girls, too, for some reason, and the episodes are called dumb things like "Friendship Mountain" or "The Good Ship Friendship."

But the ponies never go on adventures. They don't really even have problems. They never get lost in the desert or caught in an avalanche, and not one of them ever had a seizure in a school lunchroom. It seems like all the ponies ever do is go on picnics, style each other's manes, and put on fashion shows.

They also eat a lot of cupcakes.

Oh, sure, they ran out of feathers once during a hat-decorating contest. That was a big emergency. Another time they got worked up about a missing tiara. And in one episode, Pink Pony thought everyone forgot her birthday when really they were planning a surprise party all along. Her feelings got hurt for about five seconds, but then the friendship music started to play, and everything turned out okay.

But you know what? In real life, there is no friendship music. Everything doesn't always turn out okay. Sometimes ponies move away. Sometimes they mess up your club. Sometimes they make a new pony friend and don't even miss you!

Pink Pony is showing Saffron how to do figure eights now. "Didn't they already go roller skating this season?" I ask.

Rosie glances back at me. "They went ice skating."

I roll my eyes.

When Saffron stumbles, Pink Pony cheers her on until she gets the hang of it. At the end of the show, all the ponies skate in a circle together while the friendship music plays. Mom must be listening for it, because she calls for Rosie to turn off the TV.

Roger springs to his feet. "You wanna have a race now?"

"No, thanks." Rosie starts setting up her ponies on the coffee table. "Let's play ponies."

"We played ponies this morning."

"We didn't play skate ponies."

Roger doesn't seem too excited about that. I don't blame him. Racing sounds way more fun.

He tries again. "How about the *ponies* have a race? It could be a skate race. They could bash each other up like in roller derby."

Rosie doesn't look so sure.

"Or what if Pink Pony puts on magic skates that wheel her right off a cliff?"

"That wasn't in the show, Roger," Rosie says.

His face falls.

"I'll race with you," I say, getting up.

Rosie turns on me, making a sound like a growl. "He's *my* friend."

I jump back. "Okay, geez!"

Roger watches as she makes Pink Pony do a figure eight. "Can I at least be Pink Pony?" he asks.

She hands him the red one. "You can be Scarlet."

I pick up Saffron, twirling her by the tail. "I'll play, too, if we can do the roller derby thing."

Rosie glides Pink Pony across the table. "No, thanks. But if we have a pony picnic later, we'll let you know."

My eyebrows shoot up. She doesn't want me to play? She usually begs me! I drop Saffron and wander into the kitchen, stunned.

"What's up, sport?" Dad asks. He's chopping vegetables at the counter while Mom unloads the dishwasher.

I slide into a chair. "Why does Rosie have to spend all her time with that kid?"

"That kid was here this morning, and you weren't," Mom says.

"I'm here now."

"Now she's busy. She's not at your beck and call, you know."

"She used to be," I mutter.

I twist the metal washer on my shoestring

necklace. I made Rosie one just like it because we're *sisters*. Doesn't that count for anything? I thought it was like having permanent dibs on each other!

Mom sets a stack of plates in the cabinet. "Why don't you and Rosie come with me to the Parks and Rec office? Roger's dad wants him home in a few minutes anyway, and I have to pick up a key for the softball shed."

"What for?"

Her eyes gleam. "For your coach."

I whip my head around to look at Dad. "You signed up?"

"Not me, champ." He jerks his thumb at Mom.

I gasp. "You?"

"Why not me?" She puts her hands on her hips. "I'll have you know I was a starting catcher in my day."

"But this is the fun league!"

"So?"

"So you aren't exactly the Queen of Fun."

Dad starts to laugh, but when Mom shoots him a look, it turns into a cough instead. "I'm fun enough," she says.

I cross my arms. "Your favorite game is See Who Can Pick Up the Most Toys."

Mom closes the dishwasher. "I thought you'd like it if I were your coach."

I don't know what to say to that. I love my mom,

but she turns everything into a job. When I was in the class play, she was always making me run lines. When I was learning to ride a bike, she made me practice every day. And when I started having seizures, she wouldn't even take me to the pool unless I checked in with her every five seconds.

"I just don't want you to take the fun out of it," I say.

She sits down across from me. "Well, I can't back out now. And it hasn't been that long since your last seizure, so I'd feel better if one of us were at the field with you." She takes a deep breath. "But I can go easy."

I raise my eyebrows at her. "You won't make me practice?"

"I will at practice."

"What about at home? You won't make me play catch after school or come up with a schedule to work on batting or any of that stuff?"

Mom looks a little sad. "Not if you don't want me to."

I squint at Dad next. "What about you?"

"Who, me?" He tips an imaginary cap. "I'm just your pitching coach and snack supplier."

"Ooo!" I perk up at that. "Can we get rainbow freeze pops?"

"How about fruit?" Mom asks.

"Fruit isn't a treat."

"It's nature's dessert," she insists.

Dad gives me a wink. "I'll take care of it."

Mom gets to her feet. "Then let's go get the equipment."

The softball field is behind the outdoor swimming pool, down a winding road we've never taken before. We pass soccer fields on the way. They make me think of Sofía and Elena in their matching jerseys, and my chest gets tight again.

Then we round a bend, and a long stretch of grass opens in front of us.

Rosie trails after Mom as I climb out of the car. The softball diamond is way fancier than the kick-ball field at school. That's just trampled grass with some bare spots instead of bases. This place reminds me of the big-league stadium we went to once. It had a huge video screen and a mascot shooting T-shirts out of a cannon. . . . There was so much going on that I didn't even watch the game!

I stop to take everything in, tucking it away to tell Sofía later. There's a dirt infield and a tall chain-link fence that reaches from first base, behind home, and all the way to third. There are real dugouts, too. They look like big rabbit cages with metal benches inside. And behind home plate—

I suck in a breath. Bleachers.

Holy hot dogs, I forgot about fans!

I bet there will be food vendors, too—the kind that walk through the stands yelling, "Peanuts! Popcorn! Get your ice cold drinks here!"

"Meena!" Mom sticks her head out of the shed. "There's some loaner gear in here. Come see if you can find a pair of cleats."

Rosie has softball gloves on both hands when I get inside. There's a big shelf of second-hand equipment, even a whole row of shoes with those nubs on the bottom like real ball players wear. Most of them are pretty beat-up, though. "Aren't you gonna buy me a new pair?" I ask.

Mom shrugs. "Why buy what you can borrow? You'll outgrow them by next season anyway."

That's when I see them: a bright orange pair of cleats. My favorite color! They're dusty and a little too big, but I bet I can make them work. I put them on and run out of the shed. The little nubs grip the grass. I race around the bases next. The shoes make a clomping sound, but I feel lightning fast in these!

Back at the plate, I scuff my cleats in the dirt and pretend to take a few swings. There's no outfield fence, so I'm not sure how everyone will know when I hit a home run. I don't see a video screen, either. Maybe people watch the replays on their phones.

Rosie appears at my elbow. "Whatcha doing?"

"Practicing."

"Want me to pitch?"

I scowl. She's only asking because Roger isn't here. But it's still nice to have someone to play with. "Fine."

She does a little hop. "Where's the ball?"

I hear a loud clatter as Mom thunders around in the shed. "Let's just pretend," I say.

Rosie scurries to the white rubber pitching strip. She jumps right on top of it and turns to me, beaming.

I hunch over the plate and narrow my eyes.

Rosie pretends to throw. I make a big, slow-motion swing, imagining how it must feel to hit for real. "There it goes!" I shield my eyes and picture the ball soaring deep into center field. "Back, back . . . and it's outta here!"

I drop my invisible bat and jog around the bases, shoulders back, head high. While Rosie jumps and cheers, I envision the crowd roaring and fireworks exploding. When I cross the plate, Rosie runs in to give me a high five.

I stand with my hands on my hips. The wind whips through my hair as I gaze across the field, thinking about how I'll describe it all to Sofía.

But then I wonder: Why do I keep saving up things that I never get to tell her? What's she saving for me, anyway?

Maybe I won't tell her about any of this.

I picture myself opening a trunk in my mind

then. I imagine the other things I haven't told her: *Those socks don't go with your sneakers. Your cat isn't the cutest in the world. Sometimes I forget to miss you.*

I tuck softball in next to them—one more thing I'll keep all to myself.

9

We bring home all the equipment with our team name on it. We're called the same thing as the trucking company that pays for our stuff: L & M Distribution.

I like trucks and all, but it doesn't exactly have a nice ring to it.

While Mom sends our practice schedule to the other parents, I strap on the catcher's gear. I bet I could fight a dragon in this! I run around the yard, swinging my bat like a sword. *Slash! Slash! Slash!* Bird feeders bounce off my face mask as I pretend to do battle, scattering seeds everywhere.

Then, on Sunday afternoon, the whole family heads back to the diamond for our very first practice.

We haul equipment to the dugout together. Dad hangs bats on the rack. Rosie walks along the bench like it's a balance beam. I feel like a real professional in my outfit. Rosie's pants are squeezy, my yellow glove is grippy, and my orange T-shirt matches my cleats.

I'm about to go run around the bases when Mom pulls me aside. "I was going to borrow a mitt from the shed for you," she says, "but I thought you might like to use this instead." She hands me a brown leather glove. It's wrinkled and worn and looks a little dirty.

"It's kind of beat-up," I say, turning it over.

"That's because it was mine when I was your age." She has a misty look on her face.

I slide my hand inside the mitt. It feels soft and bendy, and the leather smells like warm mud. I smile up at her. "Thanks, Coach."

Mom gives me a quick hug, wipes her eyes, and starts greeting girls as they arrive.

Players pair off to warm up. A few parents hang around. I see a lanky girl with a long, black ponytail walking over from the parking lot.

Brooklyn.

I groan. Avery is with her, too. They're in full gear with special bags slung over their shoulders, a bat sticking out of each. Brooklyn clips her bag to the dugout fence and looks me up and down. "Nice shoes," she says.

I point my toes to show them off. "Thanks! They're really fast."

She nudges Avery.

I get an uneasy feeling in my stomach. Their pants look brand-new—bright white with black belts and matching stirrups. Their cleats are shiny black, too, and their socks are high and tight, not slouchy at all. I bend to pull mine up.

Brooklyn gasps. "Oh, my gosh, is that a dish glove?"

Avery snorts. "What are you, our mascot?"

"We should call her Flash," Brooklyn says, "since she's so fast." They head into the field, laughing.

I look down at my outfit. My cleats look like clown shoes now, and my socks are already slouching again. I peel off my yellow glove and stuff it into a trash can.

"Meena!"

I turn to see someone running up to me. "Lin?"

She has the same gear as the other girls, but her face is as bright as a lightning bug, like she's actually glad to see me. "Are we on the same team?" she asks.

"I guess so!"

She stops short then and looks me up and down. I freeze. Rosie's pants feel like they're squeezing the air right out of me. "Nice glove," Lin says.

My hand clenches inside Mom's mitt.

But then Lin meets my eyes. "It looks like it's seen a lot of action."

I let out a big breath and smile. "It has."

"Wanna play catch?" she asks.

"Yeah!"

"Hey, girls." Mom waves us over. "This is Sadie. She's a third grader, too." The girl next to her is scrawny with sandy brown hair. She looks as thin as a piece of paper.

I lift my hand. "Hi."

Lin doesn't say anything, but she doesn't look too impressed.

Mom gives Sadie a ball. "Why don't the three of you go warm up together."

We spread out in the grass. Sadie makes a wimpy throw that lands way in front of me. I throw to Lin, who whips the ball back to her. Sadie flinches and has to chase it to the parking lot.

"Great," Lin says. "She can't throw *or* catch."

I cringe. "That's mean."

"It's true."

Sadie hurries back and throws again. This time, the ball lands closer to her than it does to me! "Sorry," she mumbles, picking it up.

Lin holds up her own glove. "Try again," she says, "but step into it this time. Use your whole body, not just your arm. Throw as hard as you can."

Sadie shrinks back. "I don't want to hurt you."

"You're not gonna hurt me. I'm gonna catch it." She smacks her fist into her glove. "Right here."

Sadie bites her lip and throws again. Lin has to reach a little but snags it in the air. "That's it!"

Sadie smiles.

"Heads up," Lin cries and fires the ball right at me.

I hit the ground as it sails over my head. "Hey! I wasn't ready!"

"You should have been."

"Huddle up, girls," Mom calls.

I shake my head and fetch the ball. For a second there, I was actually glad we're on the same team. But *this* is the Lin I know from school—the one who bosses people around and only cares about sports.

When we join the circle, Mom has us go around and say our names. Besides the kids I already know, there's a red-headed fifth grader named Grace. Carmen and Yolanda are fourth-grade twins who joke with each other in Spanish. The other two fourth graders have their arms linked together. Jada is a Black girl with a puffy bun and looks excited to be there. Hailey is a sunburned white kid who doesn't.

"How many of you have played before?" Mom asks. "Softball, T-ball, coach-pitch?"

Everyone raises a hand except me.

"Kickball?"

I stick my hand in the air.

Mom smiles. "Most of the rules are the same," she says. "We'll go over the differences later, but today I thought it'd be more *fun* to get into some game scenarios."

She winks at me.

"Hailey, why don't you go pitch to Mr. Zee for a bit. Yolanda, grab a bat, and the rest of you, take the field!"

I sprint for center field as everyone scrambles for a position. I'm the first one there! But when I turn around, Brooklyn looks smug at first base and Lin is standing proudly at second. Don't they want to play outfield? I got a double play in kickball right from this spot!

Well, it's all mine.

Yolanda steps up to the plate. Mom carries a bucket of balls into the pitching circle. "Run at the crack of the bat, just like you would in a game," she says. "Got it?"

Yolanda nods and raises her bat.

Suddenly, from the top of the bleachers, Rosie starts strutting around and cheering in rhythm. "Go, Yolanda! Go, go, Yolanda!" The other girls smile and giggle, like they think it's the cutest thing in the world.

I crouch, down and ready. I feel like a slingshot that's about to fire.

Yolanda swings and misses a few times, then *bloop!* She hits a dribbler to second. Lin scoops up the ball and throws it to Brooklyn for a force out at first.

Grace comes up to bat next. *Crack!* She hits down the third base line. After a few swings, *smack!* Carmen hits a single into the left field hole.

New girls keep coming up to bat. Rosie cheers, and the ball zings, but it doesn't come anywhere near me! After a while, I start kicking dandelion puffs. I think about what to make with my yogurt lids. I wonder if birds might be robots, but nobody knows since we don't see them up close.

Finally, Mom calls for me to cover second while Lin heads in to bat. *Pow!* She hits the very first pitch over the shortstop's head! She blows through first and stops at second. "Nice hit," I say, holding my hand out.

"Thanks!" She slaps it so hard, it stings.

I shake out my hand as Sadie tiptoes to the plate.

Lin rolls her eyes. "This might take a while."

It does. Sadie misses one pitch after another. The whole infield starts looking bored and saggy. After about a zillion swings, *plink.* Sadie taps a little grounder my way.

Finally! When the ball stops in front of me, I scoop it up, thinking fast. The force out is at first, but Lin is right here, charging for third! For a split second, I flash back to Nora, running away from me on the kickball field. Then I make up my mind and throw.

Bam! The ball hits Lin square in the back. *Yes!*

Her body goes rigid. Then she whips around and everything goes still.

"You *hit* me?" Her eyes are wide with shock.

I take a step back. "Well . . . yeah."

Brooklyn snorts. Avery slaps her hand over her mouth.

Lin's whole face is turning red now. "Don't you know anything? You don't throw at people in softball!"

Oh, no.

Mom touches her shoulder, but Lin shakes her off and stomps toward third base.

Mom cringes at me then. "Maybe we should have gone over the rules after all." She nods toward the plate. "Your turn."

My ears are ringing as I head in to bat. Lin is glaring at me. Brooklyn is snickering. Rosie sits on her hands at the top of the bleachers and doesn't make a sound.

I'll show them. I'll wallop the ball right out of the park! I'll break a window a mile away! I'll send the outfielders running so far that they won't get back until Tuesday!

I grab the bat out of the dirt and hold it high over my shoulder, like a sword.

"Bring it down a little," Mom says from the pitcher's circle.

I do.

"Now lift your elbow. No, your other elbow."

I grip the bat tighter. "Just throw it."

Mom sighs and does a gentle wind-up. The ball sails toward me. I squeeze my eyes shut and swing as hard as I can.

Whiff!

Mom reaches into the bucket and throws again.

Whiff!

"Outfield," she calls, "you can come in a little."

Hey! Whose side is she on?

I bang my bat against the plate. *Bam, bam, BAM!* It feels good to hit something.

Mom holds up the bright yellow ball like maybe I really do have weakling eyes. "Keep your eye on the ball, honey," she says.

"I am!"

But she keeps throwing, and I keep missing. Jada looks at her fingernails. Grace sits down on third base. Brooklyn tucks her glove under her arm like she knows she won't need it.

Finally, Mom gives me an I'm-sorry look and drops the ball into the bucket. "That's okay," she says, a little too brightly. "We're all just here to have fun, right? Head in, everyone."

Dad passes out freeze pops from the cooler,

but I don't even take one. Mom talks about practice times and rainout alerts, but I can't hear a word she's saying, because Brooklyn is smirking at me, Sadie looks like she feels sorry for me, and every time I try to catch Lin's eye, she looks like she's grinding her teeth.

When Mom finally says, "See you Tuesday," Lin grabs her bag and stalks toward the parking lot.

"Lin!" I run after her. When she doesn't stop, I circle around in front of her. "I'm sorry I hit you. I didn't know that was a rule."

She pushes past me.

"Hey!" I hurry alongside her now. "I said I was sorry. What's the matter?"

"What's the matter?" She turns to gape at me. "You're terrible! You're *actually* terrible! I thought you were pretending at the evaluation, but you were just lying to me!"

I take a step back. "I wasn't lying. I didn't know!"

"Well, it's true. You're the worst one on the team."

She storms off. And I don't do anything except stand there in my phony gear, watching her go.

10

I'm quiet on the drive home. Rosie hums a little tune next to me while I stare out the window, my heart stinging like my hand did when Lin slapped it.

"I think we have a good team overall," Mom says as she pulls onto our street.

"Your pitching is decent," Dad says.

"And we've got some solid hitters. Did you see Lin up there? She's only a third grader!"

Dad clears his throat.

Mom glances at me in the rearview mirror. "But the important thing is that everyone had fun."

Dad turns around in the passenger seat. "Did you have a good time, slugger?"

I wince. "Don't call me that. I didn't even get a hit."

"You hit Lin," Rosie says.

I groan. "I wasn't supposed to."

"Oh, sweetheart." Mom says. "That was my fault. I should have started with the basics."

I sink lower in my seat. "I don't get it. How can I be bad? I'm great at kickball."

"But you've never used a bat or a glove before," Mom says. "You just need practice."

Dad winks at me. "And maybe a few pointers on the rules."

"How about we work on your batting after school tomorrow?" Mom says. "I know some drills we could try. I'll bet if we practice every day, just for an hour or so—"

Here we go. "Mom. You promised."

"But I didn't know that—" She stops.

I cross my arms. "That I'd be bad?"

There's a long pause, like she has to think hard about her next words. "I was forgetting that you're new to the game," she says. "The other girls are a little ahead of you, that's all."

"It's this gear." I kick my heel against the floor. "I look like a baby in Rosie's leggings."

"I'm not a baby!"

"And how am I supposed to catch anything with this worn-out glove?"

"It's not worn out," Mom says. "It's broken in."

"Well, I hate it!" I slam the mitt against the seat.

Dad gives me a warning look. "Meena."

When I glance at the rearview mirror, Mom's eyes look hurt, but only for a second before they flick away again.

★ ★ ★

I'm dreading seeing Lin at school on Monday, but she doesn't even talk to me.

When I go around collecting worksheets, she shoves her paper at me without looking up. When we both get up to use the pencil sharpener, she hurries to beat me there. When she sees me peeking out of the slide during first recess, she scowls and turns away.

Whatever. I don't even know why she wanted me to play softball in the first place. It's not like we're friends or anything. She's mean and bossy, and she hates art. She used to ask for Sofía's rainbow candies at lunch, too, even though she knew Sofía shared them with *me*. And one time, when I got stuck with Lin as a science partner, she kept rolling her eyes and huffing out breaths so I'd know she didn't want to be with *me*, either.

So when I hear her trying to get another kickball game going after lunch, I decide I won't play unless I'm on the other team.

So I can beat her.

Only it turns out, nobody wants to play.

Eli stays in for Catch Up Club. A bunch of other kids gather around a picnic table while Pedro and Aiden slap down battle cards. Maddy and Nora are playing horses on their usual bench. It'd be nice if they asked me to join, even though I don't want to, but when I take a step toward them, they huddle closer together, ignoring me.

Anger sparks in my chest. Sofía would never do that. She included everyone. It could be kind of annoying, actually. That's why we spent so much time in the tube slide. I liked to go where no one could see us so they wouldn't ask to join in. Sometimes I even saw Lin peeking inside. I knew she was just hanging around the slide, hoping for an invitation, so I made sure Sofía didn't turn around and see her.

I suck in a breath.

Whoa. That was mean.

And it's exactly what Maddy and Nora are doing to me.

I look around the playground. Lin is hitting a tennis ball against the building by herself for the second time today. She doesn't even need a racket or any other players. She hardly ever misses.

I have to admit, she really is awesome at sports. Everyone always wants her on their team. But if we aren't in the middle of a game, I don't think she has anyone to play with.

I know what that feels like now.

So even though she's still mad at me, and she probably doesn't even like me, the next thing I know, I'm striding up to her.

She hits the tennis ball with her bare hand. It smacks the wall and bounces back to her. Then she

hits it again, counting under her breath. "Three . . ."
Smack, bounce. "Four . . ." *Smack, bounce.*

"Hey," I say, right behind her.

She catches the ball, whirls around, and
frowns.

I scratch the back of my neck. "I'm sorry."

"For what?"

It turns out there are a few things I should be
sorry for. But I clear my throat and say, "I'm sorry
you're stuck on my team. I know you wanted to be
with good players."

She squints at me. "You really didn't know you
were bad?"

I feel the tips of my ears start to burn. "What
difference does it make? It's just the fun league anyway."

Lin rolls her eyes. "What's fun about losing?
What's fun about doing your best and having someone else screw it up?"

The heat in my ears spreads down my neck. "It
isn't my fault I'm not as talented as you."

"You know what?" She smacks the ball against
the wall and catches it. "Everybody thinks if you're
good at sports, it's because you're born that way or
something. But it doesn't just happen. I work at it."

I blink at that. "Do you think I could get better too?"

"Not if you don't try."

"But if I work at it?"

She shrugs. "Probably."

I think about that. If I ask my mom for help, she'll have me practicing every second. But recess is short, and I have nothing to do.

I stand up straighter. "Then help me."

Her eyes get big. "Me?"

"Why not? You helped Sadie the other day. All you did was give her a couple of pointers, and she started throwing better. Can't you do that for me?"

Lin looks me over. Hair is falling in her eyes, so she takes out her clip and pins it back again. Then she starts bouncing the ball against the blacktop. "You'd have to do what I say," she says.

"Okay."

"Every recess."

"Every recess but one," I add.

She squints at me. "Why should I?"

"Because you want to win." I cross my arms. "And so do I."

11

We start practicing at the very next recess. On our way to the playground, Lin grabs a few things from the equipment rack. "Bring the orange bat," she says.

I reach for it . . . then yank my hand away. It's big, fat, and plastic—a toy bat. "That thing is for little kids!"

"Well, you hit like one. Come on."

I follow her into the grass, grumbling the whole way. "Just throw slow," I say.

"I'm not gonna throw at all." She drops a plastic home plate onto the ground and attaches a long post right into the middle of it. Then she nestles a plastic ball into the little cup on top.

"No." I take a step back. "No way."

"What? You said you never played T-ball, right?"

"No, but—"

"Then we have to start at the beginning." She stands back. "Go ahead."

I roll my eyes, lift the bat, and swing. *Whiff!*

And it turns out the only thing worse than hitting with a little kid bat is missing with one.

I grimace. "I was just warming up."

"Uh-huh."

I swing again, as hard as I can. The bat makes a whistling sound as it whips through the air . . . and makes contact! I see the ball land at my feet. "I knew I could hit it!"

"You hit the post," Lin says. "The ball just fell off."

"Darn it!" I bang the bat against the ground.

"Do you want to know what you're doing wrong?"

"It's not me! It's this stupid bat!"

Lin puts her hands on her hips. "If you can't hit with a fat bat, you don't stand a chance with a skinny one."

I feel my shoulders slump. "Fine. What?"

"For starters, put your hands together. And lower the bat. It's not a lightsaber."

I do what she says.

"Now move back a little. You're crowding the plate." When I'm in position, she nods. "Okay, try again."

This time, I swing so hard that a big *oof* comes out of me, but the bat just breezes through the air.

Lin groans. "Watch the ball."

"I am watching it!"

"No, you're not! You close your eyes when you swing."

I blink at her. "I do?"

"Every time!"

The front of my neck gets hot. "Well, so what? I know where it is!"

She tips her head back and sighs. "Try again," she says slowly. "But this time, watch the ball until the bat actually touches it, okay?"

I plant my feet and bounce my knees until I feel nice and loose. Then I crouch a little, check my hands, and glare at the ball. It looks like it's daring me.

"Nice and easy now," Lin says.

I force my eyes open as wide as I can. Then I take a big breath and grit my teeth. When I swoop the bat around, it almost feels like I'm moving in slow motion.

Tap.

The ball bloops off the tee and onto the ground. I gasp. "I did it! I actually saw it hit that time!"

"Finally." Lin smiles. "You're not good, but you might not be hopeless."

I work with Lin again on Tuesday.

She's not too happy that I spend our first recess in the tube slide, but after lunch, I get more hits. By last recess, I'm even hitting with the skinny bat!

Tap. The ball bloops in front of me.

Tap. It bounces across the grass.

Tap. It rolls all the way to Lin! I mean, she's not standing very far away, but still.

We don't have time to try it without the tee, but I'm still feeling pretty good when we get to practice that night.

After warm-ups, Mom hands out our team hats. They're just plain white visors, but they make me feel a little more official. Next, she goes over some of the rules. I know most of them from kick-ball, but she looks right at me when she explains how to tag a runner with the ball instead of throwing it at them.

"Can we steal bases?" Lin asks.

Mom shakes her head. "Not until middle school."

Brooklyn snorts. "The club team does."

"Well, this is the rec league," Mom says. "We're here to learn and have fun."

And to win. I don't say it out loud, but Lin and I trade a look.

"One more thing," Mom says. "We field nine players, and there are only ten of you, so we really need everyone here on game nights. If we only have eight players, it's an automatic forfeit."

"What? Why?" Lin asks. "We could still win with eight!"

"League rules." Mom claps her hands. "Okay! We have a couple of parent helpers today. Brooklyn, go pitch to Mr. Zee for a bit. The rest of you, go with your coach when your name is called."

The parent who calls my name introduces herself as Coach Woo. She's Lin's mom! I recognize her from school pickup. She has us practice running to first while she stands by the base and gives us a signal. If she points, we run straight through. If she holds up a hand, we round first and stop. If she windmills her arm, we run all the way to second.

After that, we switch to fielding ground balls. Coach Woo rolls the first one my way. I wait for it to stop then pick it up and throw it back. Easy!

"Don't just stand there," she says. "Charge the ball."

But when I try, I can't get my glove to work. The more pointers she gives us, the harder it gets. *Stay in front of the ball. Watch it into your glove. Trap it.*

You try doing all those things at once!

So the next time the ball is rolling toward me, I yank off my mitt and scoop it up with my bare hand. *Clunk!* It knocks against my thumb and sends a zing of pain up my arm.

"Oy," Coach Woo shouts. "That's a good way to break a finger, Meena."

Switching to fly balls isn't any better. The sky is so bright that it makes my eyes water, and I keep losing the ball in the air! It hits the ground next to me every time. *Thump. Thump. Thump.*

Maybe Lin and I should have practiced catching first.

Finally, we join back up for batting practice. Rosie brought her pom-poms today. She stands in the bleachers, shaking them and cheering for each girl. Every few pitches, Mom stops to talk about what we'd do in a real game. "Where are the force outs? What will you do if the ball comes to you on the ground? What if it's in the air?"

When it's my turn, I get into my batting stance like Lin showed me. *Hands together. Eye on the ball. Nice and easy.*

But when Mom pitches, everything feels different. The ball is too fast. The bat is too heavy. I forget everything Lin taught me and just swing, hard and wild. *Whiff! Whiff! Whiff!*

Finally, Mom gives me that too-bright smile from the pitching circle. "Good try, Meena. Jada, you're next!"

I take Jada's spot at second. Lin is playing shortstop next to me, but I can't even look at her. I bet she's mad. Or embarrassed. She probably thinks she's wasting her time with me.

I'll show her. I adjust my visor and punch my

fist into my glove. *Stay in front of it. Watch it into your glove. Trap it.*

Mom pitches. Jada pops up. The ball spikes high, headed my way!

I catch kickballs. I can do this! I raise my mitt as the ball starts to drop, closer and closer. I squeeze my eyes shut.

Thwap!

Did I catch it?

Then I look and see Lin standing over me, and the ball is in *her* glove.

I suck in a breath. "That was my play."

She shrugs. "You would have missed it."

"You don't know that!"

"You had your eyes closed."

"Huddle up, everyone," Mom says.

The whole team jogs to the pitching circle.

"Listen," Mom says. "Our first game is only a week away, and the most important thing is that we work together and have fun. It's okay if we make mistakes. Let's just do our best, and cheer each other on. Can we do that?"

I glare at Lin. She's not cheering for me. She's stealing my plays!

Then Rosie starts stomping on the bleachers, pumping her pom-poms in the air.

> "We've got spirit!
> Yes, we do!
> We've got spirit!
> How 'bout you?"

A couple of girls giggle. Rosie grins. "That could be our cheer," says Hailey.

"Sure!" Mom smiles. "How else can we show our team spirit?"

"Could we wear braids for our games?" asks Carmen.

"Absolutely. What else?"

"A pizza party?" Jada suggests.

"I'll host," Coach Woo offers.

I stare at Lin's white visor, already streaked with dirt, like a real ballplayer's would be.

And that's when I get an Inspiration.

"Let's decorate our hats," I say.

"Great idea," Mom says. "You can show them off at the pizza party. Now let's do our team cheer. Hands together!"

When I reach into the circle, I see Lin giving me a squinty stare. And maybe it's not very team-spirity of me, but I stick out my tongue at her.

She might be better at softball, but I'm better at art.

And I'm gonna make the best visor on the team.

I want to work on my visor as soon as we get home.

Mom has other ideas.

"What do you say we have a little batting practice before it gets dark?" she asks. "Just for *fun*." The word sounds sharp, like a knife scraping against a plate.

I start to slink away. "Wow, almost bedtime already!"

"Meena Zee." She puts her hands on her hips. "I know we made a deal, but you're obviously struggling. Would it kill you to practice a little?"

I groan. "I've been practicing at school! I'm still not any good."

She blinks. "At school?"

"I asked Lin to help me at recess."

"But you didn't ask—" She gives me a weak smile. "Well, that's great, honey. I bet she's giving you lots of good tips. And I'm glad you found someone to play with. I know how much you miss Sofía."

I do miss Sofía. Even though I'm still mad at

her, and I'm definitely not telling her about softball, I feel the secret sitting inside me like a lump. For a few minutes, when I'm in the slide on Wednesday, I close my eyes and picture Sofía climbing in. I imagine telling her all the things I'm saving up, like I used to.

She isn't the only one I miss, though. It seems like I never play with Rosie anymore. I don't even care that she can't climb trees without a boost. And I haven't played with Eli since our last club meeting. He hardly talks to me at school, either—not even when we're allowed to visit during art time later that morning.

We're supposed to create something that makes you think "spring has sprung." Pedro is using white chalk to draw a soccer ball on black paper, but I can't tell what Eli is making. He's just shredding a piece of brown construction paper into bits. Finally, he starts pasting them onto another paper in the shape of—

"A nest!" I lean over his shoulder to take a closer look. "Hey, that's cool."

He smiles a little. "Thanks." For a minute, I'm worried that he won't say anything else, but then he asks, "What are you making?"

"A field of tulips. Mrs. D says I can't paint any more pictures of the dump." I finish the grass and squeeze out a blob of red for the flowers. "Are you gonna put a bird in your nest?" I ask.

"Just eggs, but I need more paper."

"I'll get it!" I jump up, happy for a chance to do something nice for him. "White?"

"Blue."

Huh. I grab a few different shades from the art cart. Heading back, I spot the paper on Lin's desk. She painted a page of green grass like I did, and she's squeezing out a blob of red.

I stop short. Is she copying me? The tulip field was my idea!

I hand Eli the papers and sit back down. While he starts cutting, I keep a close eye on Lin. Sure enough, I catch her looking at my painting! I scowl and wrap my arm around it to block her view.

"What kind of birds have blue eggs?" I ask, trying to keep Eli talking.

"Robins." He lights up a little. "I found an empty shell yesterday that fell out of a nest."

"Cool! Are you bringing it to our club?"

"Maybe." He shifts in his seat a little. "Do you think we could have the next meeting at your house?"

I look at him. "We always do it at yours."

"Only because the clubhouse used to be there."

I feel a sharp pang at the thought of our old milk jug igloo. "But why—" I stop, thinking of something. "Are you trying to keep me away from

your rabbits?" I ask. "Because I'm really not trying
to hog Stewart."

Eli frowns. "Stanley."

"Yeah, him. I bet he doesn't even like me as
much as you say." I grin. "He probably just thinks
I'm a giant carrot since I wear so much orange."

Eli doesn't even smile. "So can we?" he asks
again.

I feel my heart sinking. "If you want."

We don't talk after that. I fill in the white space
on my paper with red tulips, careful not to smear
the green paint. Mrs. D strolls by and nods at our
work. Then she passes Lin's desk and stops. Lin isn't
painting anymore. She's just sitting there with her
arms crossed. Mrs. D looks at her paper and sighs.

When the bell rings, we all jump up. "Please
put your projects on the rack in the hall," Mrs. D
calls. "Lin, would you stay for a minute?"

I leave my painting to dry, grab my lunch, and
head for the cafeteria. It's a few minutes before Lin
slams her tray onto the table. I turn away, pretending
to actually care about Pedro and Aiden talking about
their dumb battle cards. But when I stop at my cubby
on the way to recess, Lin is right behind me. There's
no way I'm practicing with her, so I turn to leave.

Then I hear her say, "I can't help you today."

I stop and stare at her. "Hang on. You're ditch-
ing *me*?"

She looks away. "Mrs. D is making me stay in to redo my project."

I get a prickly feeling. "Because you copied me?"

"What? No! She thinks I didn't put in any effort because it's messy. But I did! It just didn't turn out."

I look at the drying rack. "Which one is yours?" She tries to block me, but I spot her name and pull the painting out of its slot. *Whoa!* It's a mess. It looks like a little kid made it—a little kid who really likes brown. "*This* is a field of tulips?" I ask.

She sighs. "Yeah."

"Why does it look like a field of mud?"

She grabs the painting. "Because I can't make anything good, okay?"

"Wait a sec." I keep hold of a corner and take a closer look. "Did you put the flowers on top of the grass? While it was still wet?"

"I guess. "

"Well, if you mix red and green, it makes brown. Look." I pull out my painting and hold it up next to hers. "I left white space for the flowers so the paints wouldn't bleed together. See?"

For a few seconds, she studies them both. Then she huffs out a breath. "Whatever. It's not my fault I'm not as talented as you."

I get another one of those mixed-up feelings when she says that. I mean, I like being better than her at something. I'm *glad* she thinks I'm good at art.

But I'm also sorry that she doesn't think she is.

I'm more sorry, actually.

Just then, Brooklyn walks by with a group of fifth graders. Her eyes flick from Lin to me. Even though I'm not exactly wild about her, we *are* on the same team, so I give her a little wave. She gives me a dirty look and keeps walking.

"What's her problem?" I ask when she's gone.

"She's just mad to be stuck in the rec league," Lin says. "She played club softball last year, but when they had their spring tryouts, her arm was still in a cast."

"Oh, right," I say. "She broke it on a trampoline."

Lin shifts on her feet. "My trampoline."

I gape at her. "You and Brooklyn are friends?"

"Not really." Lin looks away. "She lives across the street from me, but she only comes over when she doesn't have anything else to do."

"Oh." I blink. "That isn't very nice of her."

"It's what everybody does." Lin kicks at the floor. "But whatever. She doesn't come anymore."

I open my mouth to say something, then stop. I wouldn't have started spending recess with Lin, either, if I'd found someone else to play with.

Am I as bad as Brooklyn?

Lin slides her painting out of my fingers. "I gotta go."

"Hang on," I say. "How about I stay in with you?"

She stops. "What for?"

I rock back on my heels. "Maybe I could give you some pointers."

She shakes her head. "It won't help."

I squint at her. "You know," I say slowly, "everyone thinks if you're good at art, it's because you're born that way or something. But I work at it. I bet you'd get better, too, if you made more projects."

She tilts her head at me. "You really think so?"

"Sure." I smile. "I mean, you're not good. But you might not be hopeless."

Lin's next field of flowers looks a lot better than her first.

She paints dandelions this time instead of tulips. Some are yellow stars. Others are white circles. I do give her a few tips, but mostly, I just sit next to her and say things like, "Nice!" and "Pretty!" and "Good job!"

A few times, she gets the yellow paint a little too close to the green, and my hands get itchy to take the brush and do it for her. Then I imagine her taking the bat away from me, and I stop myself.

By last recess, I don't have any mad-at-her left inside me, so we practice softball after all. "Can we work on catching today?" I ask when we stop at our cubbies.

"You still can't hit off a pitcher," she says.

"You don't think I can't catch, either, remember? You made my last play for me."

She looks a little embarrassed. "If you can't catch," she says, "your mom can stick you in right field. Hardly anyone hits out there anyway. But everyone has to bat."

She grabs her own bat out of her cubby and hands it to me. The metal barrel is covered with tiny dings and scratches, but underneath, it's shiny and bright blue. "Come on," she says. "We can't score if we don't get on base."

We find a spot on the playground away from everyone else. Lin pitches slow, without any wind-up, but the ball still feels like it's hurtling toward me. *Whiff!*

"Watch the ball," she says, for the zillionth time.

But as soon as it's coming at me, I lose track of it again. *Whiff!*

"Right here, Meena," She grabs another ball and holds it up, like she's giving me a chance to memorize it.

I glare at it like I'm trying to beat it in a staring contest.

She throws. The ball comes toward me in a gentle arc. For a second, I can actually see it turning in midair as I bring my bat around.

Tap.

Lin gasps. "You hit it."

I look at where it landed at my feet. "I did?"

"You got a piece of it, yeah!"

"Not a very big piece."

But I get a few more pieces after that. I start to

find a just-right spot on the ball that makes it zing into the air. By last recess on Thursday, I even hit it over Lin's head!

When we get to practice that night, my fielding still isn't great, but I'm sure I'll do better at the plate. Then Mom waves us in for batting practice and calls out, "Brooklyn, come in and face a few batters."

I suck in a breath. "Aren't *you* pitching to us?"

Mom smiles. "Welcome to the big leagues. Let's hear it for our first pitcher, team!"

The other girls cheer as Brooklyn jogs to the pitching circle, looking smug. I clap a little, but it's hard to feel much team spirit for her.

She scuffs her cleat in the dirt and throws a few warm-up pitches. They rocket into Avery's glove. *Thwap! Thwap! Thwap!*

"Dang, girl," Avery says, shaking out her hand. "You throw hard!"

"That's because I played club last year," Brooklyn says. "All the best pitchers do."

I see Lin press her lips into a thin line.

Carmen bats first. She misses a lot. Everyone does. I know I should be happy that our team has such a good pitcher, but I feel sorry for the batters instead. They all get a hit eventually, but nobody hits as hard or as far as usual. Even Lin only gets a single.

I chew on the laces of my glove, dreading my turn. Every time Mom calls a new batter, I hold my breath and think, *Not me, not me!*

When I finally hear my name, something amazing happens.

"Lin," Mom calls. "Come take a turn pitching."

Yes!

I practically skip to the dugout. I know I can hit off of Lin. I did it all recess!

I trade my glove for a batting helmet as she heads to the pitching circle. Brooklyn keeps throwing. *Thwap. Thwap. Thwap.* Lin glances at the coaches, but they're looking at a clipboard and don't notice.

"Excuse me." Lin sounds annoyed. "Can I pitch?"

Brooklyn rolls her eyes. "Probably not, but you can try." She drops the ball in the dirt and strolls away.

Wow.

While Lin throws a few warm-up pitches, I grab her blue bat and head to the on-deck circle. With each practice swing, I imagine hitting the ball all over the field. *Crack*—into left! *Whack*—up the middle! *Bam*—down the third base line!

Then Lin gives me a nod.

I stride to the plate and get into my batting stance. *Hands together. Eye on the ball. Nice and easy.*

Her eyes narrow.

I give her a wink.

Then she pitches—hard.

Whiff.

I stare at my bat. Is there a hole in this thing?

She pitches again. The ball rockets toward me.

Whiff!

"Want me to get you a tee?" Avery mutters behind me.

My cheeks start to burn. She wasn't throwing like this at recess! My ears start to ring as the balls come in, faster and faster. I swing all over the place. I can't help it! But for once, Lin doesn't even look annoyed.

She looks proud of herself.

Girls start chatting in the field. "Look alive out there," Mom says from the dugout. "Last pitch."

I step out of the batter's box, my eyes stinging with tears. Lin thumps the ball into her glove a few times, her jaw tight. I give her a pleading look. *Please, give me an easy one,* I beg silently. *Just one.*

Then I step up to the plate and lift my bat. *Hands together. Eye on the ball. Nice and easy.*

She throws.

For a split second, I track the ball as it barrels toward me. Then I swing so hard that I spin all the way around and land right on my butt!

WHIFF!

Mom claps from behind the fence. "Nice try, Meena. Come on in, everyone."

Girls head into the dugout. A few start chanting our team cheer. I just sit there in the dirt, my pride hurting as much as my backside.

Then suddenly, Lin is standing over me, offering her hand.

I stare up at her. "Why did you pitch like that?"

She gives me a funny look. "That's how I pitch."

"Not to me. Not at school."

"That's just practice."

"*This* is practice." I feel my lip start to tremble. "You knew I'd never hit it."

She lets her hand drop. "What do you think happens in a game? The other team won't go easy on you just because you're a rookie."

I grit my teeth and scramble to my feet. "You just wanted to get back at Brooklyn," I say, jabbing my finger at her. "You want everyone to think you're the best, but they just think you're a show-off!"

Lin leans away from me, eyes wide. "Is that what *you* think?"

"I think I'm done practicing with you." I turn away and bend to brush the dirt off myself, ignoring her.

For a minute, Lin's cleats stay planted on the ground next to mine. But I just keep swatting, dust filling the air between us, until they're gone.

14

I stay away from Lin on Friday. It's easy, so she must be avoiding me, too.

After school, Eli leaves on his bike without me. When I get home, Rosie and Roger are having a pony picnic under the bird feeders. I hang around the sand tire for a while, watching. Roger looks pretty bored, so they probably aren't playing anything I'd like, but Rosie doesn't even invite me.

My own sister.

When I go inside, Mom is on a video call. She gives me a little wave as I kick off my shoes and head upstairs to my workshop.

There's plenty of space to make projects in here since we cleared out some of my trash collection. The team pizza party is this Sunday, so I guess I should start decorating my visor, but I don't feel sparkly or creative. I plop down on my spinny office chair and kick myself in a slow circle. Sofía and I used to have sleepovers in this exact spot. We'd giggle and talk until way past our bedtime, and

I'd drift to sleep with a warm-happy feeling in my stomach, knowing she was here.

When I close my eyes now, I can still hear the sound of Sofía's laughter in my head. But I don't remember everything. I know her eyes are a mix of brown and gold and green, but I can't quite picture them anymore. It's like my full-color memory of Sofía is turning to black and white.

My heart feels squeezy when I think of that. I get up and rummage through my bins for the can tabs she gave me, then turn the jar and watch them tumble inside. There are hundreds of them— one for every day we ate lunch together. But if I had one for every day we were friends, there'd be thousands of them. I'd still be collecting them. Wouldn't I?

I wonder how long it's been since she moved away. I count up the days in my head and take out one can tab for each day she's been gone. I feel like there should be enough to fill the whole room—to fill the whole world—but they actually fit in my hand.

What does Sofía do with her tabs now? Maybe she's saving them up to send to me.

Or maybe she just throws them away.

I close my eyes and grip the tabs so tightly they bite into my palm.

"Meena?"

Mom is peeking in the door. And all of a sudden, the sadness filling up my body makes me feel so heavy that I go slump into her arms.

Mom squeezes me tight. "What's up, sweetheart?"

I don't know where to start. I'm so tired of being alone—in the slide, in my workshop, in my own backyard. But all I can manage to say is, "We always had playdates on Fridays."

Mom looks down and gives me a sad smile. "I know you did. And I had an idea about that." She tucks a piece of hair behind my ear. "How would you like to see a friend?"

"That'd be nice." If only I had any.

"Good. Because I talked to Lin's mom, and it's all arranged."

"What is?"

"A playdate at her house."

I jump back. "At Lin's house?"

"Why not?"

"We're not friends!"

Mom looks confused. "You said you've been spending recess together."

"Only to practice softball!"

"I know it's not the same as hanging out with Sofía." Mom rubs my arms up and down. "It's probably a little tricky, too, since you're so much alike."

I suck in a breath. "I am nothing like Lin."

Mom chuckles. "You're not stubborn and out-spoken and competitive? You don't like to be in charge and do things your own way? You don't forget other people's feelings sometimes?"

I open my mouth to argue, but then stop.

She ruffles my hair. "Listen, if you don't have a good time, you don't have to go back. But give it a chance, okay?"

I scuff my foot against the carpet.

"Besides . . ." Mom winks. "I hear they have a trampoline."

The first thing I notice at Lin's house is the crying.

The second is the baby gates.

There's one at the stairs leading up. There's another at the stairs leading down. There's a third one straight ahead, in the kitchen doorway.

"Thank you so much for having her," Mom says behind me.

"Our pleasure." A woman I've never seen before opens the kitchen gate for me as the crying gets louder. "Lin is out back. I'm just going to get her brother." The woman closes the gate behind me, gives Mom a wave, and hurries up the stairs.

"I'll be back in a couple of hours," Mom says.

"Wait," I say as she starts to leave. "Who was that lady?"

"Lin's mom."

"I thought Coach Woo was her mom."

"Ms. Hoye is her mom too."

I let out a breath. "Geez, I thought you were leaving me with a stranger."

Mom blows me a kiss and pulls the door closed behind her.

Two hours. *Ugh.* I should have brought my walkie-talkie so I could call Mom to pick me up sooner.

I creep across the kitchen and peer through the screen door. The backyard is small with a high fence all around, but it's jam-packed with things to do. I spot the trampoline in the corner, but there's also a climbing rope, a zip line, and even a punching bag.

Lin is standing in the middle of it all, facing a big net in an upright frame. She scuffs her foot in a bare patch of grass, flicks a softball into her glove a few times, then throws. It hits the net right in the center of a square and bounces back. Lin catches the ball easily and starts the glove smacking and feet scuffing again. Then I hear her talking to herself. "We're one out away from victory, folks, and a new batter is stepping up to the plate. The pitch . . ." She throws. "Swing and a miss. Strike one."

I hear the gate open behind me. Ms. Hoye is holding a bundle of kid, his face buried in her shoulder.

"Who's she talking to?" I ask.

Ms. Hoye smiles. "Nobody. She plays through whole games like that. It's pretty impressive, really. Go on out." She grabs a sippy cup and slips away again.

I stay put, watching. Lin keeps throwing the ball, calling out imaginary plays. "Foul to the right . . . high and outside . . . a bouncer toward third, out of play." After a while, I can even picture it: the field, the batter, the runner on first.

The count is full now. I hold my breath as Lin winds up, hands twitching at my sides.

"The runner is going." She throws, and the ball bounces high. "Line drive to the pitcher!" She snags it in her glove. "And he is outta there! Lin Hoye-Woo has thrown her first shutout of the season!" She thrusts her fists into the air.

I start clapping. "Yay!"

Lin looks right at me.

I freeze. Her face reminds me of the pain chart in the doctor's office—the face you point to when you hurt but not enough to frown.

I step outside, trying to think of something to say. "What is that thing?" I ask, nodding at the frame.

"It's a pitchback net." She looks suspicious. "Why? You wanna practice on it?"

I hold up my hands. "Nuh-uh. No softball."

Her eyebrows shoot up. "You really just came over to play?"

"I guess."

She breaks into a huge smile then.

Hang on. She's *glad* I'm here?

I look around, trying to think of something to say. "Do you use that thing for batting, too?" I ask finally.

"Nope, I use that." She points to a sock on a string, dangling from a tree. "There's a tennis ball inside," she says. "If it wraps around the branch once, it's a single. Twice is a double. Get it?"

"What about bases?"

She points around the yard. "The water meter is first, the tree stump is second, and that bush over there is third."

"But you play by yourself?"

Lin frowns. "Who else would I play with?"

"I don't know. Your moms, maybe?"

"They don't have as much time since Gilbert came along. He's my baby brother."

"Yeah, I heard him."

She brightens. "He's awake? Come and meet him!" She hurries into the house, leaps over two baby gates, and slides down a set of carpeted stairs into the living room. Ms. Hoye is on the floor with Gilbert. She's a white lady with light brown hair, but he looks more like Lin and Coach Woo—short black hair, light skin, and eyes that are a little different shape from mine.

"Hey, Gilbert," Lin says gently. "Come here, sweetie."

His whole face lights up as he toddles over. She swoops him into her arms and gives him a bunch of kisses on his chubby cheek. "Good job, Gilly. You're getting so strong!"

Ms. Hoye gets up. "Can you watch him for a few minutes?"

Lin nods and dances her brother around. "I asked for a puppy," she says as her mom heads upstairs, "but this is better."

I smile. "Is Coach Woo his real mom?"

Lin stiffens. "They both are."

"But who did he live inside before he was born?"

Her face hardens. "It's rude to ask that, you know."

"It is?"

"What difference does it make, anyway?"

I blink at that. "None, I guess. I'm sorry." Gilbert rests his pudgy little face on her shoulder, his whole body relaxing. It makes me feel warm and squishy inside. "He's cute," I say.

Lin's face softens again. "Watch this." She lays him on the carpet and raises her eyebrows at him. He lifts his shirt, and she blows a raspberry on his belly. He squeals and squiggles his feet in the air, patting his tummy for more.

We're all laughing now. I watch Lin play pat-a-cake with his feet. She looks even happier than when she kicks a home run at school. We start playing together then, bustling Gilbert back and forth between us while he giggles and shrieks.

"I barely remember when Rosie was this little," I say.

"I read him stories and tuck him in at night sometimes, just like my moms do," Lin says. "And I'm the only one who can get him to eat his peas." She gives me a shy smile. "We all take care of him, but I think I'm his favorite."

My heart squeezes a little. "Well, enjoy it while

it lasts, because someday he'll make a friend of his own, and you won't be anymore."

She stares at me. "That would break my heart."

I look away. "Yeah."

When Ms. Hoye comes and scoops Gilbert up again, Lin turns to me. "Wanna see my room?"

She leads me through four baby gates, up two little flights of stairs to a navy blue room with clothes all over the floor. The wall is mostly covered with sports posters, but I see the dandelion project she made hanging right above her bed.

I bump my shoulder against hers. "Nice painting."

She smiles. "Thanks. I tried to make another one, but it didn't turn out."

"How come?"

"I don't know. I thought if I used every paint color in the set, it'd be awesome. But it was just a mess."

I nod. "That happens to me, too."

She looks surprised. "It does?"

"It's kind of like . . ." I stop and think about it. "Remember in first grade when you dressed up as a vampire for our Halloween party?"

She blinks. "You remember that?"

"Oh, yeah. You had black clothes and vampire fangs with a trickle of fake blood out the corner of your mouth. It looked really cool."

She blushes a little. "Thanks."

"So the next year, I wore fangs too. But I also wore clown makeup and a skeleton suit and werewolf paws and a witch's hat—"

"I remember!" Lin giggles. "I couldn't tell what you were."

"Nobody could." I look at her painting again. "Some things turn out better if you don't overdo it." I rock back on my heels and look around. "So you like sports, and it seems like you're starting to like art. What else are you into?"

"Um . . ." She thinks about it. "I like bumper cars."

"Yeah?"

"All that smashing and bashing?" She nods. "Definitely."

"Do you ever watch monster truck rallies?" I ask.

"I love monster trucks," she says.

"Me too! We should watch together sometime!"

"Totally," she says.

That makes me smile. Sofía used to watch monster trucks with me sometimes to be nice, like I tried to care about birds for her, but smashing and bashing were never really her thing. "What else do you like?" I ask.

She hesitates. "You won't laugh?" When I shake my head, she gets down onto her knees, pulls a shoebox out from under her bed, and opens the lid. "Baseball cards."

I lift one out. It's a picture of a player with facts on the back. "I've seen these at the comic book shop. Are they worth a lot?"

"Nah. I get them when my moms stop at garage sales. They're usually free, because I only collect players nobody remembers."

"Why?"

"Somebody should." She peers down into the box. "I mean, some of these guys didn't get many hits or only played for part of a season. But I think it's sad that nobody wants them. I bet a lot of them were good parents or siblings or friends. You shouldn't just like someone because they're good at sports, right?" She gives me a worried look. "Do you think that's weird?"

I think about my trash collection—how I keep things other people get rid of, to give them another chance. "I don't think it's weird at all."

She gives me that shy smile again. I wonder why I never noticed it before today.

And just like that, I get an Inspiration.

"You collect something," I say. "Something you find."

She closes the lid gently. "So?"

I grin. "So how would you like to join a club?"

Mom is super excited when I ask if Lin can come over for club tomorrow.

"Don't make a big deal out of it," I say. "Please?"

She makes a serious face. "I'll just take care of snacks."

I don't get my hopes up about that. She's a fruit bowl and low-salt popcorn kind of mom. Sometimes, for a special treat, she makes cookies out of oats and seeds and mashed-up fruit and then brags about how you can hardly taste the banana.

You can totally taste the banana.

So when she takes out a carton of chocolate milk and a container of store-bought mini muffins on Saturday morning, I know she must really mean business.

Coach Woo brings Lin over and stays to work on the starting lineup with Mom. Lin is wearing her visor, and she keeps tugging on the bill, looking nervous. While our moms settle in at the kitchen table, I make a big show out of pouring the milk and cracking open the muffins. But when I hold out the container, Lin only takes one.

What the heck? There are three flavors. And they have icing! I grab one of each. "Are you just being polite?" I ask. "Because next time, we'll probably get stuck with fruit."

She grins and grabs two more.

"I'm picking up your team shirts this afternoon," Coach Woo says. "We'll hand them out at the pizza party tomorrow, but do you want a sneak peek?"

I gasp. "We're getting outfits?"

"Uniforms," Lin says.

"Take a look." Coach Woo swipes on her phone and holds up a picture of a plain white T-shirt with the letters *L & M* printed across the back.

My heart sinks. "They're white?"

"What's wrong with white?" she asks. "It's classic."

"It isn't even in the rainbow!" I get an idea. "Could we dye them orange?"

"MacIntosh Floral is orange."

"What about some other color?"

"The fire department is red, Humphrey Landscaping is green. . . ." Coach Woo shakes her head. "I think all the other colors are taken."

"You can make your visors any color you want," Mom suggests.

Lin takes hers off and sets it on the table. "I thought we could decorate them together," she says.

"Cool! Come see my supplies." We polish off our blueberry muffins and chug the last of our milk. Then I lead her into the garage, past lawn games and softball equipment to the bins where I keep my trash collection.

"This is all yours?" she asks.

"The rest is upstairs in my workshop."

She rummages through milk jugs, egg cartons, and toilet paper rolls, then picks up some of the shiny strings I collected from Rosie's pom-poms. "What are you gonna do with these?"

"I don't know yet. Maybe I'll thread them into my hair when we do braids for our game."

Her face falls. "Oh."

I cram the lemon muffin into my mouth. "What?"

She scowls and points to her head.

Oh! Her hair is too short for braids. I guess nobody thought about that.

"Whatever." She kicks at the floor. "I don't care."

But you know what? I'm starting to know her different faces, and I think she *does* care. "Maybe . . ." I reach for her head and stop.

"What?"

I unfasten her clip and lift the hair that falls

across her forehead. "This part might be long enough. Let me try."

I eat my chocolate muffin in two bites and grab a rubber band from one of my bins. Then we go out back, and I have her sit on the edge of the sand tire. Braiding her hair isn't easy. It's short and slippery, and I keep forgetting which section I'm on. But she nibbles on her muffins and sits very still. Sometimes I pull too hard, and she winces a little, but she never complains, even when I have to start over.

"What's with all the bird feeders?" she asks after a while. "They kind of take up the whole yard."

"I know." I get a little squeeze in my chest. "But they remind me of Sofía."

Lin is quiet for a minute. "That's why you sit in the slide for first recess every day, too, right?" she says. "Because it was your place. Yours and hers."

I stop braiding, surprised. "You knew that?"

She shrugs.

I finish the braid and tie the end with the rubber band. When I pin it back with her clip, it makes a pretty frame around her face. "Go look."

She checks her reflection in a window and smiles wide. "Can you do it on game day?"

"Sure."

"I'm here!" Eli comes around the side of the house, carrying a cardboard box. He stops when he sees Lin.

"We said other people could join the club, right?" I ask.

"Right." He looks surprised for a second then nods. "Okay, cool."

I point to the box. "Are those your treasures?"

"Not exactly." He sets down the box in the middle of the sand tire. "Yesterday, I had my rabbits in the tub again, and Mom started vacuuming in the hallway, and Vernon and Stanley got all huddled up. So I looked it up, and it turns out it helps rabbits bond if they get a little stressed out together."

"Really?" I ask.

"I guess. And Vernon gets nervous whenever I take him somewhere, so I thought if I brought them along, maybe . . ." He lifts the lid. Sure enough, Vernon and Stanley are nuzzled together in a corner.

Lin gasps. "Oh my gosh, they're adorable!"

"You can pet them if you want," Eli says. But the look he gives me says, *You can't.*

Seriously? He's the one who brought them to my house!

But he isn't kidding. He even looks a little worried. So I hold up my hands and make sure he sees me stuff them into my pockets.

No rabbit petting here. No sir, not me.

Meanwhile, Lin starts stroking the top of Stanley's head. "Hey, you," she coos. "You're a little cutie pie, aren't you?" She lets him sniff her fingers. Then she picks up little bits of hay and giggles when he munches it out of her hand.

It makes me smile. She's so gentle. And yesterday, she was really sweet with her brother. She doesn't seem like herself at all—or not the way I think of her, anyway.

I like it.

Eli sits back on his heels. "You wanna see something else I learned?"

"Sure," Lin says.

He pulls a banana out of his back pocket, peels it, and mashes a bit between his fingers. Then he smears a glob behind Vernon's ear. Stanley's nose twitches. He nuzzles even closer to Vernon . . . and starts nibbling the banana off him!

"What's he doing?" I ask. It tickles my neck just watching them!

"Grooming him. The banana gives him an extra nudge, but they only groom each other if they're starting to bond."

"I thought rabbits liked carrots," Lin says.

"Not as much as they like bananas." He smears some behind Stanley's ear next. This time it's Vernon's nose that starts to twitch, and pretty soon, he's licking the fruit off Stanley!

We all giggle. Lin looks at me, her eyes shining. A loose hair slips out of her braid, and for the first time, I wonder if maybe there *is* room for someone new in the space Sofía left.

I mean, it's not like Lin is perfect or anything. She can be bossy and snappy and kind of a show-off. But I think back to our last club meeting and realize that sometimes *I'm* those things, too.

Maybe I do want another friend besides Sofía. Maybe I even want it to be Lin.

Then all of a sudden, Stanley nips at Eli.

Lin jumps back. "Did he bite you?"

Eli sits up and rubs his finger a little, looking stunned. "Sort of. I should probably take them home. I think they've had enough for today."

"But you just got here," I say.

"Sorry." He puts the lid back on. "Tell Sofía I'll see her next week, okay?"

Lin and I trade looks as he picks up his box and heads across the grass. But just then Mom comes out the back door, waving her phone.

It's time!

I turn to Lin. "Got your baseball cards?"

She nods and pats her back pocket. I check mine for this week's treasures. When I take the phone and see Sofía's face, it's like a cork pops in my chest, and a bunch of feelings come fizzing up. The missing-her feeling gets sharper, but something in me relaxes, too.

Sofía.

She isn't wearing my hoodie, and her hair is in those pigtails again, but when Lin comes and sits on the sand tire beside me, I don't feel as jealous or as left behind as I did before.

"Who is that?" Sofía asks, squinting at the camera.

Lin scoots in closer, and I hold the phone back so they can see each other. "It's Lin from school."

Sofía looks surprised. "Oh, hi!"

Lin gives a little wave. "Hi, Sofía. Hi, California."

"Eli had to go home," I say, "but Lin wants to join the club, if it's okay with you." I feel so full and happy saying it that I even ask, "Elena's coming, too, right?"

Sofía hesitates. "I thought maybe you didn't want her to."

"It's fine," I say. "Get her."

Maybe it really is okay. Maybe I can finally be happy that they're doing each other's hair and playing on the same team. After all, Lin and I are doing those things, too. Sofía will be happy for *me*. I'm sure she will. And just because I wore my hoodie almost every day doesn't mean she has to. She has other clothes, too, just like we both have other friends.

I smile at Lin as Sofía calls to Elena. "That's her cousin," I explain. "It's Elena's turn to be president, but you can do it next."

Lin pulls the baseball cards out of her back pocket. "Okay."

There's a tumble of movement as Elena settles in. Then the screen goes still, and I gasp.

No. I squeeze my eyes shut. *Let it be a filter. Please, please don't let it be real.*

But when I look again, I see Elena, clear as anything.

And she's wearing my rainbow hoodie.

The rainbow colors seem to explode through the screen. It feels like they're burning my eyes.

"Why is she wearing that?" I ask, my voice tight.

Sofía smiles. "We traded for the day." She shows us the T-shirt she has on. It's a marbled design in black and white—the exact opposite of rainbow. "Do you like it?"

I feel my throat closing. "Don't you have to wear your soccer jerseys?"

"We don't have a game today," Elena says.

I can't stop staring at those rainbow stripes, each color blending into the next. The hoodie is supposed to remind Sofía of me. I sent it all the way across the country with her, even though it was my favorite thing in the world.

Is it just another shirt to her? Are we still best friends? *Can* we be when she's so far away?

Hurt flares inside me, bright and hot like a sparkler. "I gave that to you," I say. "You're not supposed to pass it around to just anyone."

Sofía's eyes widen. "Elena isn't just anyone. She's my best friend here."

I clutch the edge of the sand tire. Her best friend? What am I?

"Are you okay?" Lin asks quietly.

I'm not okay. My head is spinning, and my stomach is squeezing, and the sparkler inside feels like it's spraying tiny flames that prick and burn. "Start the meeting," I mutter.

Elena glances at Sofía then hits something against the railing of the balcony. *Clang, clang, clang!*

I flinch.

"Order, order," Elena says. "The Finders Keepers Club is now in session. First up, snacks."

Sofía holds up two crinkly, pink rolls. "We brought conchas."

I feel a new shock at that. We used to eat those at her house on Friday afternoons, just the two of us. I look again at Elena, eating my snacks, wearing my hoodie, taking my place at Sofía's side.

All this time, I've been worried I'd forget Sofía. But she's the one forgetting *me*.

And all at once, the flame inside me blazes so hot and wild that I feel like I'm shooting sparks. "Well, Lin and I already had snacks," I snap. "We had chocolate milk and muffins from the store—three kinds, with icing. Because this is our first playdate here."

"Oh," Sofía says. "Cool."

Cool? Doesn't she care?

I keep going. "But it's not our first playdate ever. We had one yesterday, too." I look right at Sofía. "On Friday."

She frowns a little but says nothing.

Elena looks back and forth between us. "Treasures next?" she asks.

"Lin has treasures," I say. "And they're way better than birds or soccer moves or sea glasses." I give her a nudge. "Show them."

She doesn't answer. When I turn, she's shaking her head, clutching her baseball cards so tightly they're starting to bend.

"*Show* them," I say again.

She looks at me, blinking fast. Then she gets up and hurries away.

What the heck? "Where are you going?" I yell. "Come back!"

But she doesn't stop. She runs across the yard, smacking bird feeders out of her way.

"What's going on?" I hear Sofía ask.

"I gotta go." I end the call and weave through the jugs to chase after Lin. "What's the matter?" I shout.

She whirls around to face me. "Did you invite me here to make Sofía mad?"

I pull back. "What? No!"

But her face is a crinkled mix of anger and hurt. "I never asked to join your dumb club, you know."

I feel that like a slap. Didn't she want to come? Don't *either* of them want me?

I draw myself up straighter. "Well, I only went to your house because my mom made me. She thought we were friends."

"We're *not*," Lin says.

I suck in a breath. We're not?

But we did art together. We jumped on her trampoline. I braided her hair!

She stuffs the bent-up cards into her pocket. "I only hung out with you to practice softball," she says, "and it didn't even help."

I feel my chest getting hot. "I can hit a little."

"You can't catch."

"I can too!"

"Prove it."

Lin stomps into the garage and comes back with a bucket of balls. She tosses me my mitt, but I drop it. She snorts.

The heat spreads from my chest to my cheeks. I grab my glove, wheel around, and tromp across the grass.

"Not there," she says. "The jugs are in the way."

I move to a new spot, then another, but the bird

feeders get in between us no matter where I stand. "Just try," I say.

She throws. The ball smacks a jug and sends it whirling.

"We have to take them down," she says, reaching for one.

"I'm not moving them!"

She shakes her head and picks up another ball. "Fine." For a split second, as she winds up, a breeze blows all the feeders to the side, and I can see her clearly. Then she throws, the jugs drop between us again, and I lose the ball until I feel it sail past my ear.

"You said you could catch," Lin snaps. "So catch." She throws again.

Bang! The ball hits a feeder. She fires another.

I reach out at random and feel it nick the tip of my glove.

"Watch the ball," she taunts, launching another one.

I jump out of the way.

"Get in front of it," she says.

"I'm trying!"

She lowers her glove, disgusted. "This is stupid," she says. "You can't even see it."

I grit my teeth. I'll show her. *Down and ready. Eye on the ball.* I raise my mitt and say, "Just throw it."

"But you can't—"

"I said throw it!"

Lin glares at me. She winds up, her jaw set.

For a split second, as the jugs spin, I see the ball careening toward me. Then—

CLUNK!

"Ouch!" I touch my forehead and sway on my feet. When I look at Lin, she's staring at me, eyes wide, a hand over her mouth.

"Are you okay?" she asks, taking a step toward me.

Before I can answer, I feel a big throb between my ears and drop to my knees.

"Coach Zee!" Lin cries. "Coach Zee, come quick!"

The last thing I see is Lin knocking over the bucket of balls as she runs for my house.

I hear the back door smack open and Mom's voice, high and sharp. "Meena?" I open my eyes and see her running over. She kneels next to me.

"I missed the ball," I say.

"Yeah, well, it didn't miss you. Can you sit up?" When I do, my head starts to pound. I moan. "Easy does it now," Mom says.

For a few seconds, the trees seem to swirl around me, and the edges of the world get dark. Then everything gets still and bright again. I take a breath.

Dad is hurrying through the grass now. "Hey there, ace." He presses an ice pack to my forehead, and pain shoots all the way down to my toes. "That's quite a goose egg you've got there."

"A what?"

He taps his own forehead. "A lump."

I touch the throbbing spot on my head and feel a big bump. "Whoa. The ball did that?"

"Looks like it."

I'm dizzy when I get to my feet, but I can walk. I brace myself to face Lin telling me everything I did wrong, but when we get inside, the kitchen is empty. "Where's Lin?" I ask.

"Her mom is taking her home," Dad says.

I glance out the front window in time to see them pulling away. She didn't even say she was sorry!

I slump into a chair. Lin's visor is still on the table. I scowl at it.

"Are you okay?" Dad asks, touching my shoulder.

I press the ice pack against my forehead and nod, but I'm not sure which hurts more, my head or my heart. "You don't have to stare at me," I tell him.

Dad starts to clear our snack dishes. Mom is already clicking on her computer across from me. After a few minutes, she leans over and peers into my eyes.

"What are you doing?" I ask.

"Checking to see if your pupils are the same size. How's your vision?"

I look around. "Same as always."

"Do you feel sleepy at all?"

"No."

"Does your head still hurt?"

I poke at my lump. "It does when I touch it."

She checks her screen again. "Well, I hope you don't have a concussion. You didn't lose consciousness, and so far you haven't thrown up or had a seizure." She tilts her head. "What about an absence seizure? Do you feel like you had one of those?"

"The space-out kind?" I shake my head. "I don't think so."

Mom closes her computer. "Then I'm not going to rush you to urgent care, but I'll call and check in with your doctor." She gets up, her eyes resting on my forehead. "Just stay where we can see you today."

Dad winks. "And don't take any more balls to the head."

For the rest of the day, Mom and Dad are pretty jumpy. They give me extra cuddles and peek through doorways at me, just like they did after my first seizure.

I keep checking Mom's phone. I'm positive Sofía will send a message to ask what happened. Or maybe Lin will check to see if I'm okay. I could be in the hospital, for all she knows, getting stitches or X-rays or a brain transplant.

But Mom's phone stays dark all afternoon.

I don't want to think about it. So I decide to decorate my visor instead. I grab it off the hook and get out my yogurt lids. Then I spot Lin's visor on the table again. She won't have a chance to decorate it before our pizza party tomorrow, I realize.

Serves her right.

A whole conversation starts in my head.

Nice Me: Maybe you should give it back.

Mad Me: What for? She hit me in the head!

Nice Me: She didn't mean to.

Mad Me: But she said we're not even friends!

Nice Me: You didn't tell her you wanted to be.

I pick up Lin's visor and trace my finger along the bill. I didn't tell her. Not exactly. But I invited her to our club and helped with her painting and did her hair. Isn't that the same thing?

I give my head a shake. Then I grab her visor and hang it up behind my jacket so Mom won't see it and get any ideas.

From now on, I'm only thinking about my own visor. I run my fingers through the pile of foil disks. Then I turn them all face up, separate them by color, and start cutting them into smaller shards, waiting for Inspiration.

Suddenly, the back door slams open, and my nice little piles scatter like leaves.

"Hey," I cry as Rosie stomps into the kitchen. "You're messing up my supplies."

She kicks off her shoes and sends them sailing against the wall. *Bang! Bang!*

"What's the matter with you?" I ask.

She smacks Pink Pony onto the table. "Roger is the matter."

I roll my eyes. "You mean your best friend in the whole wide world?"

"He's not my friend! I'm never playing with him again!"

I lower my scissors. "Geez, what happened?"

"He called me a bossy boss." She plops down in a chair. "And a pony hog."

I grin. "Was he mad, or was he trying to be funny?"

"He was mad that I wouldn't let him be Pink Pony." She kicks the leg of the table. "But I'm mad too! We used to make the ponies skate and go on picnics, but he never does what I tell him to anymore."

"What does he want the ponies to do?"

She makes a face. "Crash cars. Fight monsters. Go skydiving."

Huh. Roger sounds like my kind of kid. "So why don't you?"

"They don't do any of those things in the show."

"Well, who says you have to play like the show? Just take turns."

"You don't." Her lip quivers. "You never play ponies with me unless they do what you want, even though they're *mine*."

I shift in my seat. "That's different."

"And now I finally have someone to play my way, and he won't."

I glance at Rosie's necklace and finger the matching one around my neck. I made them to remind us that we're not just sisters. We're friends, too. And we're supposed to look out for each other.

Okay, fine. I made them to remind me.

I let out a big breath, pick up Pink Pony, and twist her tail around my finger. "You know who you two remind me of?" I ask.

"Who?"

"Vernon and Stanley."

"Eli's rabbits?"

"Uh-huh. One minute they're getting along, and then all of a sudden, *whamo!* Somebody bites."

Rosie looks a little guilty.

"It's okay," I say. "Eli says it's like that when two rabbits are becoming friends."

"You and Sofía don't get into fights."

I wince. "We're kind of in a fight right now."

Rosie's eyes go wide. "You're not friends anymore?"

"I *think* we are, it's just . . ." I scratch the back of my neck. "I guess nobody gets along all the time. That doesn't mean you stop trying."

She crosses her arms. "Well, Roger shouldn't call me names."

I nod. "You should tell him that."

She jumps up and turns toward the door.

"Hang on." I grab the tail of her shirt. "Are you gonna tell him anything else?"

"Like what?"

"Like anything *you're* sorry for?"

She slumps back down and kicks the legs of her chair.

I brush hair away from her forehead. "Like maybe if you've been a teeny, tiny bit of a pony hog?"

She hangs her head.

"What do you want more?" I ask. "To take

turns letting Roger pick, or to get every pick all by yourself?"

"Every pick with Roger," she grumbles.

"Now you're being a stubborn bunny." I poke her in the side.

She smirks and swats at my hand.

"Aren't you?" I start to tickle her. "Aren't you being a stubborn bunny?"

She giggles and squeals until I let her catch her breath. "I'm a nice bunny," she says.

"What would a nice bunny do?"

She sighs and gets up. "Talk to Roger."

"Okay." I hand her Pink Pony, feeling a twinge in my heart. "He's your best friend, isn't he?"

She looks up at me with big eyes. "He's only one of them."

Something inside me goes soft then. I pull Rosie into a hug and hold on tight—my own sister. "The next time we play ponies, it's your turn to pick, okay, squirt? The next bunch of times."

She squeezes me back for a minute then runs out the door.

The rest of my foil shards flutter to the floor. I look out the window and watch her go to Roger, still sitting in the sand tire. At first, he seems stiff and grumpy, his arms crossed.

Then Rosie holds out Pink Pony to him. His face lights up. And the next thing I know, they're giggling and dive-bombing ponies into the sand, one color after another. It makes me smile all the way down to my toes.

I thought everything was so easy for those two. But I guess even Rosie and Roger need practice. Maybe everyone does. Maybe that's how you get good at being friends with new people.

And just like that, I think of the hurt look on Lin's face when she stormed out of club today, and I feel a nip in my stomach. I know she was mean to me. But I guess I was mean too—to everyone at our club. And Lin might have clunked me in the head, but I'm the one who wouldn't move the bird feeders. I'm the one who told her to throw.

Maybe our fight was a teeny, tiny bit my fault too.

I turn away from the window and see my colorful foils scattered all over the floor. Then I start scooping them up.

Because I finally have my Inspiration.

When Mom and I get to Lin's house for the pizza party on Sunday, girls are already chasing each other up and down the stairs. The baby gates are gone, and Ms. Hoye is setting Gilbert in the middle of his own personal playland.

"What is that thing?" I ask.

"An exercise saucer," says Ms. Hoye.

"Like for baby workouts?"

"Pretty much."

Gilbert spins around, batting at little toys that are attached in a circle around him.

"I think he likes it," I say.

"Lin did, too." Ms. Hoye smiles. "It was the only thing that kept her in one place long enough for me to make a sandwich—until she figured out how to climb out of it, that is."

Coach Woo comes in the front door just as Jada and Hailey thunder past. "Outside, everyone," she calls, setting down an armload of pizza boxes. "Hey, Meena. How's the head?"

I whip off my visor to show her. The lump is sort of blue in the middle now with a circle of red around it. "Cool, huh?"

She nods. "Very impressive. Nice visor, too."

"Thanks!" It wasn't easy gluing all those shards into rainbow stripes, but I love how the foils sparkle. "I brought Lin's visor. Is she in the back?"

"Yep, head on out," Coach Woo says. "We'll be there in a minute."

It seems like the whole team tumbles through the door at once. I follow everyone outside and spot Lin at her pitchback net. While the other girls start jumping on her trampoline, hammering on her punching bag, and taking turns on her zip line, Lin keeps throwing and catching by herself. When I'm sure she's not looking, I step up to the picnic table, find her softball-shaped name tag, and set her visor right next to it.

I hope she likes it. Her hat is just as colorful as mine, but I arranged the foil shards in a spiral across the brim. I'm pretty proud of both of them, but I'm not gonna lie: Lin's is my favorite. I hope when she sees it, she'll know I'm sorry for yesterday. I hope she'll apologize, too, and we can be friends after all.

Mom and Coach Woo bring the pizza out then. Everyone crowds around the table and finds their spots. While we fill plates, we *ooh* and *aah* over each other's visors—which is very team-spirity of us, if you ask me. All the visors are pretty cool. Hailey covered hers in stickers. Jada glued a big fake rose to the side. Even Brooklyn and Avery wrote their names across the bills in puffy paint.

But if there were a prize for best visor, Lin's would totally win.

Not that it's a contest or anything.

She's still throwing at the pitchback net, though. "Lin! Come and eat," Coach Woo finally calls. Lin glances over but throws three more strikes before dropping her glove and heading over. I watch while she gets a slice of pizza, finds her spot . . . and goes still. For a long moment, she just stands there, staring. I hold my breath.

Then she picks up her visor and pulls it on.

Yes! I smile wide, waiting for her to look at me.

But she doesn't. She doesn't apologize, either. She doesn't say anything all afternoon, not even when we play sports charades, and I'm sure she knows the answers. And when we huddle up for our team cheer at the end of the party, I can tell she's only mouthing the words. She moves her lips without even looking at me, like she's making a point.

But why? Is she still mad at me? I'm the one with a goose egg!

It's only when Mom asks Coach Woo to get our team shirts that Lin suddenly blurts out, "No!"

Everyone turns.

"We'll bring them on game day," Lin says, her cheeks turning pink.

Coach Woo looks surprised. Mom seems confused, but she shrugs and says, "Tuesday it is. See you all then!"

Lin practically sprints into the house.

We might have matching visors, but it doesn't even feel like we're on the same team.

Over the next two days, the lump on my head turns purple with a yellow ring around it. I spend one whole recess showing it off and letting kids poke it. Otherwise, I sit in the slide.

Now that our first game is almost here, I'm really starting to dread it. I just know I'll strike out or drop a fly ball or let a grounder slip between my legs. I'll probably do all three.

It's bad enough making mistakes in practice. I don't want to do it in front of a crowd!

I'm so nervous when game night arrives that I can't even think of anything fancy to do for our team-spirit hair. I grab a handful of colorful rubber bands from my supply bin but just do two quick braids on our way to the field. Dad sings "Take Me Out to the Ballgame" while he drives. Rosie shakes her pom-poms next to me. Mom scribbles on a clipboard in the front seat.

"I've been thinking, Meena," she says, turning around. "You're a rookie out there, and your control of the ball is still . . . improving."

I frown. That sounds like a new way of saying that I'm bad.

"So I'd like you to wear a batting helmet tonight."

"I do."

"But only when you bat."

I stare at her. "You want me to wear it in the *field*?"

Dad glances at her. "Did the doctor recommend that?"

She hesitates. "It just seems like a good idea."

"But I'll be the only one," I say.

"I'm sure nobody will notice."

"Of course they'll notice. They'll think I look silly!"

"They'll think you look safe."

I groan. "See, this is why I didn't want you to coach. You make such a big deal out of every little thing."

"Little?" Mom sits up straighter. "You call traumatic brain injury little? Listen, kiddo. You've already got a neurological condition. I'm not risking a concussion, too."

Dad glances at her. "Do we know for sure that helmets prevent concussions?"

"I mean, it depends." She looks away. "The science is a little fuzzy on that."

"Then why do I have to wear one?" I demand.

"Because it'll make me feel better, okay?" Mom's eyes are flashing now. "I'm not sending you out there to get clobbered. We've been through enough!"

I cross my arms. "Then I quit."

Her eyes go wide. "You what?"

"The team doesn't need me. Some of them don't even like me. I'm the worst one out there."

"But it's game day!"

I slouch down in my seat. "Please . . . I don't want to play."

Mom shakes her head. "No way. You made a commitment to your team."

"But—"

She holds up her hand. "And I didn't become a coach only to have my own daughter quit on opening day."

As soon as we're parked, I get out and slam the door. Then I stomp into the dugout and feel even worse. Everyone's team-spirit hair is better than mine. Jada's mini braids are capped off with clicky white beads. Brooklyn and Avery have matching fishtail braids. Sadie has her hair braided into a circle that looks like a crown. They all crowd around as Coach Woo strides into the dugout and opens a big cardboard box.

"It took some doing," she says, reaching inside, "but as long as our team shirts were white, Lin figured why not do—"

I gasp. "Rainbow!"

The shirt Coach Woo holds up is a bright burst of tie-dye. When she flips it around, our team initials stand out in bold black: *L & M*.

She starts checking the tags and handing the shirts out, each more colorful than the other. When she tosses one to me, I stare at the rainbow in my hand. It's like the hoodie I gave Sofía but crisp and new, the tie-dye in a spiral instead of stripes.

It's like the hat I made for Lin.

I look around. Lin is standing just outside the dugout. She looks worried, chewing on the tip of her water bottle. Her hands are sort of grayish purple—from the dye, I realize.

Then suddenly her eyes flick to meet mine, and I realize . . .

This is her apology, like decorating her visor was mine.

I pull the shirt on over my tank top. The smallest size is still pretty big on me, but it feels good to be covered in rainbows again. And when I glance around at the other girls in our matching shirts and braids, I see that we finally look like a team.

Maybe I do want to play.

But hang on. I turn back to Lin. She doesn't have a braid.

I take a big breath and step toward her. "Do you still want me to do your hair?" I ask.

She looks down and shrugs. "I don't care." But she's making that face—the one that means she does care but doesn't want to show it.

"Come on," I say.

While everyone else goes to warm up, we hide behind the bleachers and get to work. Her long swoop of hair seems more slippery than before, and for a while, I can't keep hold of it. "Darn it," I mutter after a few tries.

Lin stiffens. "You don't have to do it if you don't want to."

"I want to," I say.

Her shoulders relax a little. Then she opens her sport bottle and squirts water on her head. "Try it now."

And you know what? It's way easier to braid wet hair! In a couple of minutes, I'm finished. And when she puts her visor back on, I can still see the braid peeking out the top. "How do I look?" she asks.

I nod. "Like part of the team."

Mom calls everyone into the dugout. Grace is in the pitching circle, warming up. MacIntosh Floral is getting ready to bat in their bright orange shirts. The ump leans against the fence while families fill the bleachers and lounge in lawn chairs.

Then Mom starts reading from her clipboard. "Starting lineup: First base, Brooklyn. Second base, Lin." She rattles off the whole team until I hear, "Right field, Meena." We huddle together for our team cheer. Then the circle breaks up, and I grab my glove. If I can just slip out of here before Mom sees me, maybe she won't—

"Meena Zee!"

Oh, no.

She strides over, lifts off my visor, and squishes a batting helmet onto my head. Sadie gasps. Brooklyn smirks. Avery stops strapping on her catcher's gear to stare.

I give Mom a pleading look. "Please," I whisper. "I'll keep my eye on the ball."

She shakes her head. "I'm not risking it. Hustle out." Then she and the other coaches head to the plate to confer with the ump.

The dugout starts to empty. Brooklyn wraps her knuckles against my helmet—*knock, knock, knock.* "Nice gear, Flash."

I clench my fists and watch her strut to first base. Then I pull off the helmet and throw it against the fence.

"What are you doing?" I turn to see Lin standing behind me.

I plop down on the bench and cross my arms. "I'm not playing."

Her eyes go wide. "You have to."

"I don't have to do anything."

The helmet spins slowly in the dirt. Lin shifts from one foot to the other. "But my mom said Carmen is sick."

"So?"

"So there are only nine of us here. We can't field eight. If you don't play, we have to forfeit."

I stare at her.

"If you don't play, we lose."

"Play ball," the ump calls.

My eyes sting. "We might lose anyway," I say. "And if I strike out or drop the ball . . . then it will be my fault."

"At least give us a chance," Lin says.

My lip starts to quiver. "I'm the worst one out there. I can't be the only one in a helmet, too."

Lin is quiet for a few seconds. Then she takes off her visor, grabs a helmet from the rack, and puts it on. "Then you won't be." She grabs my helmet out of the dirt and tosses it to me.

I catch it in the air.

"Ready?" she asks.

I blink back tears, take a big breath, and nod.

She nods back.

Then we take the field.

A few things I notice at my first-ever softball game: Nobody sells hot dogs, sets off fireworks, or shoots a single T-shirt out of a cannon.

But the chalk lines are crisp and fresh. The fans cheer for both teams. And you know what? Other kids drop the ball sometimes, too.

I spend most of the game sweating under my helmet in right field, hoping the ball doesn't come to me.

I also strike out. Twice.

But I cheer for Grace when she gets behind in the pitch count. I give Sadie a high five after she fields a grounder. I yell things like, "We've got this," and, "Any base!" Even though we lose by one run, Lin doesn't look mad when we do our team cheer at the end.

Still, I'm surprised to find her waiting by the playground door after lunch on Wednesday. She holds up a pair of softball gloves, like she's asking a question.

I don't want to tell her no—not if she actually wants to play with me again. But I don't want her to get her hopes up either. "I'm not getting any better," I warn her.

"Says who?"

"I'm at the bottom of the batting order. I'm stuck in right field. And the last time I tried to catch a ball, I almost got a concussion."

She shrugs. "So you need more practice."

I give her a doubtful look.

"Hey, if I can tie-dye," she says, "anything is possible."

I laugh. "I can't believe you did a craft on purpose."

"Yeah, it took me a while," she says as we cross the grass. "The kit came with only three dyes, and I kept trying to keep them separate, like with my painting. But it turns out you have to mix the colors if you want the whole rainbow."

When we make it to the other side of the playground, she hands me a mitt. "So catching is like batting," she says. "You have to keep your eye on the ball."

"Eye on the ball," I repeat.

"It doesn't matter if it's in the air or on the ground. Stay in front of it, watch it all the way into your glove, and then trap it with your other hand."

"Got it."

She jogs away from me and turns. "Nice and easy now. Ready?"

"Ready."

She makes a gentle underhand toss.

But as soon as the ball starts to arc toward me, I panic. I yelp and cover my head with both arms until the ball thumps to the ground.

When I open my eyes, Lin is giving me a funny look. "Okay, um . . ." She scratches the back of her neck. "So you took your eye off the ball."

I finger the lump on my forehead. It's not as big as it was, but when I press on it, it still hurts. "I'm scared it'll hit me."

"It won't if you catch it."

And I want to catch it. I want Lin to be glad we're on the same team.

But Mom is wrong. We're not alike. Lin isn't afraid of anything.

"All right, try this," Lin says, punching her glove. "Hold up your—"

"I can't." I pick up the ball and lob it back to her. "I'm sorry. I don't want to get hurt again."

Lin doesn't look for me at our last recess. After school, Eli gives a quick wave before hurrying off to his rabbits. Rosie and Roger are running races in the yard when I get home. For a minute, I think about joining them, but I don't want to barge in.

I glance up at the empty window in the house next door. I'm glad Rosie has a new friend. She deserves one. I just wish there were someone for me, too.

When I head inside, Mom isn't working on her computer like usual. She's sitting at the kitchen table, rubbing her softball glove with a yellow sponge. "What are you doing?" I ask.

"Oh, just cleaning this old thing. It's been a while." I almost ask if I can call Sofía to apologize for our last meeting, but then I remember the time difference again and plop down across from Mom.

"Still mad at me about the helmet?" she asks.

I pick up the little bottle of leather cleaner and shrug with one shoulder.

"I wouldn't blame you," she says. "I'm sorry I made you wear it."

I sit up straighter. "You are?"

"It wasn't my most rational decision."

"Then why did you do it?"

Mom flips over the glove and starts rubbing the sponge on the other side. "For the same reason I keep such a close eye on you in the pool. Because I want to protect you. I can't always keep things from hurting you, and sometimes I shouldn't, but . . ." She sighs. "You've been through so much this year."

She's right. A few months ago, I didn't know I had epilepsy, and I never dreamed my best friend would move away. But then I look at the crinkle in Mom's forehead and the way she's scrub, scrub, scrubbing that glove, and I realize . . .

I'm not the only one who's been through a lot. The things that hurt me hurt her, too.

And maybe sometimes getting hurt makes you scared—scared enough to make your kid wear a helmet in the field.

Or to refuse to play catch with someone who's trying to be your friend.

I think of Lin, holding out that glove to me at recess, and my stomach starts to pinch.

"Anyway," Mom says, tossing the sponge onto the table, "I hope I didn't ruin softball for you. I used to love playing." She looks sad then. "And I wanted to spend time with you."

And suddenly, instead of Lin, it's my mom I picture holding out a glove to me. I remember the look on her face when she gave me her old mitt. She didn't decide to coach so she could boss me around, I realize.

She wanted to play with me.

I reach for her hand. "I want to spend time with you, too," I say. "Maybe after dinner, we could practice a little."

She looks up, surprised. "Really?"

I smile. "It'll be fun."

She laughs, her eyes full of tears. "I'd love that."

"But right now," I say, "I know it's only Wednesday, but I was wondering . . ." I get up and rock back on my heels. "Can I have a playdate?"

"There's fruit in the bowl if you're hungry."

I give Lin a look as Mom slips on her gardening gloves and heads outside. "I told you it's not all chocolate milk and muffins around here."

She smiles and looks around nervously.

"Come on. Let's make something." I lead her into the garage and wave toward my storage bins. "Anything you want."

She cringes. "I don't have any ideas."

"Then we'll wait for Inspiration."

We stare into the bins for a long time, until Lin gives me a sly look and says, "Anything?"

"Yep."

She grabs two milk jugs and the rest of my yogurt lids plus a couple of sacks from our beanbag toss. "Scissors?" she asks. We head back to the kitchen, and I find her a pair. She cuts the bottom off her jug and hands them back. "Now you."

After I cut my jug open, she shows me how to hold it by the handle so the big hole is on top. "Catch," she says, lobbing a beanbag into the air.

I don't even think. I reach my jug out and let

the beanbag drop right into it. "Cool!" I toss it back. It makes a nice scratchy sound as it thumps into Lin's scoop. "Now let's decorate them."

I use the foils to make rainbow stripes that match my hat. Lin makes a rainbow swirl to match hers, and I'm not gonna lie: It's a little messy and she uses too much glue, but her art has come a long way! Pretty soon, we're back on our feet, tossing the beanbag across the table and catching it in our scoops. We get another bag going then and try to keep them in the air at the same time. One goes sideways, but I lunge and snag it with my scoop before it hits the floor.

"Nice," Lin says. "Next time, move your body in front of it so you're not reaching."

Hang on.

I catch the other bag in my jug and stop. "Did you just trick me into playing catch?"

She grins. "I'm the guest. I get to pick what we do."

"But—"

"And you can't get hurt." She throws the other beanbag right at her own head! It bounces off and lands on the table.

I grin. And the next thing I know, we're shrieking and laughing and pummeling each other with beanbags. Lin runs to the other side of the kitchen and holds up a bag. "Watch it all the way into the scoop," she says.

I bend my knees a little and lock my eyes on the bag as it arcs through the air. It flips like a pancake as I step forward and watch it drop right into my scoop. *Swish!*

Lin grabs a grapefruit from the fruit bowl and lobs it to me next. She tosses an orange. She throws an apple overhand. Fruit flies back and forth across the kitchen—harder, faster, squishier—until suddenly Mom is calling, "Whoa, whoa, whoa!"

The grapefruit hits Lin in the chest and drops to the floor.

Mom points to the back door. "Take it outside, you two."

We clamber out the door just as Rosie and Roger run in. "Come on," Lin says. "Let's try it with gloves." She ducks into the garage and comes back with two mitts and a tennis ball.

I take a step back. "There isn't room."

"You've got this whole yard."

But the bird feeders are still dangling all around us, twirling, taking up space. I give her a pleading look.

Her face falls. "Can we go around front?"

"I'm not allowed to play by the street."

"Can we take down a few?" she asks. "We

could put them back when we're done."

I bite my lip and look away.

We're both quiet.

"Come on, Meena, please?" Lin says, holding out a glove.

I shake my head. "I can't. I made them—"

"—for Sofía. Yeah." She kicks the side of the sand tire. "She was always nice to me, you know. But whenever you were in the slide together, you were the one who wouldn't let me in. Now she's gone, and you still won't."

She turns and stalks across the grass.

"Hey," I call after her. "We're having a play-date! You can't go play by yourself!"

She throws down the gloves. "Don't worry. I'm used to it."

20

Lin disappears behind the house. When I peek around the corner, she's hitting the ball against the garage. It smacks the big door and bounces on the driveway, then she slaps it back, like she did that day at recess. I hear her counting under her breath. "One . . ." *Smack, bounce.* "Two . . ." *Smack, bounce.* "Three . . ."

I stomp away. If she wants to play alone, then fine. See if I care.

I slump onto the sand tire. I do care. That's the problem.

Leaves rustle in the trees above me. The feeders sway and spin in the breeze. You'd think birds would flock to our whole yard, but they usually stick to the rainbow jug by the garden. Maybe they're leaving space for Rosie and Roger.

But the birds might start feeding from my other jugs, right? I mean, you never know. And seeing them makes me feel like I'm saving a spot for Sofía, the same way I used to save her a seat at lunch. It's the reason I don't want anyone sitting at her desk. It's why I still spend one recess inside the tube slide every day.

But she isn't coming back. I get a sinking feeling in my stomach. I can save all the space I want for her, but it'll stay empty.

What if I let someone else fill it? Would that mean one friend is as good as another—that Sofía isn't special to me? I twirl my bracelet around my wrist, wondering until my head and my heart both hurt. Then I scuffle into the house.

The kitchen is empty, the fruit back in its bowl. The grapefruit looks bruised and dented now—like the lump on my forehead turned inside out. On the counter next to it, Mom's phone lights up. It's a notification from Sofía's dad. When I tap on it, a picture fills the screen: Sofía, smiling with a bunch of kids in soccer uniforms.

My chest tightens. It doesn't seem like she's saving any space for me. She looks busy and cheerful, like she's part of a team.

I want to be happy for her. I'm trying to be. But I miss her too. I still wish she were here. I want to reach into the photo and drag her back. For a few seconds, my finger hovers over the screen.

Then I tap.

The phone makes a *dee-doo* sound. Then Sofía's face flickers onto the screen, so real and close that I catch my breath. "I thought that might be you," she says. "Did you get my picture?"

I nod. "Where are you?"

"I just got home from school."

Home. The word makes my skin prickle.

"What are you doing?" she asks.

I sigh. "I'm supposed to be having a playdate with Lin."

Sofía's face goes so still that for a few seconds, I think the screen has frozen. But then she says, "Oh," in a quiet voice. "Where is she?"

"Outside. We're kind of in a fight. But she started it," I add quickly.

"What happened?"

I pick up Mom's glove and slip it on. "It's just that she wants everything her way, and she's always getting her feelings hurt, and—"

Sofía gives me a faint smile.

"What?"

"She reminds me of someone else."

"You sound like my mom." I look at the hollow palm of the glove—soft and worn from use. "Can I ask you something?"

"Yeah."

I meet her eyes. "Do you like your new home better than you like it here?"

She looks thoughtful. "I like some things better. The ocean. Being so close to my cousins. I like that we can go to church in Spanish and have big family get-togethers all the time."

"Do you miss anything?"

Her expression softens. "I miss Eli's chickens. And the desks at school. They use tables here, so I don't get my own little compartment anymore. I miss all the grass, too. Our whole playground is concrete. It's good for four-square and jump rope, but I fell when we were playing tag the other day, and look."

She pushes a sleeve up and shows me a scrape on her arm, red and raw. I wince.

Her face gets sad then. "But I miss the people most of all. Eli and Rosie and Mrs. D. And you. Especially you." She blinks fast. "When I'm not mad at you, I mean."

I feel a big whoosh of shame at that. "Is that why you don't wear my hoodie?"

She looks surprised. "I do wear it. I wore it every day at first. But sometimes . . ." She takes a big breath. "Sometimes it makes me miss you too much."

I think of the bird feeders out back. They make me miss her. Isn't that a good thing?

"And when Elena wears it . . ." She meets my eyes again and shrugs. "It kind of feels like having you here."

I trace the worn lacing of the glove with my

finger. "Lin made us tie-dyed shirts," I say, "but they don't make me feel like you're here." I shake my head. "Lin is nothing like you."

"She is in one way," Sofía says. "She wants to be your friend."

My eyes sting with tears, and her face goes blurry. "You're my friend."

"You don't have to pick between us. You can be friends with us both."

I blink hard. "Won't that mean our friendship isn't special?"

"It won't mean that to me."

I feel a flash of panic, and my heart starts to beat faster, like something hard and fast and scary is coming at me. I want to cover my head and duck out of the way, because I've been clunked before, and I know how much it hurts.

"But what if—" My voice quivers. "What if I try to be friends with Lin, and it doesn't work out? Or what if it does, and she leaves too?"

Sofía gazes back at me. "I guess that could happen."

I finger the lump on my forehead. No. I should protect myself—put a helmet on right over my heart. It would be safer.

But would it be better? Or would it just hurt in a different way?

I think of sitting alone in the tube slide. I think

of Lin playing handball by herself and calling out games with no other players.

"We're on a softball team together," I say quietly.

"Really?"

I nod. "I wanted to tell you, and then I wanted to keep it secret, and then I sort of . . . forgot. I lost track of a lot of things I was saving up for you." I frown at her. "What if I forget you, too? What if we lose all our memories of each other?"

Her eyes go soft. "Then we'll make more."

I gaze at her through the screen. For a few seconds, the missing-her feeling seems to fill every bit of space inside me. But when I take a big breath and let it out, some of the hurt goes with it. "I want us to have other friends," I say. "But sometimes, I still want it to be just you and me, like right now. Is that okay?"

Sofía smiles. "I'd like that."

I cringe a little then. "I'm sorry I've been so mean to you and Elena. I really am glad you have each other. Will you bring her to club again on Saturday so I can tell her that?"

Sofía nods. "Will you bring Lin, too?"

"I'll try, but I don't know if she'll come." My shoulders sag. "I've been a pretty stubborn bunny."

I hear the ball banging against the garage as soon as I step outside. I circle around the house and stand at the edge of the driveway, where the grass meets the cement.

At first, Lin ignores me. "Three . . ." *Smack, bounce.* "Four . . ." *Smack, bounce.* Then she gives me a side-eye.

"I'm sorry," I say.

"For what?" *Smack, bounce.*

"For picking Sofía instead of you."

She hits the ball harder. "You always did." *Smack, bounce!* "You always will." *Smack, bounce!*

The garage door is clanging so loudly now that my ears are ringing, and I have to shout. "You can't take her place. But the thing is—"

SMACK, BOUNCE! Lin hits the ball harder. *SMACK, BOUNCE!* The door bangs louder. *SMACK, BOUNCE!* She raises her arm.

So I reach in and grab the ball. *Thwap!*

Everything goes quiet. Lin stares at me, her hand paused in midair.

"The thing is," I say again, quietly this time, "Sofía can't take your place either."

For a few seconds, Lin's eyes are bright. Then her expression hardens. "You're only saying that because she's gone."

I suck in a breath. It feels like she's smacking *me* now.

For a second, I want to storm back into the house and leave her out here by herself.

Then I see how stiff and straight she's stand-ing, crossing her arms in front of her like a shield—like something hard and fast is coming at her, and she doesn't want to get hurt.

She's scared too, I realize. Just like I am.

But if you stay away from all the things that could hurt you, then you miss out on a lot of good stuff, too. Like playing catch. And making new friends.

"You and Sofía aren't playing against each other," I say. "You're on the same team. You're both my friends. At least I want you to be."

Lin wipes her eyes on her shoulder and looks away.

I step closer. "But I don't want to squish you into some Sofía-size hole. You have your own shape. I like you that way."

I hold my breath, waiting. What about me? Am I the right shape for her?

Then I see the corners of her lip turn up a little. "Look." She points with her chin.

I follow her gaze to the glove on my hand. The tennis ball is nestled right in the pocket.

"You caught the ball," Lin says.

My jaw drops open. "I caught the ball."

She laughs and gives me a little shove. "I told you you'd get better!"

"You did," I stammer. "And I did!"

For a few seconds, we just stand there grinning at each other. Then she gives me that shy smile I'm starting to know so well. "I want to be your friend too," she says.

A flood of feelings bursts through me: relief, excitement, joy. They blend and mix inside me, swirling like a kaleidoscope and making the whole rainbow. "Then will you help me with something?" I ask. "Since we're friends, I mean."

Lin raises her eyebrows. "Catching or batting?"

I laugh and reach for her hand. "Help me take down some bird feeders."

The whole yard opens up when we take down the jugs. It feels good to make space for other things—and for other people.

We leave the one by the garden, though. It's the busiest feeder anyway. Maybe the birds like it because it's out of the way or because it's covered in rainbows.

I like it because Sofía has the matching jug, on her little balcony in California.

When we're finished, there's plenty of room in the yard to play catch without banging into anything. We throw the tennis ball until I start to get the hang of it. After dinner, I try using a real softball with Mom.

But I don't practice during recesses on Thursday. Lin and I feel like playing kickball instead—as long as we can be on the same team.

I'm a mix of nervous and excited for our next game, like green and yellow making . . . well, greenish yellow.

Aunt Kathy and Eli come to watch. Carmen is back, and Lin is our starting pitcher. She looks very focused, warming up with Dad. Coach Woo looks on from the dugout. Ms. Hoye watches from a lawn chair, bouncing Gilbert in her lap.

When the other team takes the field, we huddle together for our cheer, and then Mom calls out the batting order. "Avery, Brooklyn, Grace, Lin!" Avery picks up a helmet, but when she sees the other pitcher, she stops. "Oh, no."

We all press against the chain-link fence as the girl takes a few practice pitches. She's lean and wiry, and she has a snap like a slingshot.

"Didn't she win the championship game last year?" Grace asks.

Lin nods. "I heard she went to a special pitching camp."

"She throws wild sometimes, though," Brooklyn adds. "My friend said she hit three batters in her last game."

The girl fires in another pitch. The catcher

leaps for the ball, but it smacks against the back-stop. *Clank!*

"Play ball," calls the ump.

Avery shoots Brooklyn a grim look as she steps into the batter's box.

I hold my breath and lace my fingers through the fence.

The first pitch hurtles inside. Avery jumps back. Our whole team gasps.

Mom claps. "Good eye."

But Avery looks spooked after that. She flinches at a ball down the middle and strikes out swinging at an outside pitch. Brooklyn and Grace don't do any better. They step up to the plate like they're walking the plank, and they both strike out.

Three up, three down.

"Hustle out, girls," Mom calls.

I grab my mitt and jog to right field. Lin strikes out the first batter. The second girl pops up to the shortstop. When the next kid steps up to the plate, Lin turns and looks right at me. "She's a lefty, Meena! Be ready!"

I get down low and zero in on the ball, rocking from one foot to the other.

And maybe all that concentrating is like making a wish, because the batter hits a fly ball right to me! I charge forward and watch it drop. *Eye on the ball. Stay in front of it. Trap it in your glove.*

Thwap!

I suck in a breath and stare at my mitt.

Holy homers, I caught it. She's out!

I try to act nice and casual as I jog to the dugout, but it's hard with my team cheering, Rosie jumping up and down, and Lin yelling, "You did it! You did it!" When I turn and look at the bleachers, I even see Eli, pointing his mom's phone at me and grinning. I wave for the camera, my whole body zinging with excitement.

Then the pitcher starts warming up, and everyone gets quiet again. Lin pulls on her batting gloves as she steps into the on-deck circle.

"Are you scared?" I ask her through the fence.

Lin's eyes flick to mine. "Her pitches aren't that fast," she says. "Just her wind-up. Look."

I watch the next pitch and see what she means. The girl's wind-up is a blur of motion, and her release reminds me of a snapping turtle, but when I lock my eyes on the ball, I can track it through the air just fine.

"Batter up!"

I grit my teeth as Lin takes the plate. If anybody can hit against this pitcher, it's her.

The throw: Lin slices her bat through the air. *Ping!* The ball slams into the fence above the catcher.

I clap. "Way to get a piece of it!"

But the next pitch gets a piece of Lin. It slides inside and plunks her right on the shoulder! She winces. Everyone gasps. The ump pulls off his face mask. When Lin nods, he yells, "Take your base."

Our next batters are even more freaked out after that. Yolanda and Hailey strike out flinching. Jada and Sadie lean back from the plate but draw walks. It's two outs now, and the bases are loaded.

I'm the last one to bat.

For a few seconds, as I step up to the plate, I'm almost glad that nobody's gotten a hit, because then it won't seem so bad when I don't.

But then the other coach calls, "Come in closer, outfield," and I feel a spark of anger in my chest. I lift my bat as the outfielders move to the edge of the grass.

Hands together. Eye on the ball. Nice and easy.

The pitcher winds up. She throws. The ball rockets toward me. I feel it breeze past my chin as I swing.

Whiff!

Darn it! I bang my bat against the plate. When she throws again, I swing even harder.

WHIFF!

Voices explode all around me: "Nice pitch!" "One more strike!" "Easy out!"

Another voice taunts in my head even louder: *You're the worst one here.*

But then Lin calls from third base, her voice cutting through all the others. "You've got this, Meena! You can do it!"

I take a deep breath and lock eyes with the pitcher, sweat trickling down my back. I can do it.

She brings her hands together and throws.

I keep my eye on the ball and bring my bat around, nice and easy.

And I don't hit it out of the park. I don't even hit it out of the infield.

But I do make contact. *Tap.*

The ball dribbles to the ground in front of me. The crowd erupts. "Go, go, go!"

I charge for first, my feet pounding the dirt. When I round the base, I see the pitcher and catcher both fumbling for the ball as Lin crosses the plate.

Our dugout goes wild! Lin is jumping up and down like I hit a home run.

Then Avery is strutting up to the plate again, the top of the batting order. "Come on, team," Brooklyn calls from the on-deck circle. "If Flash can hit this girl, anyone can!"

And you know what? I'm not even offended, because I started a rally!

Avery singles. Brooklyn hits into the left field hole. Grace brings me home. But when Lin clears the bases with a drive up the middle, I throw my rainbow hat in the air and cheer louder than anyone.

"That's my friend out there!"

As soon as we finish shaking hands with the other players, Rosie jumps into my arms. "You won! You won!" I lift her off her feet and twirl her around until she shrieks and giggles. Then I run to join my team behind the dugout.

Everyone is jumping up and down and squealing. Even Brooklyn and Avery are slapping hands with the other girls. I look around at all those bright faces. We're ten players—tall and short, bold and shy, with fancy gear and hand-me-down gloves. But we played like a team. As long as we do that, maybe it doesn't matter if we win or lose.

Although winning is pretty great. Lin smiles at me then, and I know she's thinking the same thing.

Mom makes a little speech. Coach Woo goes over a few of our plays. Then we all grab hands across the circle and shout our cheer as loud as we can.

"Now can I call you slugger?" Dad asks as the dugout empties.

I link arms with Lin and look right at Brooklyn. "You can call me Flash."

Brooklyn rolls her eyes and grins.

Eli strolls over from the bleachers then. "Good game, you two," he says.

"Thanks!" Lin taps the bill of my visor. "I taught her everything she knows."

"Did you get a video of my hit?" I ask Eli.

"Nope, sorry," he says.

"But you were pointing the camera right at me!"

"That's because I wasn't alone. Look!" When he lifts the phone to show us, rainbow tie-dye fills the screen.

"Surprise!" a voice says.

I gasp. "Sofía? You were watching?"

"The whole time!" Her forehead crinkles with worry. "Are you okay, Lin? I saw you get hit."

"I'm fine. Do you think it'll bruise?" She pulls up her sleeve and looks eagerly at the red spot.

I peer closer. "I bet it's purple by club day."

"Can we meet at my house?" Eli asks. "We can move Vernon and Stanley into the new hutch."

"Are they ready?" Sofía asks.

"Yep! No bites all week. They even took a nap together."

I squint at him. "You don't mind if I'm around your rabbits?"

"Nah," he says. "Stanley and I are good now."

"How can you tell?"

Eli's ears go a little pink. "He licked banana off my face."

I laugh. "He *what*?"

The rest of Eli reddens. "You're the one who gave me the idea!"

"Me? How?"

"You said Stanley thought you were a giant carrot." He shrugs. "So I made him think I'm a big banana."

Lin starts to giggle. "You did say bananas are their favorite."

I bump my shoulder against Eli's. "They're one of my favorites, too."

He grins.

"Okay, everyone," I say. "Club this Saturday at the Big Banana's!"

Lin pulls the phone a little closer. "Is Elena coming?"

Sofía's face falls. "Yeah, but we can't stay for very long. We have an early game."

"Oh." My heart starts to sink.

But then Lin says, "How about we come and watch?"

We all look at each other. "That's right," I say, perking up. "You came to our game, so we'll go to yours!"

"Yes!" Sofía claps and squeals. "We can be a *fan* club!"

"I wanna join a club." Rosie wedges her way into the circle. "Can I come?"

"Of course you can, squirt," I hug her from behind. "You can even invite Roger."

"Time to go, kids," Mom calls from the parking lot. "School tomorrow."

For a minute, we all press together to wave and shout our goodbyes. Then Sofía's face disappears and a picture of Vernon and Stanley fills the screen. They're curled up together, a sleeping pile of fur that makes even me feel a little melty.

"They're so cute," Lin says, tracing the screen with her finger. "I'm glad they're finally friends."

Eli snorts. "Took them long enough, the stubborn bunnies." He pockets the phone. "See you tomorrow."

Everyone runs across the grass to join their families then. Aunt Kathy puts an arm around Eli. Dad opens the car door for Rosie as Mom lifts the last equipment into the trunk. Lin takes Gilbert by the hand and helps him toddle along between Coach Woo and Ms. Hoye. Watching them all, a plain old one-color feeling spreads through me like sunshine.

Happiness.

I finger the beads of my friendship bracelet. Sofía was my best friend for a long time. And she'll always be special to me. After all, she's one of a kind—like the bright yellow bead in the middle of my bracelet.

But Lin is special, too. So are Rosie and Eli. Each one of them is a color all their own. It feels good to let them mix, though. Lin is right. That's how you get the whole rainbow.

I gaze at the swirl of tie-dye on the back of her jersey. Suddenly, the big black letters on the back of Lin's shirt jump out at me: *L & M*. I suck in a breath.

Our initials. They were there all along, just like she was.

"Hey, Lin," I call after her. "You wanna play during first recess tomorrow?"

She turns around, surprised. "First recess? Are you sure?"

"I'm sure." I smile at my friend. "Let's meet in the slide."

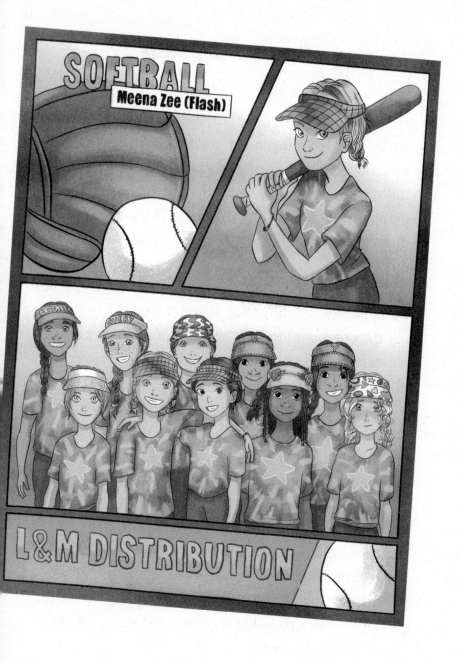

Acknowledgments

I come from a ball-playing family. When I was little, my dad played on a slow-pitch team made up almost entirely of his extended family and a town team that changed its name to match a misprint on their T-shirts. A while later, he and my mom played together on yet another team with our church.

I won't lie. I didn't particularly like going to their games. I thought it was hot and boring, and my parents wouldn't let us buy anything from the concession stand. But in my family, when anyone played, performed, or presented, we *all* showed up.

As we grew, my siblings and I got our own chances to play. Dad coached every one of us while Mom kept the scorebook, made rain-out phone calls, and washed uniforms over and over. My softball career ended after sixth grade, but the biggest thrill of my childhood was a family trip to see the Cubs play at Wrigley Field. It was a six-hour drive—the farthest we ever traveled together. My parents still wouldn't let us get anything from the concession stand, but it was free hat day, and Ron Cey hit a grand slam.

So when I call to mind the many people I have to thank for this book, I think of my family first. Team Manternach, thank you for a lifetime of love and support, in and outside of sports. Team Zanin, I may have been a late recruit, but I've always felt lucky to be one of you!

Thank you to the whole team at Simon & Schuster Books for Young Readers. My lovely editor, Krista Vitola, is unfailingly responsive and kind no matter what else is on her plate. Book designer Tom Daly and illustrator Mina Price have always welcomed input while creating wonderfully vibrant art. Copy editor Beth Adelman caught mistakes I didn't even know I was making.

Thank you to my agent, Emily Mitchell, softball mom and fellow Cubs fan who held my feet to the fire about some of the finer points of the game.

Thank you to writing friends Lizzie Cooke, Jane Kelley, L.M. Klein, Lindsay Lackey, and C.C. Harrington for keeping me connected and motivated in what is otherwise an awfully solitary job.

Thank you to my local Parks and Recreation Department for giving my own kids a place to play and for supplying opportunities for "research" when I needed to refresh my memory.

Thank you to the teachers and readers who continue to welcome me into your classrooms, both virtually and in person. You are the reason I do what I do!

Thank you to Anna Johnson Manternach for answering my questions about athletic injuries and to Erika Edberg Manternach for giving the book a final once-over.

Most of all, thank you to Brian, Amelia, and Mara. You are my All-Star Team, now and always. I love you!

Comedy in Action

Elmer M. Blistein

Comedy

in

Action

Duke University Press
Durham, N. C.   1964

For permission to quote material in copyright I am indebted to many people:

Mr. George Abbott for permission to quote from *Damn Yankees;*

Mr. S. N. Behrman for permission to quote from *Amphitryon 38;*

Mr. Sammy Cahn for permission to quote from his song "The Innocent Standerby" from *High Button Shoes;*

Mr. J. R. Hale for permission to quote from his translation of Machiavelli's *Mandragola;*

Samuel French, Inc. for special permission to reprint the selection from Sidney Howard's *They Knew What They Wanted,* copyright 1925 by Sidney Howard, copyright 1952 (in renewal) by Polly Damrosch Howard;

Mr. Garson Kanin for permission to quote from *Born Yesterday;*

Doubleday and Company for permission to quote from *The Life and Times of Archy and Mehitabel* by Don Marquis;

J. B. Lippincott Company for permission to reprint the selection from "The Magic Box," from *More in Anger* by Marya Mannes, copyright © 1958 by Marya Mannes; copyright 1953, 1954, 1956, 1957 by Marya Mannes; published by J. B. Lippincott Company;

The Public Trustee and The Society of Authors for permission to quote from *Pygmalion* by George Bernard Shaw;

Mrs. E. E. Cummings for permission to reprint the section from the Preface to George Herriman's *Krazy Kat,* copyright 1946 by E. E. Cummings.

Music Theatre International for permission to quote from *Guys and Dolls,* copyright © 1951 by Jo Swerling, Abe Burrows, and Frank Loesser. All preforming rights of *Guys and Dolls* are controlled by Music Theatre International, 119 West 57th Street, New York 19, N. Y.

Portions of this book have appeared in modified form in *The South Atlantic Quarterly, The Western Humanities Review,* and *The Brown Alumni Monthly.* I am grateful to these periodicals for granting me permission to reprint the material.

*For **Sophia Schaffer Blistein** who knows
how, where, and when to laugh*

Preface

Prefaces, acknowledgments—call them what you will—are occasionally considered disingenuous or bromidic. Recently, as a case in point, a highly respected periodical saw fit to publish a devastating parody of what its author considered a typical university-press-book acknowledgment. Yet the life is so short, the craft is so hard to learn, and so few of us are self-taught that acknowledgments are not only necessary but desirable, motivated not only by honesty but by gratitude.

A grant from the Faculty Research Fund of Brown University was most helpful. I am grateful to the staff of the Film Library of the Museum of Modern Art, particularly to Richard Griffith, Margareta Akermark, Eileen Bowser, the ever-helpful Jo-Ann Ordano, and that most knowledgeable of all projectionists, Arthur Steiger. Beaumont Newhall and James Card quietly and efficiently made available to me the tremendous resources of George Eastman House in Rochester, New York. David A. Jonah and his staff at the John Hay Library of Brown University invariably and cheerfully produced whatever book or article I sought. For advice, suggestions, encouragement, and stimulation, I am indebted to Jess B. Bessinger, Hyatt H. Waggoner, Richard L. Grossman, and all the students who saw fit to take a course entitled "Comedy and Laughter" with me.

A person should never acknowledge indebtedness to his family for two very good reasons: his acknowledgment would inevitably be inadequate, and the individual members may at some time seek an impossible-to-produce *quid pro quo*.

E. M. B.

Brown University
Providence, Rhode Island
February, 1964

Contents

*Finish the tragedy! No. I have finally understood. Certainly
everything is ugly, everything is sad, and afterwards we know
it. But the soul must be purged by laughter. The only virile
attitude to take in the face of the human condition is to laugh
at it. And that is comedy.*

—JEAN ANOUILH, *La Petite Molière*

Introduction

At the conclusion of Plato's *Symposium*, that convivial, intellectual treatise on love, the convivial finally overcomes the
intellectual because, we are told, someone had neglected to
close the door. We can accept Plato's reason, even though we
may be beset by doubt, because Socrates, alone of the company, remains in character:

Agathon arose in order that he might take his place on the
couch by Socrates, when suddenly a band of revellers entered, and

spoiled the order of the banquet. Someone who was going out having left the door open, they had found their way in, and made themselves at home; great confusion ensued, and everyone was compelled to drink large quantities of wine. Aristodemus said that Eriximachus, Phaedrus, and others went away—he himself fell asleep, and as the nights were long took a good rest: he was awakened towards daybreak by a crowing of cocks, and when he awoke, the others were either asleep, or had gone away; there remained only Socrates, Aristophanes, and Agathon, who were drinking out of a large goblet which they passed around, and Socrates was discoursing to them. Aristodemus was only half awake, and he did not hear the beginning of the discourse; the chief thing which he remembered was Socrates compelling the other two to acknowledge that the genius of comedy was the same with that of tragedy, and that the true artist in tragedy was an artist in comedy also. To this they were constrained to assent, being drowsy, and not quite following the argument.

We can sympathize with Aristophanes and Agathon. Drowsy or alert, we too are often "constrained to assent" when the theorists of tragedy tell us that tragedy and comedy are the same thing, that they do not need to discuss comedy when they have already discussed tragedy. They overpower us with the convincing respectability of an ablative absolute. "*Mutatis mutandis*," they say condescendingly, "what is true of tragedy is also true of comedy." And off they go to contemplate the eternal verities, not bothering, as George Gordon remarks, to tell us what are the things that ought to be changed. Aristotle is guilty, Coleridge is guilty, Lamb is guilty, and Bradley is guilty. When gold rusts, what can you expect from iron?

If the critics would stop with their erroneous but innocuous statement about the similarity of comedy and tragedy, we should have no complaint. After all, they are not required to develop theories of comedy, or to meditate on the sources of or the reactions to comedy; they are not even required to like comedy. But most critics not only dislike but actively distrust that which they are unable to understand. I do not know whether Plato understood comedy—I feel he did not, but I cannot prove it—but he certainly disliked and distrusted both comedy and laughter:

> Our guardians ought not to be overmuch given to laughter. Violent laughter tends to provoke an equally violent reaction. We must not allow poets to describe men of worth being overcome by it; still less should Homer speak of the gods giving way to "unquenchable laughter" at the sight of Hephaestus "bustling from room to room." That will be against your principles.

His distrust seems to be born of an uneasiness in the presence of comedy, a fear of the effect that comedy can have on an audience, even though he realized, reluctantly, that the whole man should know about comedy:

> For serious things cannot be understood without laughable things, nor opposites at all without opposites, if a man is really to have intelligence of either; but he cannot carry out both in action, if he is to have any degree of virtue. And for this very reason he should learn them both, in order that he may not in ignorance do or say anything that is ridiculous and out of place—he should command slaves and hired strangers to imitate such things, but he should never take any serious interest in them himself.

The principle enunciated here may be accurately, if inelegantly, summed up, "Hang your clothes on a hickory limb, but don't go near the water."

Plato is not alone in regarding comedy as an entertaining but not quite respectable member of the literary family. Aristotle admits, somewhat apologetically, that comedy exists; Matthew Arnold's attitude toward comedy is made explicit when he relegates Chaucer to the Limbo of those who lack "high seriousness"; Chaucer himself demonstrates a certain uneasiness about his comic creations when he seeks spiritual respectability in his Retraction; even so great a master of the comic art as Molière wistfully remarks that making good people laugh is a strange undertaking. For frequently this apologetic, almost condemnatory, attitude toward comedy has been fostered by those best in a position to attack it, the practitioners of comedy. The comedians, actors and writers alike, have frequently taken a half-defensive, half-apologetic tone toward their art: the comic writer knows that his work is important, but he feels that he must write a tragedy to insure his fame; the clown wants to play Hamlet.

Such an attitude is, to a certain extent, understandable. After all, we all feel the necessity for variety and change in our lives, and we should not condemn that need in others. The need for change may be understood, but the apology for art may not be. There is, without doubt, a place for "high seriousness," a place for the tragic; but, since most of us live in the happy middle ground of life, neither too wise nor too stupid, neither too good nor too bad, neither unblemished saint nor sinner of deepest dye, there is definitely a place in our lives—and without apology—for the comic and comedy.

The critics and philosophers, the comedians and the comic writers, are not the only ones to blame for the offhand dismissal of comedy from the company of the learned, the virtuous, the respectable. All of us, readers, viewers, raconteurs, have to bear part of the blame. Most people do not believe that time spent on tragedy is wasted; they feel that eternal truths will come from such study. They may be right, but eternal truths can come from a study of comedy too. There is a further obstacle to a close study of comedy. If people do not like comedy, they may feel that to study it is to waste time; if they do like comedy they may believe that close analysis of comedy's effects is almost sacrilegious, that nothing kills a laugh more quickly than explaining a joke. While there may be some merit in such a belief, the logical conclusion to the hypothesis is that the more ignorant we are, the more we can laugh; the less we understand something, the louder we can laugh at it. Such a conclusion is untenable. Because it is untenable classical and medieval critics—some of them—sought to explain laughter and comedy on rhetorical grounds. In the past century critics have tried to explain comedy and laughter on sociological, psychological, philosophical, and anthropological grounds. Certainly Meredith, Freud, Bergson, and Cornford have much of value to offer all those interested in comedy and the comic, and certainly any attempt at a synthesis must include the medieval rhetoricians and the classical moralists, but the grave danger of working from the theorists is that the synthesis would tend to become synthetic, and genuine insight be perverted into *ersatz* cataloguing.

Therefore, there is no attempt here to write a history of comic theory. Neither is there any attempt to avoid mentioning the theorists of the past in an effort to appear autodidactic. It will be evident to anyone who reads that I am tremendously indebted to the theorists of comedy, ancient, modern, and contemporary. I did not, however, get interested in comedy because of the theorists; I became interested in the theorists because I was interested in comedy and laughter. It was not enough to laugh at something that was amusing. I wanted to know why I was laughing, why this was amusing, why that left me cold. Occasionally, I found the theorists very helpful as I attempted to soothe the annoying cerebral itch; at other times they were no help at all. I soon discovered that there was no universal theory of laughter. Aristotle would help in one place, Hobbes in another, Freud in still another, but no theorist or theory was universally applicable.

So there is one more caveat that I must issue: this book does not pretend to be a universal theory of comedy. A good working title for it might be "Some Notes toward a Definition of Comedy," or "Some Approaches to Comedy," or even "An Essay [using that word in its original sense] on Laughter and the Comic." But all of these and the title the book now bears are merely substitutes, and poor ones at that, for what, if I were permitted eighteenth-century style, I should like to entitle this book: "A Modest Inquiry into the Nature of the

Comic and the Laughable, with Some Animadversions on the Pretensions of the Comic Theorists, and Some Appreciation for the Creators and Actors of Comedy." Such a title would not be brief, but it would dispense with the necessity for a table of contents. In addition, it would be an adequate description of the book.

The world is a comedy to those that think, a tragedy to those who feel.

—HORACE WALPOLE, *Letter to Sir Horace Mann*

The drive for respectability: an aspect of the comic character

The respectable man is a serious man; the important man is a serious man. At the councils of the wise, only the serious are admitted. All these things we are told and told so often that they must be true. Yet, if they are true, how do we account for the flash of insight, the clear-eyed vision of the truth that comedy and the comedian so often provide? The critics of comedy have frequently pointed out that comedy is intellectual, tragedy emotional, as if it were possible to separate feeling from thought, the heart from the mind. But perhaps the comedian is kept from the councils of the wise just because of these clear-eyed visions of the truth. To most men, the truth is painful, particularly when they have made a mistake. Comedy has the unfortunate knack of seeing mistakes through masses of verbiage, storms of emotion, and clouds of rhetoric. The Fool in *King Lear* has taxed the old king with some home truths, and has been warned that the whip awaits him if he keeps on. His answer is perceptive, true, and couched in most homely terms: "Truth's a dog must to kennel; he must be whipp'd out, when Lady the brach may stand by th' fire and stink." The truth and the comedian are frequently tactless.

In an effort to account for the comedian's ability to see to the heart of the matter when many of the wise and serious so often fail, many critics and commentators have noted the salient fact that comedians tend to be, in their private lives, quiet, retiring, even morose. By so doing, the critics can be happy since they have maintained their formidable equations: seriousness equals respectability; seriousness equals importance. They not only provide the equations, but also provide the proof. The proof, strangely enough, takes the form of an anecdote about a clown. The story has been told about Grimaldi, about Rich, about Chaplin, about Will Kemp, about, I suspect, every great comedian. William Makepeace Thackeray, writing on Swift in his *English Humourists of the Eighteenth Century*, tells the story more economically and more universally than most:

> Harlequin without his mask is known to present a very sober countenance, and was himself, the story goes, the melancholy patient whom the Doctor advised to go and see Harlequin—a man full of cares and perplexities like the rest of us, whose Self must always be serious to him, under whatever mask or disguise, or uniform he presents to the public.

Even if this poignantly ironic anecdote is omitted, some other mention is generally made, in order to prove the equations, about the two faces, one private, one public, of the comedian. Gene Fowler, writing on Jimmy Durante in *Schnozzola*, and obviously writing before the first successful lunar probe, waxes mystical as he presents his proof: "The public knew nothing of Jimmy Durante's burdens. Laughing strangers care little about the private woes of their clowns. Who has looked upon the other side of the moon?"

The critics, the commentators, the theorists have frequently described, then, what may be called the Pagliacci Syndrome. The comedian is represented as a Janus-like character, wearing the mask of comedy on his obverse, the mask of tragedy on his reverse. But despite the descriptions, the equations, the syndrome, the proof, we are not happy. Too many obstacles have been placed in the path of true comedy, of joyous laughter. But haven't we made a mistake? Haven't we depended too much on the theorists, on the commentators, on the critics? What does comedy itself have to say?

So we turn from the theorists to comedy itself, and particularly dramatic comedy. When we think of dramatic comedy, the great comic characters come to mind, and they bring with them an obstacle which we anticipated but which optimism seemed to preclude: the obstacle, unfortunately, of conscience, of what the other fellow thinks, of propriety, of respectability. Seriousness, not laughter, has been traditionally equated with dignity; dignity is the *sine qua non* of propriety; and we all yearn and strive for propriety. Our equations are still with us. Not all comic characters worry about propriety, to be sure, but those who do not are generally the characters we laugh at rather than with, the characters whose discomfiture delights us, the characters who are, in short, the comic villains or the comic antagonists. With them I am not at this moment concerned. I am concerned with some of our favorite comic characters in the drama who are not completely immune to this infection of propriety. Even Falstaff, that "trunk of humours," that "huge bombard of sack," briefly contemplates reform and propriety: "If I do grow great, I'll grow less; for I'll purge, and leave sack, and live cleanly, as a nobleman should do." But, perhaps fortunately, the pun on *great* and *less* is too tempting to leave alone, and the prospect of reform is, in fact, dispensed with before the possibility of reform is completely voiced. But the prospect was, albeit briefly, in mind.

Sir Toby Belch and Feste bravely taunt the complaining respectable who take a dim view of tinkers' gabble and coziers' catches late at night, but cakes and ale and even hot ginger inevitably seem to lead to a broken head, a bedside but respectable marriage, and Sir Toby's most terrible out-of-character line, "I hate a drunken rogue." Feste manages to remain in character—he even insists on his part in the plot: "I was one, sir, in this interlude; one Sir Thopas, sir. But that's all one." But Feste is comic only on the periphery of his being. In the center he is more suited to the concert stage than to the burlesque house; he is more singer than fool, more philosopher than clown, more dignified in motley than most men are in morning coats and striped trousers.

Touchstone, that rarest of fools, presses in "amongst the rest of the country copulatives" to achieve the propriety and respectability of marriage. He plans to make a lady out of his Audrey, "A poor virgin, sir, an ill-favour'd thing, sir, but mine own." He doesn't even wait until he is married to begin the lessons, "(bear your body more seeming, Audrey)" for the courtier's spirit is strong within him: "I have trod a measure; I have flatt'red a lady; I have been politic with my friend, smooth with mine enemy; I have undone three tailors; I have had four quarrels, and like to have fought one." Pygmalions never learn to keep their Galateas safe in stone or safe in the forest of Arden or even safe at 27A Wimpole Street; once stone has been exchanged for living flesh, and the forest for a Duke's court, and Wimpole Street for a splendid formal reception, the creator becomes the victim, if not the butt, of his creation.

Alfred Doolittle, the magnificent dustman, knows so clearly that the difference between five pounds and ten pounds is the difference between fun and respectability: "Ten pounds is a lot of money: it makes a man feel prudent like; and then goodbye to happiness." Firm in his determination to remain one of the undeserving poor, he successfully withstands the blandishments of the extra five pounds: "You give me what I ask you, Governor: not a penny more, and not a penny less." A man of such moral courage will not leave us, we feel sure; a man of such conviction will remain faithful to his station, faithful to his trust; a man of this stature will have no contemptible middle-class notions of respectability and propriety. The end of the play, however, finds him the tragic victim of an annuity of 4,000 pounds, clothes of proper cut, and the respectability of an impending marriage. Middle-class morality, a patently absurd synonym for propriety, has done him in. I call him a tragic victim because, like Othello, he is so aware of what has happened to him:

Thats the tragedy of it maam. It's easy to say chuck it; but I havnt the nerve. Which of us has? We're all intimidated. Intimidated, maam; that's what we are. What is there for me if I chuck it but the workhouse in my old age? I have to dye my hair already to keep my job as a dustman. If I was one of the deserving poor, and had put by a bit, I could chuck it; but then why should I, acause the deserving poor might as well be millionaires for all the happiness they ever has. They dont know what happiness is. . . . Intimidated: thats what I am. Broke. Bought up. Happier men than me will call for my dust, and touch me for their tip; and I'll look on helpless, and envy them.

A slight touch of his former carefree character is evidenced a moment later when, in reply to Higgins' statement, "Doolittle: either youre an honest man or a rogue," he replies (the stage direction says, "tolerantly"), "A little of both, Henry, like the rest of us: a little of both." But respectability and propriety are not to be denied. As he leaves Mrs. Higgins' flat to go to the church where his spirit-broken wife-to-be awaits, he may be heard musing, "Bridegroom. What a word! It makes a man realize his position, somehow."

So money or marriage or sometimes a combination of the two tends to make great comic characters achieve respectability. Unfortunately, respectability seems to be—at least to these people—a synonym for seriousness. But money and marriage, alone or in combination, are not the only sobering influences. I am not making an attempt at alliteration here, but surely music should be added to money and marriage. A hint in this direction was dropped earlier when the honey-voiced Feste was claimed as a philosophically serious character rather than a clown. Surely, too, the example of Harpo in the Marx Brothers' movies is another case in point. The ineffable Harpo exploits to the fullest most of the resources of comedy that do not require speech. His horn, his genius for pantomime, and the well stocked pockets of his great coat even enable him to create visual puns and visual wit. This zany is, in turn, buffoon, roué, pantomimist, defender of the oppressed, oppressor of the powerful, chaser, and chased. Then, suddenly, a change occurs: just as comic relief is considered by many to be essential to tragedy, so the Marx Brothers seem to feel that serious relief is necessary to comedy. That's when Harpo makes a serious appearance. It is not always prepared for, to be sure, but it is always present. Sometime, generally at the height of the foolishness, a harp appears—*materializes* would be a better word. At least once—this in *A Day at the Races*—and possibly one other time, the harp is a remnant of a torn-apart concert grand. At that moment a change comes over Harpo: his face mirrors delight; lechery disappears from his eyes; deviltry disappears; his features soften and his mood changes. His onslaught (no other word seems appropriate) on the harp may be terrifying and unorthodox, but the result is startling. Caught in a snare of his own contriving, he is oblivious to the world. He becomes a lonely, romantic, almost tragic figure. Music has had this effect on him, as it has had on other men, and women too. It would almost seem that the effects of money and marriage are slowly deleterious to the comic character, while music is startlingly swift in its sobering effect.

Not perhaps so swift as music, but definitely rapid in its effect on the comic character is important position in life. Even Falstaff briefly considered reform when the prospect of high station was before him. But perhaps it would be better to take another character, not necessarily a comic one, to see the effect of exalted position on him. Prince Hal, for example, with the responsibility of Shrewsbury upon him is a far cry from the cruelly comic baiter of Francis, the tavern boy, a far cry from the vicious prankster of Gadshill. At Shrewsbury he has no time for laughter. He must fight, and to fight he needs a weapon. When Falstaff's "pistol" turns out to be a bottle of sack, the borrowing Prince has time only for the bitter line, "What, is it a time to jest and dally now?" before he is off to perform the duties that responsibility and position demand of him. We are not surprised at the Prince's reformation. Indeed, we are not even sure that a reformation was necessary despite the cynical comments of Hotspur, despite Henry's sorrowful laments about his prodigal son. After all, we have heard his soliloquy at the end of the play's second scene; we have been adequately informed that the "vile politician, Bolingbroke" has a crafty politician son. The critics may tell us that Hal's soliloquy is an offense against dramatic propriety, and perhaps it is, but it makes explicit what men of action and affairs have always known: there is a time for a holiday humor, and a time for responsibility:

> If all the year were playing holidays,
> To sport would be as tedious as to work;
> But when they seldom come, they wish'd-for come,
> And nothing pleaseth but rare accidents.

Hal is not, of course, a comic character even though his comic scenes outnumber his serious scenes and the lines in his comic scenes far outnumber the lines in his serious scenes. He is, in effect if not in conception, a character who is his own foil:

> So, when this loose behaviour I throw off
> And pay the debt I never promised,
> By so much shall I falsify men's hopes;
> And like bright metal on a sullen ground,
> My reformation, glitt'ring o'er my fault,
> Shall show more goodly and attract more eyes
> Than that which hath no foil to set it off.
> I'll so offend, to make offence a skill,
> Redeeming time when men think least I will.

If we take his remarks literally, we are forced to the conclusion that his characteristics really do not change no matter how much his character seems to develop and mature and mellow. In this sense we may say that the same spirit motivates his treatment of Francis in *1 Henry IV* and Michael Williams in *Henry V*. In the former, he produces and stages the entire episode; in the latter he takes advantage of a circumstance which he has, in a larger sense, also produced and staged. Francis, though the son of a woman, may have fewer words than a parrot, but Michael Williams has the words and the wit to turn a promised beating into a glove full of crowns:

WILLIAMS: All offences, my lord, come from the heart. Never came any from mine that might offend your majesty.

KING: It was ourself thou didst abuse.

WILLIAMS: Your majesty came not like yourself. You appear'd to me but as a common man; witness the night, your garments, your lowliness. And what your Highness suffer'd under that shape, I beseech you take it for your own fault, and not mine; for had you been as I took you for, I made no offence. Therefore I beseech your Highness pardon me.

KING: Here, uncle Exeter, fill this glove with crowns
And give it to this fellow.

It must be passing fair to be a king, even if you do not ride in triumph through Persepolis but merely wander through the camp and note the qualities of people. Henry is in good company when he does so. Antony and Cleopatra, Vincentio, the Duke of Venice, and Haroun-al-Raschid all found it salutary to wander in disguise among the common people in order to discover their thoughts, deeds, and emotions. Note well, however, that although Henry had appeared to Williams as a common man, he did not take the chance of receiving a box in the ear according to the provisions of their agreement in the night. After all, it would have been beneath his kingly dignity to do so, just as it was beneath his princely dignity to permit the sheriff to arrest his associates, or to permit the Lord Chief Justice to jail Bardolph with impunity. In the Williams case, Fluellen, the magnificent Welshman, is the gull. By appearing as his own foil, Henry had provoked the quarrel. Williams was rewarded with gold; Fluellen received a box in the ear and tried to pay a shilling for the honor. But Falstaff had been rejected and, indeed, was dead by this time, and the desire for low comedy, so essential a part of Henry's character, still required satisfaction.

But Hal, or Henry, as I mentioned earlier, is not a comic character. He is serious, aware of his responsibilities, aware of war and statecraft and rule. But he turns from the serious not merely to observe but actually to engage in the comic. He baits Francis, he robs Falstaff, he makes a butt of Fluellen, he courts the princess all in an attitude of rich comedy. He takes, despite Plato's dictum, a serious attitude toward the comic and comedy. He is a participant, not merely an observer. Therein lies his greatest strength or his greatest weakness: he is a serious character who finds in the comic a reason for being if not a reason for doing. Important position, both when he anticipates it and when he actually possesses it, takes him from the realm of the comic, just as it has taken other, more genuinely comic characters. He enters the ordinary, everyday, comic realm in order to establish a contrast, or in order to render bearable the terrifying loneliness of kingship, of responsibility, of important position. Perhaps for the same reason Abraham Lincoln read Artemus Ward to his Cabinet.

While important position often tempers and even destroys the comic, when it lapses from position into mere officialdom it can, and frequently does, create the comic. Bergson, who insists on automatism as one source of the comic, says:

> But complete automatism is only reached in the official, for instance, who performs his duty like a mere machine, or again in the unconsciousness that marks an administrative regulation working with inexorable fatality, and setting itself up for a law of nature.

It is occasionally hard to decide where important position leaves off and officialdom begins. Most of the time, however, the decision is not hard to make. We may have doubts about Polonius, but we don't have any about Dogberry. Even Cassio provides one of the rare moments of comedy in *Othello* when in his drunknness he lapses into officialdom and insists on maintaining the official lines of demarcation between ranks:

> CASSIO: For mine own part—no offence to the general, nor any man of quality—I hope to be saved.
> IAGO: And so do I too, lieutenant.
> CASSIO: Ay, but by your leave, not before me; the lieutenant is to be saved before the ancient.

The prospect of salvation is not normally considered a humorous subject, but the rank-pulling of officialdom succeeds even in this rarefied atmosphere. Even the theologians who discuss the angelic hierarchies have never envisioned cloud-soft wings decorated with chevrons or other insignia of rank derived from a former, lower existence. Malvolio, too, probably belongs in the category of officialdom, but it is difficult to decide whether his position molded his character or his character made his position inevitable. In addition, he is a comic antagonist, not a sympathetic comic character.

It is the literality of the official mind that produces the comic effect. Bergson calls this literality *rigidity*, and equates it with his catch-all definition of the comic, "the mechanical encrusted on the living." There is something about officialdom that imposes on officials a fixed, rigid routine. This routine, in its place, has undoubted benefits. If the policeman follows a fixed order in trying all the doorknobs of the shops on his beat, he is probably more efficient than his colleague who tries doorknobs at random. If we, in our own homes, follow a fixed routine of locking one door and then the other, adjusting the thermostat, setting the clock, turning off lights before we get into bed, the chances are that we do not toss and turn with worry about an unlocked door, an unset clock, an overheated bedroom. In other words, there is a time when not comedy but efficiency is obtained when the mechanical is encrusted on the living. Comedy arises, however, when routine is imposed upon actions which do not require routine, or when the wrong kind of routine is established. Policemen *should* stop speeding drivers, and they *should* prevent loiterers from leaning against buildings, and undoubtedly there is a proper routine for performing both of these tasks. I feel sure that the proper routine does not include asking the speeding driver if he is going to a fire, does not include asking the loiterer leaning against the building if he is holding the building up. The officials' questions are, of course, rhetorical, expecting the answer, "No," and the comic character, aware of the rhetoric, can create comedy for the audience by using the official not as the creator of laughter but as the butt. At the beginning of the Marx Brothers' film, *A Night in Casablanca*, Harpo is discovered leaning against a building. A policeman comes along, asks the inevitable question, but receives the unexpected answer of a smiling, vigorous, affirmative nod of the head. Outraged at the unexpected answer (his routine, you see, has been disrupted) the policeman yanks Harpo away. The building, needless to say, collapses. Our laughter is directed at the policeman, not at Harpo. Not only has the building collapsed, but, if only for a moment, the entire rigid world of officialdom has collapsed. We are delighted, not because we do not have respect for officialdom but because the official has misused his officialdom and retribution has been swift. The Dogberries of this world do not have to mutilate language to produce comedy. They can become comic by making a routine out of their authority. That is the reason, I suppose, that many people buy, read, and enjoy the detective stories which have the gifted and imaginative amateur outsmarting the rigid, routine-minded officers from the local constabulary or even from Scotland Yard. Imagine Sherlock Holmes, Lord Peter Wimsey, or Sam Spade in a policeman's uniform! The policeman's lot is frequently not a happy one—to the policeman—but it is frequently a laugh-provoking one to the audience. *The Mikado*, perhaps even the *Pirates of Penzance* and *H.M.S. Pinafore* testify to the comic effect of the triumph over officialdom.

If, then, important position, responsibility, officialdom in general are sources of the comic, how is it possible that they can, along with money, marriage, and music, have a deleterious effect on the comic character and the comic spirit? There is no pat answer to the question, but there are approaches to an answer. The sociological and psychological approaches have much merit, and I intend to mention them later, but there is a purely literary approach that deserves some consideration here. I do not want to become involved in a discussion of the essential difference between an author's intention and a work's intention. I believe that such a difference exists, that an author can have one intention for an episode or a character and have the episode or character get away from him. I believe that Shylock in *The Merchant of Venice*, Mercutio in *Romeo and Juliet*, possibly Beatrice and Benedick in *Much Ado About Nothing* are cases in point. I don't believe that there is always or even frequently a difference between the author's and the work's intentions, but I do believe that the difference is occasionally there. Frequently, however, we see another phenomenon: the author seems to contrive a happy ending for a sympathetic comic character who does not, if we accept the characterization as given, deserve a happy ending. Yet he gets one and, as Dorothy Sayers points out, we have seen a miracle:

> Mr. Wilkins Micawber . . . is favoured by a miracle at the end of *David Copperfield*. He is a "good" character—that is to say, a character sympathetic to his author—and it is desired to reward him with a "happy ending." He is therefore packed off to Australia, where in defiance of his own nature and in defiance of the nature of Australian civic life in the last century, he becomes a prosperous magistrate. However consoling this solution of the Micawber problem, a little thought convinces us that any person less suitable to prosper in these conditions than Mr. Micawber can scarcely be imagined.

Miss Sayers may be slightly harsh on both Dickens and Micawber. Dickens may have been able to see (although I doubt it) that the same quality of mind that made Micawber improvident in the handling of his own affairs may have qualified him—better than most—to sit in judgment and handle the affairs of others. But we in America have an advantage that Miss Sayers did not have when she wrote her book: we have seen the case of a man who suffered financial failure in the handling of his own haberdashery business but who was successful—eminently so, according to some—in handling the affairs of a nation. Miss Sayers may have a valid point when she says that Micawber's rising to the state of a prosperous magistrate is a reward for services rendered. It is to my mind the wrong kind of reward, but it is the kind of reward that frequently is bestowed on a sympathetic comic character: he becomes respectable. Micawber becomes respectable financially because Dickens wanted to reward him; Alfred Doolittle becomes respectable matrimonially and financially because Shaw's perverted sense of morality or humor thought that this kind of reward was in order; W. C. Fields in *The Bank Dick* gets to be respectable financially and sartorially so that he can flaunt this respectability before those who had looked down upon him and to prove that a fast wit and a touch of larceny in the heart can work miracles; and Charlie Chaplin in *City Lights* gets the respectability of recognition for a thoroughly decent and selfless act which he had performed. Micawber and Doolittle were at the mercy of their authors, and so, to a minor extent, was W. C. Fields, but Chaplin made his decision alone. These decisions typify, I believe, the desire for respectability that gnaws at the mind of the creator of the comic character, author and actor alike.

But what are the reasons for this desire, this drive, that leads the comic character to seek respectability? One reason may be implicit in a story that Danny Kaye tells when he takes a break in the middle of his performance, waves the orchestra away, borrows a cigarette from someone in the audience, and relaxes in a confidential mood. The story concerns the first time that his daughter, then a child of five, saw him perform. He knew where in the audience she was seated and, although the spotlight obscured his vision, he shaded his eyes with his hand, located her, and asked if she were having a good time. Her answer was waveringly affirmative. A short time later he shaded his eyes once more, looked in her direction once more, asked the same question, and got the same answer, but this time the wavering voice had changed to a quavering voice. He was disturbed, but finished his act. At the end he went to his dressing room and, a short time later, she showed up, smiling bravely through tears. He naturally asked what was bothering her, and the answer, spoken through a fresh torrent of sobs, was, "I don't like people to laugh at my daddy." The story may be false, but I doubt it. Kaye's five-year-old daughter typifies the reaction of the average audience to comedy and laughter. Kaye may have been able to assure his daughter that if people didn't laugh at her daddy she wouldn't be wearing shoes, but again I doubt it. To his daughter, to the audience, indeed, to society as a whole, comedy and laughter are not respectable, not proper. It may have been in an effort to justify himself to his daughter, to his audiences, to society at large that Kaye took his world-wide trip on behalf of UNICEF. Certainly he used all of his comic devices to achieve acceptance and appreciation wherever he went. Certainly his artistry as a mimic endeared him to children and adults alike. Certainly, too, the results of his trip made him a man of serious stature, of respectable position, in short, a philanthropist who dispensed laughter instead of money. His trip and the television film that was its product showed that he was capable of high seriousness as well as low comedy.

But Kaye is not the only comedian who has had similar motivation and similar desires. The sympathetic comic character, the one we laugh with rather than at, is not a fool, a buffoon, or a clown. He is a thinking man, and he is able to think clearly enough to realize that an audience, even when it is holding its sides, feels charitable, kindly, even condescending when it approves a comedian's timing, delivery, or wit. He knows, too, that an audience stands in awe as it applauds a tragedian who has just finished revealing his soul. He may find it difficult to understand the audience's reaction. What has the tragedian got that he hasn't? He admits that comedy is occasionally raucous, unbuttoned, bedraggled; but just as frequently comedy is suave, smooth, urbane. Comedy, as well as tragedy, can wear a top hat or a crown, and the top hat doesn't necessarily have to be a target for an urchin's snowball. And even motley can possess dignity as the example of Feste shows us, and as the melancholy Jaques' line, "Motley is the only wear!" implies.

And what if comedy is raucous? Certainly the mad Lear's cries are raucous too. Certainly Oedipus is not suave or smooth or urbane as he stands with blood streaming from his empty eye sockets. Willy Loman may not wear motley, to be sure, but certainly his entire wardrobe does not consist of suits of solemn black. Pagliacci's motley certainly does not render him the less tragic. The comedian finds, therefore, that the obvious, superficial differences do not account for the audience's reaction to his art, and he then is forced to look not at himself as contrasted with the tragedian, but at the audience. And when he does look at the audience, looks deeply, I mean, he sees something that causes him to despair. The audience, attired in courtly robes, dinner jackets, or sack suits, is nonetheless essentially primitive in its reactions. All the outward manifestations of sophistication and civilization may be present, but there is a primeval urge in any theater audience that demands something more than intellectual stimulation, more than entertainment, more than comedy and laughter, if it is going to do something more than applaud. In order to stand in awe it requires a victim, a victim who is destroyed. That the comedian is unable to supply, for while the tragic character as well as the audience is essentially primitive, the comic character is essentially civil. Macbeth and Brutus Jones are primitive men who are unable to keep their imaginations in check. They must be destroyed, and the audience will stand in awe. Oedipus and Othello are primitive men who are unable to control their tempers. They must be destroyed, and the audience will stand in awe. Even Hamlet, the glass of fashion and the mold of form, permits the primitive instinct for revenge to overcome him. He is destroyed and the audience stands in awe. But Alfred Doolittle can adjust, even Lady Wishfort and Mrs. Malaprop are able to adjust, to a change in circumstances. Destruction is not for them because they are flexible. The spirit of compromise, the ability to see the human situation from more than one point of view, is the mark of the comic character, and that is another reason, I suppose, that the sympathetic comic character reflects his creator's desire for respectability. For the great, sympathetic comic character, despite Bergson's theory of rigidity, does not have a one-track mind, is not equipped with intellectual blinders. Some comic characters, the butts of our laughter, the ones we laugh at not with, are so equipped, but they and the comic villain in general are a subject for another chapter. For the sympathetic comic character, however, very often the opposite is true. Far from being equipped with intellectual blinders, he often develops an intellectual squint from his attempts to see both sides of every question. So, because he is civil and intellectual, he is unable to make himself a victim, a primitive victim, if you will, in an attempt to obtain from the audience the type of approbation that he desperately seeks. Since he is unable to emulate the primitive aspect of his audience, he identifies himself—almost in despair—with the sophisticated aspect, the veneer which the audience presents to the world. And when he does that, the clarity of vision which a comedian must possess tends to disappear. He then becomes civilized rather than civil; he becomes acceptable, even respectable, in the eyes of his audience, those whom it is his duty to satirize, to poke fun at, to attack. He identifies himself with his raw material. Once he makes this identification, much of his value is lost. He can no longer be objective in his satire, wit, humor, and comedy, and the result is very often distorted and ridiculous. When tempted to his previous satire and wit, the clichés of those he has joined rise readily to his mind. He feels that he is fouling his own nest, that he is a traitor to his class and kind. Imagine Andrew Joseph Volstead writing advertising copy for National Distillers.

Certainly, then, this drive for respectability on the part of the comic character merits our study if we are to give to comedy the same sensitive consideration that we have given to tragedy. And there is no reason why we should not. Fortunately, many creators and actors of sympathetic comic characters realize the dangers present in the drive for respectability, and they attempt to confine their yearnings to their private musings. They realize, too, that the stage and life need characters to laugh with as well as laugh at if the multi-faceted sanity and reasonableness that we call comedy is to survive. What we need now are twentieth-century audiences and critics who are sensitive enough and mature enough to accept comedy for what it is: a respectable art form that creates and fosters an attitude toward life that is vigorous, corrective, and penetrating. Then, perhaps, the creators and actors of sympathetic comic characters can dispense even with their potentially dangerous private musings. Then, perhaps, Hamlet will yearn to play the clown.

Hood an ass with reverend purple,
So you can hide his two ambitious ears,
And he shall pass for a cathedral doctor.

—Mosca, in *Volpone*

The object of scorn: an aspect of the comic antagonist

At one point in "The Importance of Being Earnest," Miss Prism, the absent minded nursemaid-governess, is describing a novel she had once written. In it, she says, "The good ended happily, and the bad unhappily. That is what Fiction means." When we watch or when we read dramatic comedy, Miss Prism's mildly ambiguous definition serves to comfort us when an obstacle is placed in the path of obviously true love, or when a sympathetic comic character is placed in a situation that is surrounded by difficulties. For when we consider dramatic comic characters, our thoughts most often run to the sympathetic comic characters, the ones we laugh with, rather than at. We think of Feste and Falstaff, Charlie Chaplin and W. C. Fields, the melodramatic Cyrano whose wit conceals a breaking heart, and Billie Dawn, the twentieth-century Magdalene. We think of them because all of these characters, to a greater or lesser extent, have aspirations towards a world that is outside the comic, the world of respectability. We think of them because, although we have only a sneaking awareness that they are better than we are, we have an open awareness that they are better than they appear to be, that their comic-dom confines them to situations not good enough for them.

> gods what a terrible tragedy
> not to make good with the tragic
> gods what a heart breaking pathos
> to be always doomed to the comic

Few of the sympathetic comic characters would go so far as to echo "the wail of archy" from *archy and mehitabel,* but we frequently have the feeling that our favorite comic characters are "doomed to the comic." We will admit that there is no artistic justification for our feeling, but we will also assert that there are psychological and sociological justifications for such an attitude. That is why, despite a momentary twinge of regret, we feel pleased when the critics applaud the performance of such an inspired clown as Ed Wynn when he plays a serious role; that is why, despite slight overtones of condescension, we feel pleased when a comedian like Red Buttons wins an Academy Award for a serious role in *Sayonara.*

Although we think most often of the sympathetic comic characters, we should not confine our thinking to them. The extremely complex art form which is comedy has many levels, many avenues of approach, and the matter of character is but one. And even the matter of character is not exhausted by an exploration of the sympathetic comic character. We must keep in mind the comic butt, the comic antagonist, the comic villain. Call him what you will, he has one salient characteristic: he makes us laugh at him rather than with him. It would, however, be a fundamental mistake to assume that the comic antagonist is always a less complex person than the sympathetic comic character. Frequently such is the case, of course, and then the butt is merely a two-dimensional sheet of cardboard intended to be the target of a custard pie. Frequently, too, the butt merely has to slip on a banana peel or have a chair pulled out from behind him as he attempts to sit, and the audience, sublimating its latent sadism (as some psychologists tell us), or giving vent to its appreciation of the unexpected (as some critics of the Max Eastman school tell us), can be expected to burst forth with gales of laughter. Such characters, simple as they are, have provided enjoyment for generations of high brows and low brows. The middle brows may enjoy them and laugh at them too, but they feel, most often, insecure in their laughter, as if it were possible to lose intellectual caste by a display of emotional honesty.

But the comic butts of the slapstick school, enjoyable and laughable though they may be, do not concern us here. We are concerned with the comic butt who is more complex than the slapstick comedian, who is at times as subtle as the sympathetic comic character, who is worse than he first appears to be, who is at first in a situation too good for him. He is, in short, the reverse of the coin whose obverse is the sympathetic comic character. The drama knows characters of this nature. Such characters are Parolles in *All's Well That Ends Well*, Mr. Applegate in *Damn Yankees*, Harry Brock in *Born Yesterday*, Malvolio in *Twelfth Night*.

Parolles is more complex than the simple classical braggart soldier. The problem of Parolles is, fundamentally, the age-old one of the difference between appearance and reality. Parolles would have us believe that he is a warrior, a sophisticate, a wit, handy in battle, cosmopolitan in taste and language, dapper in dress. Many in his world believe the appearance, and some who are aware of the reality find it necessary and politic to stomach his absurdity. At his first appearance, Helena describes the conflict. She is talking of her love for Bertram when Parolles appears on the scene.

> Who comes here?
> One that goes with him. I love him for his sake;
> And yet I know him a notorious liar,
> Think him a great way fool, solely a coward.
> Yet these fix'd evils sit so fit in him
> That they take place when virtue's steely bones
> Look bleak i' th' cold wind. Withal, full oft we see
> Cold wisdom waiting on superfluous folly.

Helena is not the only one to see the reality. Old Lafew sees it also and readily smokes him out, but the rest, particularly the men, require time, much time. After all, his technique is not bad. Note him as he implies his bravery and experience in battle when some of the young nobles of France are setting off for the Italian wars. He and Bertram are to remain behind.

> Noble heroes, my sword and yours are kin. Good sparks and lustrous, a word, good metals: you shall find in the regiment of the Spinii one Captain Spurio, with his cicatrice, an emblem of war, here on his sinister cheek. It was this very sword entrench'd it. Say to him I live, and observe his reports for me.

Perhaps Captain Spurio is as illegitimate as the etymology of his name would imply (although he is mentioned once again in the play, it is significant that Parolles is the one who mentions him), and perhaps too, if there be such a person, the cicatrice on his left cheek came from a source other than the cowardly sword of Parolles, but who is to know? These nobles are young, relatively inexperienced in war and humanity, and Parolles is rapid with the convincing detail which cannot at the moment be questioned. Even Lafew thought him for two ordinaries to be a pretty wise fellow, and Lafew had age and experience on his side. How, then, can we blame the gullible youngsters?

So Helena unmasks him in Act I, and Lafew unmasks him in Act II, distilling the dram of reality from the vat of illusion:

> Go to, sir! You were beaten in Italy for picking a kernel out of a pomegranate. You are a vagabond, and no true traveller. You are more saucy with lords and honorable personages than the commission of your birth and virtue gives you heraldry. You are not worth another word, else I'd call you a knave. I leave you.

Instead of becoming infuriated at this attack, Parolles, as always, salvages the one drop of sweetness from the bitter cup: "Good, very good! It is so then. Good, very good! Let it be conceal'd awhile." The "goods" that he utters may be ironic, but the relief evidenced in the "Let it be conceal'd awhile" is genuine. Concealment of the reality and display of the appearance are ever his stock in trade. Lafew is unable to convince Bertram of Parolles' absurdity, but Bertram is a young and inexperienced man. Only older, experienced men can see through Parolles; but women of any age, Helena, Mariana, the Countess, find him transparent.

By the end of Act III, everyone save Bertram is aware of what he is. To convince Bertram of Parolles' cowardice and fraudulence, the French lords conceive a plot to expose him as a poltroon and a traitor. The plot is successful and Parolles, completely unmasked now, is left to his own devices, deserted by everyone, even Bertram:

> Yet am I thankful. If my heart were great,
> 'Twould burst at this. Captain I'll be no more;
> But I will eat, and drink, and sleep as soft
> As captain shall. Simply the thing I am
> Shall make me live. Who knows himself a braggart,
> Let him fear this; for it will come to pass
> That every braggart shall be found an ass.
> Rust, sword! cool, blushes! and, Parolles, live
> Safest in shame! Being fool'd, by fool'ry thrive!
> There's place and means for every man alive.

This speech alone, even if there were no other evidence, would enable us to see that Parolles is not the traditional, simple comic butt. Too often the comic butt is unable to understand anything, least of all himself. Parolles has no such problem. He has understood the reality of himself from the start, and this speech demonstrates conclusively his self-understanding. If he were in reality a brave man, this unmasking would never have happened. If he were possessed of a true sense of decency, such an unmasking would have destroyed him completely. He won't be a captain any more, but he'll enjoy the creature comforts as well as any captain. And his future is summed up in the key line of the speech, "Simply the thing I am shall make me live."

Parolles' hope succeeds. Lafew will take care of Parolles who, having been fooled, will thrive by fool'ry: "Sirrah, inquire further after me. I had talk of you last night. Though you are a fool and a knave, you shall eat." But Parolles must always remember what he is. Any attempted reversion to his former situation brings stern reminders:

> Good Tom Drum, lend me a handkercher. So,
> I thank thee. Wait on me home; I'll make sport with thee.
> Let thy curtsies alone! they are scurvy ones.

From artificial captain he has become a nobleman's genuine fool, and he does not mind. He is, in fact, grateful. The audience has laughed at him for pretending to be something he was not. Lafew henceforth will laugh with him for being what he is. The simple comic butt might have been ignored in the dénouement. This complex comic butt must be taken care of.

Mr. Applegate, from the George Abbott–Douglass Wallop musical comedy *Damn Yankees*, is in fast company when he is compared with the Shakespearean comic antagonists. Yet he belongs in such company if only because he manages to make the devil of the morality play into a flesh-and-blood character. If Parolles, as C. S. Lewis suggests, may be compared with Belial, Mr. Applegate definitely must be identified with Lucifer. Yet Mr. Applegate holds audience attention because he is not a type: he is an individual. He has no horns and no tail. I don't think his feet are cloven, but I must admit that after kicking a chair in a fit of temper, he does say, "Oh, my hoof!" He normally wears business suits, but in one scene he parades around in a flamboyant dressing gown. He always wears bright red socks. He has the disconcerting habit of plucking lighted cigarettes out of the air, and he explains his habit by the simple statement, "I'm handy with fire." He is able to answer the fatuous query of a couple of autograph hunters, "Are you anybody?" with the almost accurate, "Not a soul." He has the ability to be invisible when and to whom he desires, and passes off this remarkable ability with the debonair statement, "An amusing little stunt—it was all the rage in the Middle Ages." Perhaps most important of all, he appears "as if by magic" when Joe Boyd says, "I'd sell my soul for one long ball hitter." For, do not doubt it, Mr. Applegate is the devil in a twentieth-century sack suit and with twentieth-century problems. He has dispensed with some, but by no means all, of his medieval trappings. Although he first appears to the sound of "eerie music," he settles his deal with a hand shake (right *and* left hands). He thinks signing in blood is just a "phony stunt." He has more trouble with wives than with the Methodist Church, and he lets Joe Boyd, a twentieth-century real estate agent, talk him into an escape clause. His seductive agent, Lola, "a beautiful red-head, is just what the Devil ordered." But this succubus falls in love with her prospective victim, and Applegate had done so much for her too. After all, despite her youthful beauty, she is 172 years old, and had been "the ugliest woman in Providence, Rhode Island." Surely the medieval devil didn't have such troubles with his assistants.

But while he has dispensed with some of the medieval touches, and while he seems beset with twentieth-century problems, he still maintains a strong sense of history: "I am quite a famous character . . . I have historical significance too. In fact, I'm responsible for most of the history you can name." Then, when he is explaining to Lola her part in his present proceedings, he again uses historical simile:

APPLEGATE: Look, Lola, here's the tie-up. This is a mass torture deal like the thirty-years war. I've got thousands of Washington fans drooling under the illusion that the Senators are going to win the pennant.

LOLA: (*Enthusiastically*) Oh, Chief, that's awfully good. There'll be suicides, heart attacks and apoplexy. Just like the good old days.

His sense of personal history serves him in good stead when, despite all his precautions, his victim wants to exercise his option under the escape clause. He then reverts to the medieval devil: "Very well. An operation of this kind has to take place at the witching hour. So, at five minutes to midnight if you still want to go back, say the word." And the devil loses his victim, but he doesn't give up easily. His actions in the concluding scene are strangely reminiscent of those of Dr. Faustus in the concluding scene of Marlowe's play. He pleads: "It was in impulse and I regret it. But I'll make amends." He cajoles: "I'm not really a bad fellow, Joe—I'm just emotional." He rages in his frustration: "Listen to me, you wife-loving louse you belong to me. You crook, you thief, you two-timing false-faced swindler! You've robbed me, you've robbed me!" And these last lines are accompanied by his jumping up and down in rage and frustration as the curtain falls and the audience dissolves in laughter at the timeless devil, possessed of so much knowledge, frustrated by the potent power of a man's love for his wife.

Applegate is, then, an excellent example of the comic antagonist. He is more important to the plot of his play than Parolles is to his. Parolles merely seems to be domineering; Applegate is so. That is why our sympathy is with his victims, not with him. We want him to be cheated, and this play is very satisfying because he ends up cheating himself. When he makes his mistake and tries to erase the error, we are delighted that he is foiled. Martin Luther and Saint Thomas More have told us the devil is a proud spirit and cannot endure scorn, and our laughter is the more intense and the more pleased for that reason. For this devil, this Mr. Applegate, has been triply scorned: once by his minion who, contrary to all the laws of demonology, has been able to drug him and thus place him in an impossible predicament; once by his victim, who manages to elude his clutches; and finally by the audience, which enjoys his discomfiture. Luther and More may be right when they tell us that the devil cannot endure scorn, mockery, or laughter; C. S. Lewis is certainly right when he makes it clear in *The Screwtape Letters* that the devil can neither understand nor tolerate love.

Both Parolles and Mr. Applegate have a superficial smoothness, a veneer that is thin, to be sure, but that nevertheless exists. Harry Brock, the comic antagonist of Garson Kanin's play, *Born Yesterday*, has no hint of smoothness, no hint of softness about him. He has a certain rough, vulgar charm; but he has always done what he has wanted to do, despite any opposition, and he thinks that he always will. We have some idea of the kind of man he is even before his first appearance on the stage. In Washington for a brief visit, he has rented a two-hundred-and-thirty-five-dollar-a-day hotel suite. You don't have to be a communist to agree with the chambermaid who thinks that there ought to be a law against people who have that much money to spend on a hotel room—especially since she earns only eighteen dollars a week. We find out too, before his first appearance, the source of his income: "Ran a little junk yard into fifty million bucks, with no help from anyone or anything—except maybe World War II." When he first "stamps in," we discover that his name may be Brock but, according to the stage direction, "Gross is the word for him." Despite all that we have heard about him, despite his crudeness and boorishness in his relationships with other people, we may feel that he is a diamond in the rough, a magnificent example of what a man can make of himself under our wonderful system of free enterprise. We don't feel that way long. His first business venture was a paper route, surely a good American beginning. But Brock got his paper route through force: "I bought a kid out with a swift kick in the keester." His next business venture was a junk yard. He got the junk yard through stealing:

BROCK: I'll tell you. I'm a kid with a paper route. I've got this little wagon. So on my way home nights, I come through the alleys pickin' up stuff. I'm not the only one. All the kids are doin' it. The only difference is, they keep it. Not me. I sell it. First thing you know, I'm makin' seven, eight bucks a week from that. Three bucks from the papers. So I figure right off which is the right racket. I'm just a kid, mind you, but I could see that. Pretty soon, the guy I'm sellin' to is handin' me anywheres from fifteen to twenty a week. So he offers me a job for ten. Dumb jerk. I'd be sellin' this guy his own stuff back half the time and he never knew.

PAUL: How do you mean?

BROCK: (*Relishing the memory*) Well in the night, see I'm under the fence and I drag it out and load up. In the mornin', I bring it in the front way and collect . . .

PAUL: So pretty soon you owned the whole yard.

BROCK: Damn right!

Starting out with force, he soon, as we have seen, moved to theft. Then he discovered the purchasing power of money is not limited to things. Money can be used to buy people: "I never met a man who didn't have his price." Money buys the bodies of some people, the minds of others, the souls of still others. So he buys Billie Dawn; then he buys a lawyer who, before meeting Brock, had the stamp of greatness on him; then he buys a United States senator. Why shouldn't he? After all, a senator to him (he speaks relatively, of course) is "A guy who makes a hundred and fifty bucks a week." Our sneaking admiration soon turns to dismay, then disgust. We see him browbeat everyone in sight: his cousin Eddy, barbers, chambermaids, bootblacks, hotel managers, the whole *dramatis personae*. We see him use physical force on his lawyer, on his cousin, on Billie, on Paul. We are not at all impressed with the fleeting glimpses we get of the sentimental, paternalistic side of his character. We feel that it proves nothing good about him that he has provided employment for the boy whom he beat up to obtain his paper route, for the man from whom he stole to get his first junk yard. These two people, and his treatment of them, may be a sign of a sentimental character; they are, more likely, symbols of his belief that money can do anything, even turn enemies into friends.

This gross character with his rude wit, his boorish charm, must be proved wrong. He must be shown that there are some things and some people that money cannot buy, some people whom force cannot frighten. The audience must be enabled to laugh at his downfall, partly to get the aggression out of its system, partly to demonstrate its approval at the victory of virtue over vice, partly to conceal, even from itself, its fears that the attitudes which Harry Brock represents are dominant in our culture. And Harry Brock does meet his downfall. His downfall is, perhaps, foreshadowed by his defeat in the gin rummy game which he plays with Billie, but there is a major difference. Billie wins at gin rummy through luck or skill. Perhaps, in such a game as gin rummy, there is very little of the latter, but she does not use force, she does not cheat, she does not lie or steal. When Billie and Paul finally do triumph over the force that is Harry Brock, their victory is tainted, only slightly, to be sure, but nevertheless tainted, by the fact that they had to use Harry's methods to beat Harry. We are not surprised at Billie's use of such methods. After all, she has been with Harry for a long time, and has picked up some of his habits. Indeed, she has for a small portion of almost every day managed to become the dominant figure in their relationship by the simple expedient of withholding from Harry something that Harry wants but that is hers to give. As I say, we are not too surprised at Billie because reformation does not obliterate memory, but we are surprised at Paul, the twentieth-century Galahad. For Paul makes common cause with Guinevere, and turns from a Galahad to a Launcelot. Pragmatically, the end may stand clear of the means in a case such as this, but morally, of course, it cannot. Paul and Billie steal papers which are most incriminating. If the contents of the papers are revealed, the bill which Harry wants Congress to pass will have no chance of passing. It does no good to argue that Billie, on paper, owns the incriminating documents at least as much as Harry does, for Paul has no stake in them at all. Then, after stealing the papers, they use them to blackmail Harry. Blackmail is not only an ugly word, it is an ugly deed. Harry will be kept in line, we do not doubt, but his attitudes have not changed a bit. Billie and Paul have departed, leaving Harry, Hedges his senator, and Devery his lawyer, in varying stages of gloom, despair, and chagrin:

BROCK: (*Trying hard to laugh off his disaster*) How do you like that? He coulda had a hundred grand—and she coulda had me. So they end up with nothin'. (*A pause*) Dumb chump.

HEDGES: Yes.

BROCK: Crazy broad.

HEDGES: Quite right.

DEVERY: (*Toasting, his glass held high*) To all the dumb chumps and all the crazy broads, past, present, and future—who thirst for knowledge—and search for truth—who fight for justice— and civilize each other—and make it so tough for sons-of-bitches like you (*to Hedges*) and you (*to Brock*) and me. (*He drinks*).

No, Harry Brock does not reform at the end, even when confronted with necessity. He remains the same because he does not really know the difference between good and evil, between virtue and vice. Reformation inevitably implies a realization that what you were was bad. Harry does not feel that way. He still feels that he and his methods were right. He made a miscalculation, that's all. Oh, yes, the miscalculation wouldn't have been so bad had the chump not been so dumb, the broad not so crazy. Harry remains the same, and the audience is delighted not only that he has been beaten, but that he has not reformed. After all, had he reformed, the audience out of some sense of spiritual generosity or of spiritual altruism might have felt compelled to join him in a rueful smile at his past, an understanding smile at his present, a hopeful smile at his future. As it is, the audience can laugh at him, not with him, laugh heartily that this yearner after power has been frustrated in his drive, that this bully has been bullied. Laugh at him too because he has been made forcibly, if momentarily, aware that some people cannot be bought, that some things are not for sale. And while the audience laughs, perhaps it may forget that though he was beaten at his own game, the victors had to use weapons that he too would have used. We sympathize with, we laugh with, Billie and Paul; we do not have to worship them. We laugh at Harry; and, because he has lost, we no longer have to detest him.

Malvolio in *Twelfth Night* merits our displeasure from the moment that he steps on the stage. His first words show that he is sadly deficient in humor. Feste, whom we have learned to admire, has been trying to joke himself back into the good graces of Olivia, and he has been successful. Olivia asks Malvolio if he doesn't think that Feste is improving. Malvolio's answer, condescending, superior, humorless, leads Olivia to describe Malvolio in terms which we applaud: "O, you are sick of self-love, Malvolio, and taste with a distemper'd appetite. To be generous, guiltless, and of free disposition, is to take those things for birdbolts that you deem cannon bullets."

Just as he dislikes humor, and this play is a comedy, so Malvolio dislikes music, and music is very important in *Twelfth Night*. Sir Toby, Sir Andrew, and Feste are engaged in drinking and singing and laughing. Like other men, in other times, they find pleasure in laughter, in song, in wine. Perhaps they have been a little noisy; perhaps they have had insufficient regard for those in the household who were trying to sleep; perhaps they should be quieted, even silenced, but the arrogant Malvolio uses the wrong methods. Instead of trying to joke the revelers out of their revelry, he adopts a holier-than-thou attitude which a more subtle man would have realized was calculated to enrage not subdue:

My masters, are you mad? or what are you? Have you no wit, manners, nor honesty, but to gabble like tinkers at this time of night? Do ye make an alehouse of my lady's house, that ye squeak out your coziers' catches without any mitigation or remorse of voice? Is there no respect of place, persons, nor time in you?

Sir Toby at first tends to ignore Malvolio, merely suggesting that they were keeping time in their catches, and besides it might not be a bad idea if Malvolio went and hanged himself. But Malvolio continues his diatribe, and it is little wonder that Sir Toby now feels compelled to cut this pompous ass down to his rightful size: "Art any more than a steward? Dost thou think, because thou art virtuous, there shall be no more cakes and ale?" Certainly Sir Toby is probably drunk at the time, but drunk or sober he has sufficient clarity of vision to comprehend that a toady like Malvolio is not to be tolerated.

Words are not enough to destroy this time-pleaser, this affection'd ass, this fool who thinks himself "so cramm'd . . . with excellencies that it is his grounds of faith that all who look on him love him." Maria comes into the picture with a plot that will take excellent advantage of Malvolio's self-love. She will drop a letter in his path; the handwriting in the letter will convince Malvolio that it was written by Olivia; he will take the dictates of the letter to heart, and will act in accordance with them. Both his discovery of the letter, and his actions afterwards, will provide the conspirators with hilarious laughter. This customarily solemn-suited man will appear to Olivia wearing yellow stockings, cross-gartered. This customarily solemn-faced man will appear smiling to Olivia. This customarily solemn-thinking man will, suffering from delusions of grandeur, attempt to flirt with Olivia.

How good the plan is we discover when next we see Malvolio. He has not seen the letter yet, but obviously Maria has been shrewd enough to be cognizant of his inmost thoughts. When we next see him, he is meditating—day-dreaming would be a better term—on his future. He envisions himself married to the Countess Olivia. If we examine the text closely, we can readily see that love for Olivia has nothing to do with his yearnings. If love entered into the situation at all, we might be inclined to feel some sympathy for him, but his desire for marriage is not motivated by love. He is motivated solely by a yearning for the power that a husband of the Countess, a Count Malvolio, might possess. He would have power to give orders to the Countess' uncle, his mortal enemy, Sir Toby Belch; he would have power to control the household and give orders to the Fabians and the Festes and the Marias who now tend to flout him; things would be done his way. As he envisions this happy circumstance, he naturally makes derogatory comments about Sir Toby. If we, aware of the humor in the situation of the biter being bitten, laugh at the concealed Toby's reactions to Malvolio's comments, we laugh more loudly at Malvolio's presumption because we know that Olivia's affections do not incline in his direction. We laugh, too, at his gaucherie when, in his day-dreaming, he makes the classic mistake of confusing the present with the future: "I frown the while, and perchance wind up my watch, or play with my—some rich jewel." The "my" and the hesitation that follows it are important in this connection. Malvolio forgets momentarily that as Count Malvolio he would no longer be wearing his chain, the menial steward's badge of office. It is a natural mistake, to be sure, but we laugh at it because it is a mistake growing out of presumption.

But all this takes place before he finds Maria's carefully phrased letter. The timing here is most important. Had he been led to such envisionings by the discovery of the letter and the ambiguous words which it contains, we might feel sorry for him. As the circumstance exists, however, we do not feel sorry for him at all. The confidence man's cliché, "You can't cheat an honest man," helps us here. Malvolio had yearnings for power before he ever saw the letter. He asked to be duped. His thoughts were channeled in the proper direction before the trick was played on him. The letter merely confirmed his thoughts. Why shouldn't we laugh at him? Why should we sympathize with him? He asked for it.

So he attires himself as the letter suggested; he alters his solemn countenance and appears smiling when Olivia wants him. He couldn't have chosen a worse time to slough off his solemn attitude. Olivia had wanted him because she is despondent, and Malvolio, normally "sad and civil . . . suits well for a servant with my fortunes." So he prances in, gay, flirting, full of ambiguous and veiled reference to the letter about which Olivia knows nothing. It is little wonder that his behavior and appearance cause Olivia to believe that he is a victim of midsummer madness. Kind and gentle, although despondent, she asks that some of her people take care of Malvolio and she asks that Sir Toby look to him. Her reaction to his situation pleases the dupe. If no lower member of the household than Sir Toby is to look after him, surely his dreams have not been in vain, surely nothing can come between him and the full prospect of his hopes. So self-centered is his imagination that he is unable to realize that if Olivia's orders please him, they please Toby and his group even more. The nuisance, the villain, is now in their clutches. They treat him as a madman; according to the benevolent custom of the day, they throw him into a dark room, all the while abjuring him to renounce the devil who assuredly has possessed him. Once he is safely confined, they take this wonderful opportunity to play pranks on him, to torment him, to send Feste in guise of a priest to reprove him. But all will come out in the end. Feste brings him pen, ink, and paper. From the depths of his self-pity, Malvolio composes a letter part pleading, part cajoling, part injured. Feste delivers the letter to Olivia. Olivia, who has always thought kindly of Malvolio, but who always thought of him not as a husband but as a good and faithful servant, sees to it that he is released. Fabian tells all, carefully shielding Maria, as a gentleman should do, and taking all the blame on his shoulders and on the broad shoulders of Sir Toby. He does so, it must be confessed, after Olivia has assured Malvolio that he will be both plantiff and judge in his own case. Nevertheless, Fabian's speech is important. It tells us some important information, and it gives a fair account of the proceedings:

> Good madam, hear me speak,
> And let no quarrel, nor no brawl to come,
> Taint the condition of this present hour,
> Which I have wond'red at. In hope it shall not
> Most freely I confess myself and Toby
> Set this device against Malvolio here,
> Upon some stubborn and discourteous parts
> We had conceiv'd against him. Maria writ
> The letter, at Sir Toby's great importance,
> In recompense whereof he hath married her.
> How with a sportful malice it was follow'd

The object of scorn / 37

> May rather pluck on laughter than revenge,
> If that the injuries be justly weigh'd
> That have on both sides pass'd.

Fabian here demonstrates the essential difference between the sympathetic and antagonistic comic character. The plot was Maria's from the start, but he takes the blame on himself and on Sir Toby who, despite his wounds, is well able to bear it. He demonstrates completely that both sides have been wronged, and that the whole affair, seen in the proper light, is cause for laughter, not revenge. Certainly his approach is reasonable but, conciliatory though it may be, it brings from Malvolio only the bitter exit line, "I'll be reveng'd on the whole pack of you!"

How, then, are we to feel about Malvolio? The answer seems simple. If this is a play about music, he is the discord. If this is a play about laughter, he is the frown. If this is a play about unselfish, romantic love, he, selfishly, loves only himself. Despite Maurice Evans' television version of *Twelfth Night*, despite reputable critics like Mark Van Doren, Malvolio is not the center, the focal point of this romantic comedy, any more than Parolles is the center of *All's Well That Ends Well*, or Don John the center of *Much Ado About Nothing*. Malvolio is a minor obstacle in the path of true love. If the purpose of *Twelfth Night* is to get Viola married to Duke Orsino, and Olivia married to Sebastian, and Maria married to Sir Toby, why do we need Malvolio? We need him to laugh at, because we laugh with all the rest. We laugh with Feste, with Sir Toby, with Maria, with Fabian, even with the Duke in his romantic melancholia, and with Viola in her almost insurmountable problem. We laugh at Malvolio. He is opposed to culture and grace and laughter and joy and music—all the things that we care for. So we laugh at him. In a world of unselfish love, he is selfish. So we laugh at him. We don't have to call him a Puritan; we just have to call him a kill-joy, a time-pleaser, a self-seeker. He exits with our laughter ringing in his ears. If Olivia, the tender-hearted, thinks him notoriously abused, and if Duke Orsino, suddenly practical, wants peace made with him so that he can discover more information about Viola's friendly and helpful Captain, we don't mind. We really don't want Malvolio destroyed; we merely want him to be taught a lesson. If he can't learn, so much the worse for him. There will still be Illyria filled with frank and open love; and there will still be Feste making jokes, getting in scrapes, singing his lovely songs; and there will still be Sir Toby with his hatred for unfilled cans. What more do we need than love and laughter and song and conviviality? So we laugh at Malvolio's final exit because he has been foiled in his desire to substitute self-love for romantic love, a serious mien for frank and open laughter, and the conning of politic authors for the gaiety of song and conviviality.

Parolles, Mr. Applegate, Harry Brock, and Malvolio do not, of course, exhaust the roster of comic antagonists in dramatic literature. They are merely representatives of their type, but if we want to understand dramatic comedy we must understand them. I suggest that if there is a physiological theory of tragedy, and Aristotle's *Poetics* with its emphasis on catharsis is at least one such theory, then it is equally possible to have a physiological theory of comedy. This theory would also emphasize catharsis, but not catharsis of the emotions of pity and terror. The emotions that we seek to purge in comedy are those of scorn and mockery. We do not scorn, we cannot mock, the sympathetic comic character. We certainly are able to scorn and to mock the comic antagonist, the comic villain. Strangely enough, the tragic hero and the comic villain have some things in common. Both are over-reachers; both suffer from hubris; both try to possess more power than is rightfully theirs. The tragic hero is destroyed by the operation of nemesis; the comic villain is frustrated through the mockery of our laughter. The audience of a comedy does not ask that the villain be destroyed; it merely asks that he be foiled. If, like Parolles, he has a possibility of reformation, we are pleased, but not so much that we want to sympathize with him. If, like Mr. Applegate, Harry Brock, or Malvolio, he has no prospect of reformation we do not really mind. For then we can feel superior to him, and we can scorn not only his over-reaching, but also his intellectual blindness, his stiff-necked arrogance. This feeling of superiority is germane to Aristotle's theory of tragedy; it is equally germane to this theory of comedy. For we can seldom, unless we are blind, feel superior to the sympathetic comic character; we can always feel superior to the comic antagonist. And when we leave the theater or put down the copy of the play, we can have a feeling akin to that of the Greek audience which had seen an Aeschylean or Sophoclean tetralogy. The Greek audience, if we are to believe Aristotle, felt superior to the plight of the tragic hero. It reasoned, "Here is this man, noble, even regal. If such terrible things can happen to him through frailty and error, my problems are not so bad after all. I'm really better off than he." When we have seen a comic villain foiled, we can feel superior to him, wondering, if he does show symptoms of reformation, what ever made him so stupid in the first place; congratulating ourselves, if he shows no signs of reformation, on being less stupid, less narrow of vision than he. And we do not mind that the villain has not been destroyed for we generally feel, smugly perhaps, that it will serve him right to go on living with himself. His narrow-visioned pride, his selfishness, his humorlessness, his frustrations should provide him with the kind of company he deserves. The villain has become our butt—the sympathetic comic characters have seen to that—and he has served his purpose admirably well. The bogey man in the children's fairy tales takes fear with him when he is revealed as merely a shadow of evil; the comic villain takes our scorn and our mockery with him when he is revealed as easily foiled, easily frustrated. It is good that he does so. The scorn and the mockery which we so frequently feel should be directed against ourselves have found another target. We can be pleased, we can be content, we can almost feel a little self-satisfied—until the next time we do something foolish.

"You remember the time I knocked Chicago Molly down?"
"Why, you didn't knock her down—I did."
"Well, I started kicking her first."
—W. C. FIELDS in My Little Chickadee

Cruelty and comedy (1): "You beat your pate, and fancy wit will come."

The curtain rises on Act II, scene v of a great tragedy. A beautiful and imperious queen is discovered with her retinue. She is moody, irritable; she seems not to know what to do with herself; time hangs heavily on her hands. She is waiting, as we soon discover, for a message from her loved one who is far away across the sea. First she calls for music, "moody food of us that trade in love," but even before the first notes sound she has already changed her mind. Now she wants to play billiards. She asks one of her attendant ladies to play with her, but the lady, pleading a sore arm, begs off, and suggests that the queen play with her eunuch. The eunuch is willing enough to play, but by the time the queen has taken a moment to voice a mildly bawdy joke at his expense, her mood changes once more and she decides to go fishing. The thought of fishing is satisfying to her momentarily sadistic bent. She intends to "betray" the fish by having her music play far off. Her hook shall pierce their slimy jaws, and she shall call every one of them by the name of her lover as she draws them up, saying, " 'Ah, ha! y'are caught!' " Her lady-in-waiting reminds her of the time that the queen and her lover had gone fishing and wagered on the outcome. At that time one of the queen's divers had put an old salted and dried fish on her lover's hook, and the whole retinue had laughed at his discomfiture. The queen remembers that she had laughed him out of patience, and then laughed him into patience, and then drunk him to his bed. Not satisfied with that, she had dressed him in her own head-dress and mantle, and she had put on his victorious sword. At this point in the reminiscence, the long-awaited messenger arrives. He tries to give his message, but the queen's impetuosity is such that he can scarcely get two words out (or, rather, one word repeated) before she is interrupting, imagining all sorts of dire circumstances that have afflicted her lover. Finally, after many attempts and many interruptions, the messenger is able to deliver his message. It contains worse news than she had imagined. It would have been bad enough for her to have heard that her lover had been captured or was dead; it is worse to hear that he has been married to another woman. She is unable to accept the news with equanimity. We hadn't expected that she would. We might have expected that she would fall into a fit of hysterics, but she goes much further than that. She knocks the messenger down; she strikes him; she drags him up and down the room by his hair; she draws a knife on him. The messenger prudently runs away. The audience imprudently laughs, as it has been laughing all through the scene. The audience knows that it is watching the tragedy of *Antony and Cleopatra*, yet it laughs. The audience knows that it is watching a scene of cruelty and brutality, yet it laughs.

This audience is not composed exclusively of sadists. This is a very sophisticated audience attending a performance of one of Shakespeare's most sophisticated plays. It probably knows what Aristotle has said about tragedy. It may even know that Aristotle has said of comedy:

> It is an imitation of men worse than the average; worse, however, not as regards any and every sort of fault, but only as regards one particular kind, the Ridiculous, which is a species of the Ugly. The Ridiculous may be defined as a mistake or deformity, not productive of pain or harm to others; the mask, for instance, that excites laughter, is something ugly and distorted without causing pain.

But what Aristotle has said doesn't seem to help very much in this situation. The queen probably has acted in a ridiculous manner, but she has caused pain or the appearance of pain. The audience is in a dilemma. It undoubtedly feels a sense of concern, a sense of sympathy for the messenger who merely reports the news; he does not, after all, create it: "Gracious madam, I that do bring the news made not the match." It may even feel a sense of sympathy for the betrayed queen. It laughs, nonetheless, because it has witnessed a cruel and brutal comic scene. Why it laughs at cruelty and brutality is another matter, a matter which requires much thought.

For if we fail to analyze closely, cruelty and comedy seem to have little in common: one causes pain, the other pleasure; one causes moans, the other laughter; one causes sorrow, the other joy. Yet, empirically, they must have something in common, for cruelty and brutality have frequently been used as an occasion for comedy, as a source of laughter. We see them at work together in the beating that Strepsiades receives at the hands of his son Phidippides in *The Clouds*; we laugh at the wonderful domestic battle between Noah and his wife in the Wakefield *Noah* play; we laugh as the rascally Mak gets tossed in a blanket by the duped shepherds in *Secunda Pastorum*; we see them, too, in the beatings that the clever servant comes, resignedly, poutingly, to accept as his due, whether his name is Sosia in *The Amphitruo*, Dromio in *The Comedy of Errors*, Fag in *The Rivals*, or Harpo Marx as he ministers to the needs of the irascible Sig Rumann in *A Night in Casablanca*. The means and implements used by the beaters may and do change—one need only recall the open hand, the fist, the foot, the bastinado, the whip, Sig Rumann's rapier, Chaplin's cane, Mike Sacks's inflated bladder, Mack Swain's bed slat, and Mabel Normand's custard pie—but the beating remains an anticipated and comic constant.

Frequently one beating, comic though it may be, is merely the beginning of a series of beatings, each one funnier than the last. The father beats the son, the son beats the servant, the servant beats the scullery or errand boy, and the boy, finding no human being below him in the order of things, promptly kicks the dog. Bergson would probably call such a piling up of circumstance the Snowball Effect. Sheridan, in *The Rivals*, doesn't bother to name it. He merely uses the device for comedy. Captain Absolute and his father, Sir Anthony Absolute, have had, as their names might suggest, a violent disagreement. Obviously the father and son, despite their name, have been too well bred to resort to blows; threats and vituperation are more their stock in trade. The father's exit lines indicate the mood: "I'll disown you, I'll disinherit you, I'll unget you! and damn me! if ever I call you Jack again!" Although there were no blows, blows were not far from the old man's mind. Fag, the servant, enters at this point, and tells the Captain and us the Audience what old Sir Anthony did after he left the room:

He comes downstairs eight or ten steps at a time—muttering, growling, and thumping the bannisters all the way: I, and the cook's dog, stand bowing at the door—rap! he gives me a stroke on the head with his cane; bids me carry that to my master, then kicking the poor turnspit into the area, damns us all for a puppy triumvirate!

The Captain, still angered by his interview with his father, orders Fag to cease his impertinence, and pushes him aside roughly as he leaves the room. That leaves Fag alone for a moment on the stage, and he takes the opportunity to wax philosophical—until an errand boy arrives:

FAG: So! Sir Anthony trims my master: he is afraid to reply to his father—then vents his spleen on poor Fag! When one is vexed by one person, to revenge oneself on another, who happens to come in the way, is the vilest injustice! Ah! it shows the worst temper—the basest—

Enter Errand Boy

BOY: Mr. Fag! Mr. Fag! your master calls you.

FAG: Well, you little dirty puppy, you need not bawl so!—The meanest disposition! the—

BOY: Quick! quick, Mr. Fag.

FAG: Quick! quick! You impudent jackanapes! am I to be commanded by you too? you little, impertinent, insolent, kitchen-bred—

Exit kicking and beating him.

Why do we laugh at this scene when we read it or see it presented on the stage? There are probably many reasons but, when we examine the circumstances closely, three stand out. In the first place, Sir Anthony is of choleric temperament. He has been crossed, and no one crosses him with impunity. The words he has used to cudgel his son are merely substitutes—and not very satisfactory ones to a person of his disposition—for the blows that he wants to strike. But how can a man strike a fully grown son, particularly when this son is a captain? Yet the blow must be struck. So, when he hits Fag on the head with his cane, he makes it clear to Fag and the audience that the blow was intended for his son. Fag, then, becomes the innocent bystander who receives the blow intended for another. Perhaps this does not seem comic, but it may be pertinent to point out that many of the pie-throwing routines in Mack Sennett moving pictures depend upon just this device for comic effect. Chaplin is very fond of it, and he doesn't always rely upon pie throwing. He does use pie in *A Night in the Show*, but he uses ice cream in *By the Sea*, a mop in *Triple Trouble*, a sword in *Carmen*, and a fist in *His New Job*. The device, or something resembling it, appears in almost every two-reeler he made, as it appears in many of the Laurel and Hardy two-reelers.

When Jule Styne and Sammy Cahn wrote the music and lyrics for the Stephen Longstreet musical comedy *High Button Shoes*, they wrote one song, *The Innocent Standerby*, which, to the best of my knowledge, never appeared in the show. It is unfortunate that the song disappeared in rehearsal, for it is pertinent in this connection, particularly the first eight bars:

> When two guys argue and quarrel,
> Who gets it in the eye?
> Not the fellow who started the quarrel,
> But the innocent standerby.

But we need not confine ourselves to Mack Sennett, Charlie Chaplin, Laurel and Hardy, and *High Button Shoes*. The device is a staple of Jacobean and Restoration drama. It appears in Roman comedy when the braggart soldier, shown up as a coward, goes home and beats his servant. Nor does the innocent standerby have to be animate. In one of Jolita's *Little Eve* cartoons, the first panel shows Little Eve berating her silent husband; the next panels show him walking up the stairs to the attic; the last panel shows him revengefully kicking her dress form. Nor do we need to confine ourselves to

Cruelty and comedy (I) / 47

comedy. The device of the innocent bystander exists in the garb of tragic irony when Cinna the poet is destroyed by the mob in *Julius Caesar*, when Macduff's wife and children are murdered in *Macbeth*, when Satan, in *Paradise Lost*, unable to get back at God, decides to seduce Adam and Eve, two of the lower members of God's creation. But the device most often appears in comedy. When it does appear in tragedy we get not true tragedy but ironic horror.

But the innocent-bystander routine, comic though it may be, is only one of the reasons we laugh at the Fag episode. Consider another aspect of the scene. The scene contains an inevitable, though possibly illogical, series of events: the father abuses the son, and the servant in lieu of the son; the son abuses the servant, too; the servant abuses the errand boy; and the errand boy, presumably, abuses the cook's dog. We have found such a series comic since we were children. *The Farmer in the Dell* and *Old Macdonald Had a Farm* are merely variations on the theme. *The House that Jack Built*, particularly in its sixth stanza, demonstrates the technique admirably:

> This is the cow with the crumpled horn,
> That tossed the dog,
> That worried the cat,
> That killed the rat,
> That ate the malt,
> That lay in the house that Jack built.

The Hebrew Passover Seder has in it (significantly at the end so that the children who like it will stay awake during the rest of the service) the *Chad Gadya* which contains a series of violences, to be sure, but also an insistence upon the omnipotence of God:

> One kid which my father bought for two zuzim:
> And a cat came and ate the kid,
> And a dog came and bit the cat,
> And a stick came and hit the dog,
> And a fire came and consumed the stick,

And water came and extinguished the fire,
And an ox came and drank the water,
And the shochet came and slaughtered the ox,
And the Angel of Death came and killed the shochet,
And the Holy One Blessed be He came and destroyed the
                                    Angel of Death.

As can be readily seen, the *Chad Gadya* contains very little instructional matter in comparison to the great amount of pleasurable sugar coating. The little instruction that is present tends to fade into insignificance when it is mentioned that after each line of the verse the same refrain line is sung. And what is the refrain line? Has anything new been added? The answer is, of course, no. The refrain line is merely the repetition of the first two words of the song: "Chad gadya, chad gadya." Certainly the song's primary purpose is to provide, by means of a series of violent incidents, by means of repetition of the same syllables, a reason for laughter, a source of pleasure. This may seem Bergsonian, particularly when we think of his principles of "repetition," "inversion," and the "reciprocal interference of series," but it is only superficially so. When Bergson speaks of "repetition," he means "coincidence"; when he speaks of "inversion," he means "the robber robbed," or "the biter bitten"; when he speaks of "the reciprocal interference of series," he means *"a situation . . . [which] belongs simultaneously to two altogether independent series of events and is capable of being interpreted in two entirely different meanings at the same time."* In other words, Bergson is dealing with problems that are far more complex than the rather simple one proposed to us by our series of events.

In addition to the innocent-bystander device and the series-of-events technique, there is a third reason that the Fag episode is comic. And if Bergson doesn't help us too much with the second, he certainly helps us with the third. Fag has been saying, "When one is vexed by one person, to revenge oneself on another, who happens to come in the way, is the vilest injustice!" when the errand boy comes into the room. Fag immediately forgets his moralizing, forgets his philosophy, and begins to beat and kick the boy. He does so, of course, not for anything the boy has done (although he does try rationalization on this point) but simply because he has been beaten and shoved by Sir Anthony and Captain Absolute. To order an inferior to follow advice, not example, is a common enough, though deplorable, practice among teachers and parents. To reason a course of conduct and then do the opposite is a common practice of mankind. As Bergson says, "It is not uncommon for a comic character to condemn in general terms a certain line of conduct and immediately afterwards afford an example of it himself: for instance, M. Jourdain's teacher of philosophy [in *The Would-Be Gentleman*] flying into a passion after inveighing against anger." Many other examples could be added to Fag and M. Jourdain: practically all the characters in *Love's Labour's Lost*, but particularly the King and Armado, are guilty; Rosalind in *As You Like It* is guilty; Beatrice and Benedick in *Much Ado About Nothing* are guilty; I am guilty, you are guilty, he, she, or it is guilty.

Perhaps, then, it has been demonstrated that a simple comic beating is not so simple after all. There are many reasons why we laugh at a stage beating, and the three which I have given do not exhaust all of the possibilities. Nor do I believe that we are sadists when we laugh at the messenger in *Antony and Cleopatra* or at Fag in *The Rivals*. I do believe, however, the primary reason we laugh in each instance is that the beating is undeserved. If the victim had done something wrong, we might believe that the beating is both deserved and real. Since the victim had done nothing wrong, we permit ourselves to take refuge in the theatrical bromide: "they make love in jest, they poison in jest"; and we add one of our own: "they beat in jest." Since the beating is undeserved, it is obviously unreal. We can, therefore, laugh; we do not have to take action.

Perhap it was something of this nature, something of the essential unreality which underlies comic brutality, that Harold Ross had in mind in an episode mentioned by James Thurber in his book *The Years With Ross:*

He [Ross] was wary of fatality in drawings, sharing Paul Nash's conviction that "not even Americans can make death funny," and when Carl Rose, in 1932, submitted a picture of a fencer cutting off his opponent's head and crying "Touché!" Ross thought it was too bloody and gruesome, and asked Rose to let me have a swing at it, because "Thurber's people have no blood. You can put their heads back on and they're good as new." It worked out that way. Nobody was horrified.

And few people have been horrified by Charles Addams' cartoons with their emphasis on the supernatural, on organized mayhem, on the bizarre, on the exotic. Do we willingly suspend disbelief for the time that it takes us to smile, or laugh? I doubt it. We smile or laugh because disbelief is not suspended. We know we are laughing at the unreal, not the real. We are the sophisticated, so we laugh. The unsophisticated might give forth a shriek of horror. It is too simple to say, as Al Capp does, "All comedy is based on man's delight in man's inhumanity to man." Even all of Mr. Capp's comedy is not based on that premise. His Shmoos, for example, were the source of gentle laughter before he found it necessary to kill them all off. We certainly do not shed tears over a creature that wants to die, is determined to die, finds happiness in dying, if someone looks at it hungrily.

Before we leave the subject of comic beatings, it might be well to point out what a modern master of slapstick had to say on the subject. Ezra Goodman once interviewed Mack Sennett and published the result of that interview in the New York *Times.* Among other enlightening things, this is what he had to say:

What would Sennett say were the ingredients of successful screen slapstick? "Brevity is one," he holds. Another is "controlled pandemonium." "But," he emphasized, "there is one slapstick rule that is absolutely essential. Never hit mother in the face with a pie. Give it to the mother-in-law, but not mother."

Mr. Sennett's language may be slightly inelegant, but his point is beautifully clear. He holds, as do so many other thinkers on the subject of comedy, that there are some subjects that comedy should not touch. Even so learned a thinker as James Thurber has maintained that ". . . major blasphemies have no place in comedy." Leaving aside the fact that blasphemy does not admit of degree, we find few subjects from mother to God that comedy has not touched, and successfully too. Sostrata, the mother of Lucrezia, in Machiavelli's *Mandragola*, is certainly made an object of mirth. The Lawd in Marc Connelly's *Green Pastures* is frequently treated with what must be to the devout unpardonable freedom. Indeed, much comedy depends on treating a serious subject with levity. Certainly war is a serious subject, but among many other examples we have *What Price Glory?*, Chaplin's *Shoulder Arms*, Keaton's *The General*, Bill Mauldin's cartoons, and *Stalag 17* treating actual combat and imprisonment with a light touch. The political leaders and rulers of great countries should be taken seriously, but we remember with pleasure and delight the annual Gridiron Club Dinner, *Of Thee I Sing*, Chaplin's *The Great Dictator*, and *Love's Labour's Lost*. We can almost say that if a subject is unable to bear our laughter, it does not merit our serious consideration. Man's attitude toward proper objects of mirth has changed little in the millennia that elapsed between the homeric laughter of the gods at Hephaestus bustling from room to room and the laughter of the average man who could purchase a newspaper and enjoy the sight of a dwarf perched on the elephantine thighs of the late J. P. Morgan.

It should be clear by now that beatings are not the only form of physical cruelty that we have in comedy. Restraint of freedom is certainly a form of physical cruelty, and such restraint has frequently been a source of laughter. Malvolio in *Twelfth Night*, receiving the standard Elizabethan treatment for suspected lunatics, is incarcerated in a dark room; the audience laughs at him. The man or woman in puritan New England who had committed a peccadillo was placed in the stocks; the passersby, we are told, laughed at the sight. In Charlie Chaplin's *Work*, Charlie's slave-driving and irascible boss gets his head stuck in a bucket of wallpaper paste; the audience howls at his discomfiture. Sig Rumann in the Marx Brothers' film *A Night at the Opera* plays the role of a pompous impresario who loses most of his clothes and gets locked in a closet when he attempts to block the course of true love and hilarious laughter; the audience enjoys his predicament. It may well be argued that all these examples, even that of the puritan man or woman, are comic antagonists or comic butts, and that we would naturally laugh at anything which causes them annoyance or pain. That's true enough, but we also laugh at the situation of the sympathetic comic character whose freedom is restrained. And there are ways to restrain that do not involve the locked door, the iron bars, the stocks, or the oubliette. Clothes can be a restraining force. In *As You Like It*, Rosalind must wear male attire. Her transvestitism causes her many problems, problems that merit our laughter. A young girl falls in love with her; her father fails to recognize her (a minor matter, to be sure, for as she says, "But what talk we of fathers when there is such a man as Orlando?"); her true love, and this is the major difficulty, doesn't recognize her either. She is unable to act as she wants to act, speak as she wants to speak. Clothes have restrained her freedom as much as the locked closet door restrained Sig Rumann's freedom, as much as the dark room restrained Malvolio's freedom. Of course, her restraints are dissolved in the end just as Malvolio's are, just as Sig Rumann's are, just as the similar restraints of

Cruelty and comedy (I) **/ 53**

Viola in *Twelfth Night* are. But she is a sympathetic comic character, and her freedom has been restrained, and the audience has laughed.

Not clothes but a machine restrains Chaplin's freedom in *Modern Times*. He becomes its victim, its servant, its slave. The cog wheel catches him up and makes him, temporarily, a component part of the diabolical mechanism: the automatic feeder feeds him nuts and bolts. He has no freedom of motion; he has no freedom of thought. By the time that he escapes from it, the machine has imposed upon him one reflex action: with a huge wrench he proceeds, temporarily deranged, to tighten everything in sight, no matter how slightly it resembles a nut. Like Pavlov's dogs, he has been conditioned, and the audience, primitive or sophisticated, conditioned or unconditioned, laughs at this sympathetic character whose freedom has been restrained.

While clothes and machines, bear traps and paste buckets can restrain freedom, the obvious restraint is the jail cell or the prospect of a jail cell. No one who saw it will ever forget Willie Howard's plaintive but fruitless cry from the cell to his lawyer, "Pay the two dollars." Phil Silvers, in his television role of Sergeant Bilko, frequently found himself in the guardhouse. One episode is germane to this discussion. Colonel Hall has passed an anti-gambling ordinance. Bilko naturally violates the ordinance. He is, as might be expected, confined. Confinement of this most rugged of all individualists would inevitably be a source of comedy, but this confinement is more than ordinarily comic because he has sought it. He has conceived a diabolically clever plan. If things go according to his plan, Sergeants Grover and Ritzik, his two favorite poker victims, will be confined with him. In the guardhouse with nothing else to do, he will have infinite leisure to fleece them. His plan goes awry. He is confined, to be sure, but they are forcibly prevented from joining him. At this point in the script it is difficult to determine which is the most comic: their attempts to get in the guardhouse (no victims ever fought harder to be slaughtered), Bilko's attempts to get out, or the attempts of all three to play poker while he is in and they are out and the military policemen are attempting to restore order. To argue that the audience is not laughing at cruelty, to argue that it is laughing at a magnificent example of the punishment fitting the crime, is to miss the point. Bilko's freedom is restrained. He epitomizes the free spirit. Any type of physical restraint is cruel, is brutal, both to him and to his sympathetic audience. That other sources of humor are present in the episode, I freely admit. The inflexibility of the official mind is clearly portrayed by the military policemen. The eagerness of gulls to be gulled is clearly portrayed by Grover and Ritzik. As mentioned above, Bilko's predicament may well be considered an excellent example of the biter being bitten, because he has sought the imprisonment. But the physical restraint of the free spirit is the primary source of comedy in the episode.

The practical joke is another form of cruelty that frequently causes laughter. If you were to ask fifty people if they find practical jokes funny, all fifty would deny that they do, and vehemently. At least forty-nine of them will laugh when they see one. The minor reservation is necessary here because the victim rarely, if ever, laughs. Our present degree of sophistication causes us to maintain that we frown, not laugh, at practical jokes. The practical joke, we say, is low brow, is infra dig. Yet practical jokes are not now and never have been confined to the low brow. There are such elaborate, high brow, literary practical jokes as "Bunburying" in *The Importance of Being Earnest*, the disguised Rosalind's treatment of the love-sick Orlando in *As You Like It*, and the horning of Messer Nicia in *Mandragola*. Our sophisticates generally laugh at these episodes. They will laugh, too, at the clever administration of a hot foot, the dextrous removal of a chair as the victim attempts to sit, the ingenious mechanical contrivance that causes a bucket of water to inundate a victim as he opens a door. They won't admit laughing at such incidents, even though they do so, unless you follow the advice of H. Allen Smith and refer to them not as "practical jokes," but as "pranks."

Indeed, most practical jokes, literary or non-literary, do not deal in physical pain; they deal, instead, in emotional pain, in emotional brutality. But with all our newly acquired knowledge of psychosomatic medicine, we should hesitate before we draw any sharp line of demarcation between emotional and physical pain. For the practical joke, physical and emotional, has been a staple of literary comedy from *The Clouds* through *Love's Labour's Lost* and *The Jumping Frog of Calaveras County* to Sam and Bella Spewack's *Kiss Me, Kate!* And there are merely differences in degree, not in kind, when Bill Calhoun signs Fred Graham's name to a $10,000 I.O.U. in *Kiss Me, Kate!*, or when the Princess of France and her ladies exchange favors so that they can confuse the King of Navarre and his gentlemen in *Love's Labour's Lost*, or when Joe the Joker administers a hot foot in Damon Runyon's short story *Sense of Humor*.

Mention of *The Jumping Frog of Calaveras County* brings to mind the pertinent fact that the victim of comic brutality or the practical joke need not always be human. The popularity of the Donald Duck and the Tom and Jerry cartoons is proof of that. Indeed, the victim of comic brutality need not even be animate. The *Little Eve* cartoon mentioned above provides proof. Both Jimmy Durante and Harpo Marx cause laughter, despite the occasional twinge of regret that stirs in the breast of the music lover when they destroy a piano before the eyes of the audience. The destruction of a golf club or a billiard cue following a poor shot has frequently caused laughter both on the stage and in life. And W. C. Fields, operating on the theory that you can create comedy when an object that the audience expects to break merely bends, capitalized on this point with a succession of canes, billiard cues, and golf clubs. Even Fields was not totally immune to the destructive infection. In *The Barber Shop*, Fields is represented as owning a bass violin called "Lena." A man comes in and tries to sell him another bass violin which is, according to the owner's nomenclature, masculine. Unsuccessful in his attempt at a sale, he asks Fields's permission to leave his bass fiddle in the barber shop while he does some shopping. At the end of the two-reeler, Fields discovers that the two bass violins have propagated a litter of violins. In paternal outrage he destroys the masculine intruder as he kicks it out of his shop.

Despite the plethora of golf clubs and canes and pianos and fiddles that populate comedy, the victim of comic brutality is most often human or possessed of human characteristics. Al Capp's *L'il Abner* with its cast of comic brutes is a case in point. So, too, is George Willard's *Moon Mullins*, which presents in the characters of Willie and Mamie a twentieth-century version of the Wakefield *Noah* play. Of course, there is a major, twentieth-century difference: Willie, unlike Noah, never wins either argument or fight. To mention comic strips and not to mention George Herriman's *Krazy Kat* would be to lose critical franchise. *Krazy Kat* is full of poetic language, classical allusion, universal symbolism. Yet in this strip a unique form of violence is raised to high comic art. The three principal characters in the strip, Krazy Kat, Ignatz Mouse, and Offissa Pupp, have already been celebrated by such formidable intellects as Gilbert Seldes and E. E. Cummings. It would be difficult to disagree with Seldes and Cummings—even if I wanted to, which I don't—but we should not lose sight of the fact that the primary source of humor in the cartoon is a brick flying through the air. The brick has been hurled with deadly accuracy by Ignatz; its target is the loving head of Krazy, who must not, despite her pleasure at being hit, be called a masochist; the task of preventing the flight of the brick or, as is most often the case, punishing the hurler, is Offissa Pupp's. Certainly there are other aspects of comedy in the strip. It seems contrary to nature that a cat should love a mouse or that a dog should love a cat, but that's the way Herriman's world is. Cummings explains the situation as well as anyone can explain the inexplicable:

Two of the protagonists are easily recognized as a cynical brick-throwing mouse and a sentimental policeman-dog. The third protagonist—whose ambiguous gender doesn't disguise the good news that here comes our heroine—may be described as a humbly poetic, gently clownlike, supremely innocent, and illimit-ably affectionate creature (slightly resembling a child's drawing of a cat, but gifted with the secret grace and obvious clumsiness of a penguin on terra firma) who is never so happy as when egoist-mouse, thwarting altruist-dog, hits her in the head with a brick. Dog hates mouse and worships "cat," mouse despises "cat" and hates dog, "cat" hates no one and loves mouse. . . . Joy is her [Krazy's] destiny: and joy comes through Ignatz—via Offissa Pupp; since it is our villain's loathing for law which gives him the strength of ten when he hurls his blissyielding brick. Let's not forget that. And let's be perfectly sure about something else. Even if Offissa Pupp should go crazy and start chasing Krazy, and even if Krazy should go crazy and start chasing Ignatz, and even if crazy Krazy should swallow crazy Ignatz and crazy Offissa Pupp should swallow Krazy and it was the millennium—there'd still be the brick. And (having nothing else to swallow) Offissa Pupp would then swallow the brick. Whereupon, as the brick hit Krazy, Krazy would be happy.

As Cummings says, "There'd still be the brick," and this brick has lost many of its normal connotations. It is not designed to be part of a noble edifice, or of a body-and-spirit-warming fireplace, or even of a herringbone-pattern sidewalk. It is designed purely as a weapon and, as a weapon, it is, in Cummings' word, "blissyielding." How much more can you ask of an inanimate object? This brick is, in so many ways, superior to Chaplin's cane or Fields's billiard cue or Durante's piano. In *Krazy Kat* cruelty and brutality cause a type of laughter that we normally do not associate with violence: one of the highest forms of comedy, the comedy of joy. James Feibleman in his book *In Praise of Comedy* lists the names of comedy in descending order: Joy, Divine Comedy, Humour, Irony, Satire, Sarcasm, Wit, and Scorn. As Feibleman is aware, no one will agree completely with the order of his list, but he has done a brave service in preparing the order. Just as an example, I might prefer placing Divine Comedy higher than Joy, and placing Wit higher than Sarcasm, but there is some merit to his list. Certainly (remember Cummings' word "blissyielding") *Krazy Kat* belongs in the Joy category; normally comedy of brutality would be placed on a far lower plane.

There are, then, many forms of cruelty that cause laughter and comedy, and the comedy that is created is not confined to any one aspect. Cruelty can create high comedy as well as farce, sophistication as well as slapstick. The mention of farce and slapstick, however, brings to mind the formidable comic chases included in every Marx Brothers or W. C. Fields moving picture. These chases involve not only the participants but also the spectators. So comic are these chases that it might well be argued that the invention of the automobile and the motion-picture camera created a new dimension in comic horror. That there are comic chases in plays that antedate the automobile and the motion-picture camera, I am well aware; that these earlier chases, even such a brilliant one as that in *The Birds*, are limited in technique and effect, I insist. To see a chase in a Keystone Comedy or in Chaplin's *The Kid*, or in *The Bank Dick* or in *The Big Store*, is to laugh at dangers narrowly missed, to thumb one's nose at death and destruction, to achieve once more—if only vicariously—the splendid exhilaration that we knew as children when, with shirts stuffed with stolen apples, we outdistanced the heavy-

Cruelty and comedy (I) **/ 59**

footed, irascible owner of the tree. But it may be argued that the chase is not brutal or cruel. The sympathetic comic characters, admittedly, generally escape, but the threat of cruelty and brutality is always present. Fear of cruelty, fear of brutality can be as potent in evoking laughter as the fact of cruelty or the fact of brutality. As Buster Keaton has said, "The best way to get a laugh is to create a genuine thrill and then relieve the tension with comedy." The chase, then, is generally more comic if the crack-up at the end is avoided. Here is one case when the will is genuinely preferred to the deed.

Along with the chase as a source of the comic we should mention the sick joke, the cruel joke, the Bloody Mary—call it what you will—that a few years ago swept the country into its mephitic embrace. While the comic chase of the motion picture is a new dimension in comedy, the sick joke most definitely is not. It is older than Aristophanes and obligingly appears on the scene whenever the sophisticates of an age, be they the courtiers of Caesar Augustus or the glib-tongued denizens of Madison Avenue, feel that cruelty, horror, and sex should be treated lightly, coolly, as a joke. But the sick joke deserves—"deserves" is too strong a word; "requires" would be better—a chapter devoted to it alone. Its history and morphology are fascinating, repulsive but fascinating.

There are other forms of cruelty that cause comedy and laughter, but certainly we have mentioned enough forms to demonstrate that cruelty and comedy frequently have much in common. To point out that they have much in common is one thing, and an easy thing at that; to explain why they have much in common is not so easy. When we laugh at a scene of comic cruelty, we may be laughing in hysterical relief that we are not the victim. Certainly this theory has some merit. We all know about aesthetic distance; we all know that behind the footlights they make love in jest, they murder in jest, they beat in jest. We know, I say, because we are clever, we are sophisticated; but is everyone in on the secret? Constance Rourke tells of a remarkable incident in her brilliant work, *American Humor.* She is describing one member of an audience present at a performance of a melodrama in a Kentucky village. On the small stage a gambler's family was movingly portrayed as starving. This member of the audience, moved to compassion, rose and said, "I propose we make up something for this woman." Even after someone had whispered to him that it was all make-believe, he delivered a lecture on "the worthlessness of the gambler, flung a bill on the stage with his pocketbook, advised the woman not to let her husband know about it or he would spend it all on faro, and then with a divided mind sat down, saying, 'Now go on with the play.' "

Such naïveté is not confined to Kentucky backwoodsmen. George Burns described an event that happened to him in the Victoria Palace in London. He and Gracie Allen were playing to a packed house—but let him tell it:

> We had an encore that we used in case we were a hit. I would come out and say, "Ladies and Gentlemen, we would like to do a little more, but we're not prepared." Then Gracie would interrupt and say, "*I* am." Then she would talk, and then I would talk, until we were both talking competitively, and it would end with one of our big jokes.
>
> Opening night we were a hit and we were doing this encore. I said, "Ladies and Gentlemen, we would like to do a little more, but we're not prepared." Gracie said, "*I* am." She talked, I talked, we were both talking, and suddenly an English gentleman in white tie and tails who was sitting in the sixth row, and who apparently didn't understand it was part of the act, rose to his feet, snapped his fingers, and said, "See here, let the little lady carry on."

We may smile condescendingly as we hear the tale of the partly gullible, naïve, backwoodsman, or the tale of the supposedly sophisticated English gentleman, but certainly we have missed a great experience in life if we have not, at one time or another, felt such an identity with dramatic reality.

Cruelty and comedy (I) / 61

So we may laugh in relief that we are not the victims of the comic brutality, but I doubt that that is the only reason. Instead of being glad that we are not the victim, we may be identifying ourselves with the perpetrator of the cruelty. In that case, since we are humane and decent beings, the victim obviously deserves his comeuppance at our hands, and we are delighted that the ends of justice are being served. So that gives us another theory, also with some merit, that we like to see pomposity deflated, we like to see Sir Politic Would-Be in his tortoise shell, Malvolio in his dark room, Parolles blindfolded and bedevilled, and Sig Rumann, clad only in long underwear, locked in a closet.

While it is undoubtedly satisfying and laughable to see pomposity deflated, that, too, is only part of the answer. This theory, like the previous one, will not hold in all examples. We like to see comic antagonists and comic butts get what is coming to them, but how do we account for our laughter when the sympathetic comic character is beaten, gets incarcerated, or is subjected to other forms of the cruelly comic? We do laugh at the misadventures of Charlie Chaplin in the boxing ring, and in *City Lights* Chaplin is definitely a sympathetic comic character. And we do laugh at the discomfiture of Falstaff at Gadshill, and Falstaff is certainly a sympathetic comic character in 1 *Henry IV*. Bottom in *A Midsummer Night's Dream* is not a comic antagonist, but the sight of him in an ass's head is undoubtedly a source of laughter.

Our two theories, then, leave something to be desired. Each is valid some of the time; neither is valid all of the time; even if we combine them, we cannot justly claim that they will cover all the aspects of the cruelly comic. Perhaps, then, we may offer the theory that we laugh at cruelty if the pain that results from it is limited: it may hurt, but not maim; abuse, but not kill. Such discrimination requires tremendous objectivity on the part of the audience, but most audiences are able to be properly objective. Ashton Reid, writing on Buster Keaton, has this to say about timing and cruelty and comedy:

> In the gag business, timing is the difference between a wow and a flop. Mr. Keaton learned this fact the hard way. When he was a mere stripling, part of the Three Keatons routine called for Old Man Keaton to whack Buster on the seat of the pants with a broom. The kid found out that if he yelled "Ouch!" instantly, no one laughed. If he ignored the whack, no one laughed. But if he ignored the whack for five seconds and then yelled—that was funny. It was funny because it conveyed the idea that it took five seconds for the whack to travel from Buster Keaton's pants seat to his brain.

Whether or not Reid's interpretation is correct, we have concrete evidence that audiences are able to discriminate—even five seconds worth. So we are unable to say that audiences are incapable of the necessary objectivity and discrimination. We are unable to say that insufficient time is available between the cruelty and the laugh. We cannot even fall back on the snide comment that far as we have progressed in twentieth-century physiology and psychology, no one as yet has invented a do-it-yourself pain-threshold detector. But there are examples to refute such a theory. Chaplin went beyond the limits mentioned above when he made death comic at least once in *Carmen*, occasionally in *The Great Dictator*, and many times in *Monsieur Verdoux*, which he had the courage to subtitle, "A comedy of murders." The animated cartoons featuring Popeye the Sailor deal in organized mayhem: bones are broken with finesse and casualness; arms and legs are stretched so freely that it seems as if a comic procrustean bed is controlling the action; necks are twisted round and round as if some dextrous hand were winding a clock. Tom Lehrer's songs treat death as comic on at least three occasions. Jonathan Swift's *Modest Proposal* deserves mention in this connection. In other words, there seem to be no limits to the extent and kind of cruelty that can cause laughter. None of the traditional theories seems to obtain when carefully examined. Surely there must be some reason why we laugh when we are presented with scenes of cruelty, brutality, and death. Perhaps we laugh because we know, consciously or unconsciously, that what we are watching is not real. I do not forget Constance Rourke's backwoodsman. He, too, in Miss Rourke's words, was of "divided mind." I do not forget George Burns's English gentleman, so fashionably attired in white tie and tails. The point of the Burns and Allen act was to convey the impression that what they were doing was spontaneous, unrehearsed, natural, not dramatic. The English gentleman can be excused if he saw fit to protest a blatant display of what he considered to be bad manners. It is easy, too easy, for us to forget that when we applaud at the final curtain of *Antony and Cleopatra*, we are applauding the representation of an action, not the action itself. We are not applauding the act of suicide; we are applauding the stage representation of the act. When we laugh at stage or screen representations of violence, cruelty, brutality, or death, we are probably laughing at the representations of the acts, not the acts themselves; when we laugh at practical jokes that really cause pain, we take time to gasp in horror. This time that we take, unconsciously to be sure, enables us to ascertain that the pain does not exceed the stated limits: hurt, but not maim; abuse, but not kill. Perhaps it is healthy that we do so. Perhaps by so doing we are able to purge ourselves of the latent sadism that is, to a greater or lesser measure, in all of us. This theory is, to be sure, Aristotelian, but only superficially so. In actuality it is, despite all of the nasty things that Plato had to say about comedy and the comic, Platonic. The representation of a cruel act on the stage is at least two, and probably three, removes from reality. If we actually think that the cruelty which we see enacted on the stage is real, we should not laugh, we should not applaud, we should take action. Because we know that it isn't real, we are enabled to dissolve in laughter. For we know full well that after the final curtain there will be no welts on the back, no bruises on the buttocks, no more ropes or chains confining arms and legs. And in the dressing room the stage corpse and his stage murderer will be sitting side by side as they remove their make-up. What are they discussing? Not, you may be sure, the Freudian theory of tendency wit, but a far more momentous problem: where will they go to have coffee and sandwiches?

You taught me language, and my profit on't
Is I know how to curse.
                              —Caliban in *The Tempest*

Cruelty and comedy (II): *"When you say* that, *frown!"*

A few years ago, the cruel joke, the sick joke, the Bloody Mary—it had many names—rapidly made its mephitic way across the country. Even now it has not completely disappeared. It has not died. Along with the sick comedian, it is merely hibernating in poorly lighted, badly ventilated caverns which are called "sophisticated supper clubs" by those in the know. Those in the know have also spent much time in high-level debate in an effort to ascertain the origin of the sick joke.

Most connoisseurs of the genre believe that its bloodline (I use the term advisedly) is simple: by Ivy League out of Madison Avenue. Some connoisseurs, however, are far more specific in their description: by Charles Addams out of Tom Lehrer.

> *"Mother, what's a vampire?"*
> *"Shut up, kid, and drink your blood."*

Whatever the bloodline, and some case can be made for each of the theories and many more in addition, by this time the country has definitely taken sides in a slightly less high-level debate to determine the sick joke's value. Those who approve of the sick joke feel that it provides a healthy, non-aggressive outlet for our latent sadistic impulses (I doubt that Freud would call the sick joke "non-aggressive") and, besides, it's funny. Those who disapprove feel that its flourishing gives more proof—if, indeed, more proof were needed—that delinquency of the juvenile, mature, and senile varieties is rampant (I somehow remember that Milton felt that no person had ever been corrupted by a book) and, besides, the sick joke is not amusing.

> *"Mother, why do I keep turning around in circles?"*
> *"Be quiet, Herbert, or I'll nail your other foot to the floor."*

Funny or not, healthy outlet or symptom of a moral illness, the sick joke flourished, particularly in the groves of academe and in the rarefied atmosphere where dwelt the entrepreneurs of the "communications" industry. Some people hoped that if they simply ignored it, it would go away. It didn't. It may have hibernated, but it did not disappear. It would seem that it is here for a while and, if we can't avoid it, and we can't, we had better try to understand it. I don't mean the joke itself, for the joke is obvious to the point of painfulness. I mean rather its source, its origin, for the two bloodlines given above are clearly superficial and interested far more in epigrammatic utterance than in truth. I mean, too, its reason for being in such a place as this, at such a time as now. These problems lead us, inevitably but unfortunately, into such forbidding areas as the history and sociology of literary taste. By a brief examination of literary history, we can see that the emotional attitude which creates the sick joke is a recurrent, not a unique, phenomenon; by gingerly dipping a tentative toe in the gelid waters of sociology, we may be able to see why it re-arose at precisely this time and in precisely this place.

"Something in a hearing aid, Mr. Van Gogh?"

The sick joke represents, it seems to me, an attempt to attain a superior, sophisticated attitude toward violence, sex, physical deformity, revealed religion, and death. In order to attain this attitude, the normal—one could almost say the "stock"—responses must appear to be ignored. We normally respond with horror to representations of violence. The sick joke asks us to laugh. We normally respond with a feeling of awe to representations of revealed religion. The sick joke asks us to snicker. We normally respond with compassion or sympathy when confronted with physical deformity. The sick joke wants us to be amused. But laughter, and snickers, and amusement are not enough. We must be aware as we laugh that what we are laughing at is not normally considered funny by those who are not so clever as we are. We must be aware that we are the initiated, the esoteric. We must feel superior, we must feel sophisticated in the presence of violence, sex, revealed religion, death, and physical deformity.

> *"Mrs. Jones, may Johnny come out and play baseball?"*
> *"Why, boys, how can you ask that? You know that Johnny is a quadruple amputee."*
> *"We know, but we need something for second base."*

It is easy to find examples through the ages of such sophistication. We can find it in some of the plays of Aristophanes, in many of the epigrams of Martial, in some of the *Meta-morphoses* and in sections of the *Ars Amatoria* of Ovid, in parts of the *Golden Ass* of Apuleius, in *Trimalchio's Dinner* by that *arbiter elegantiarum*, Petronius. I have by no means exhausted the classical period, but a few examples should suffice. The Middle Ages offer us some of the *Lais* of Marie de France, the sophisticated attitude toward illicit love of Chaucer's Pandarus and, indeed, of the entire courtly love tradition, the sophisticated attitude toward violence and the clergy of Chaucer's *fabliaux*, and the attitude toward physical deformity which is represented by the gargoyles on gothic cathedrals.

> *"Look, kid, I don't care who your father is—you don't walk on the water while I'm fishing."*

The Renaissance, even if we exclude some of the exquisite refinements on the art of torture developed by the Inquisition, gives us a rich lode to be mined. Just by confining ourselves to one literary figure, we have the youthful Shakespeare with his sophisticated attitude toward violence and death in *Titus Andronicus*, *Henry VI*, and *King John*; his sophisticated attitude toward violence, sex, physical deformity, religion, and death in *Richard III*; and his sophisticated attitude toward sex in *Venus and Adonis*. William T. Hastings has interpreted this attitude brilliantly in his excellent essay, "The Hardboiled Shakspere." Of *Venus and Adonis* he writes:

> At mention of "the boar" Venus nearly swoons,
> "And on his neck her yoking arms she throws:
>   She sinketh down, still hanging by his neck,
>   He on her belly falls, she on her back."

There follow, as every schoolboy knows, some witty verses on the general subject of leading a horse to water. And then we pass to a dialogue between the two which rapidly develops into a debate on love, lust, and "increase." The more innocent of modern readers may forget the pose of the two debaters . . . but we can be sure that for Shakespeare and his courtly readers therein lay the special savor of the passage, than which it would be difficult to imagine anything more hardboiled.

Only the more innocent of modern readers will forget the pose of the two debaters. Hastings has caught in essence the attitude that I am trying to describe. He may call this attitude hardboiled, and I may call it sophisticated, but there is basically no difference between the two attitudes. I suppose it is unnecessary to mention either to the hardboiled reader or to the sophisticated reader that this debate episode in *Venus and Adonis* lasts from line 592 to line 810 of the poem, 219 lines of what might well be called sophisticated titillation.

"Mother, may I have a new dress for Easter?"
"No, you may not, Edward."

After the time of Shakespeare, there are the scenes of horror with which the Jacobean dramatists sought to thrill and titillate their audiences, and the smart, superior, clever, even smutty, attitudes toward love, lust, and sex which Vanbrugh and Wycherley imposed upon the audiences of the Restoration. Then there was the eighteenth century, the Age of Reason, the Age of Wit, the age of Pope and the *Dunciad*, and Swift and his scatalogical poetry. And before we leave the eighteenth century, surely we have time to mention the super-sophistication of John Cleland's attitude. According to report, Cleland, finding himself without funds, sought to rectify his impecunious situation. Unemployment insurance was unknown in the eighteenth century. He therefore set out to write a book that would be as lewd as possible. He also set for himself—so the tradition runs—an almost impossible restriction: he would use no word which could possibly offend the most proper of men and women. The result, successful if you consider his original intention, was his notorious book, *Fanny Hill, or The Memoirs of a Woman of Pleasure.* It is true that no individual word offends, but the book is indisputably salacious. How sophisticated can you get?

"Tell me, Jocasta, what was that difficulty you had with your second husband?"

Then, still in the eighteenth century but lapping over into the nineteenth, and just across the English Channel, there was Count Donatien Alphonse François Sade, better known as the Marquis de Sade. He gave three words, "sadism," "sadist," and "sadistic" to the dictionaries, and thousands of pages in which cruelty and violence and lewdness are inextricably united, to the world. His leading characters, both male and female, are always aware, intellectually aware, of what they are doing and why they are doing it. They are not immoral but amoral. They never lose themselves in complete emotional abandon as other, more normal, mortals do. Simone de Beauvoir, in her perceptive essay, "Must We Burn Sade?" describes with insight and accuracy the attitude of the Sade protagonist:

The male aggression of the Sadist Hero is never softened by the usual transformation of the body into flesh. He never, for an instant, loses himself in his animal nature; he remains so lucid, so cerebral, that philosophic discourse, far from dampening his ardor, acts as an aphrodisiac.

Mlle de Beauvoir is undoubtedly correct in her description and in her analysis. The effect of Sade's books on the reader is something else again: Sade's philosophical discourse acts not as an aphrodisiac, but as a soporific; his description of sex and violence act not as an aphrodisiac, but as an emetic.

And the same may be said of the books of Leopold von Sacher-Masoch. He, like Sade, gave three words, "masochism," "masochist," and "masochistic" to the dictionaries, but he gave, fortunately, far fewer pages and far less philosophical utterance to the world. As a matter of fact, it is doubtful that Sacher-Masoch belongs in Sade's company at all. He is far less cerebral, imaginative, and vicious than his notorious predecessor. It is customary to link the two, explaining blandly that, after all, masochism is merely the reverse of the coin of which sadism is the obverse. While there may be some degree of merit in this linking, there is, I feel, a fundamental difference implicit in these perversions. Sade's hero makes every effort to insure that his victim has no possibility of pleasure. He generally rationalizes his behavior by maintaining that if the victim derives any pleasure, the hero's pleasure is reduced by just that much. To consider pleasure in such a light seems extremely cold-blooded and dispassionate. Yet it must be remembered that the Sade hero is cerebral above all. Such calculation is part of his reason for being. Sacher-Masoch's victim-protagonist seems to take the diametrically opposite point of view: the more pleasure the tormentor gets, the more the victim-protagonist's pleasure is increased. In short, the masochist needs a morbidly cruel person for a tormentor; the sadist is far more self-sufficient in that he needs only an object, not a personality. I may be totally wrong in this judgment, but I find it hard to believe that a victim of physical cruelty is able to rise above his situation as easily as an inflictor of physical cruelty. The sadist hero, completely dominating his situation, can and does easily deprive his victim of any prospect of pleasure; the masochistic hero, completely dominated by his situation, neither has nor desires such control over his tormentor. Sade is, then, more intellectual; Sacher-Masoch is more physical and emotional. Both writers, however, demonstrate a sophisticated attitude toward violence, cruelty, religion, sex, and horror.

> "Why don't you try Carter's Little Liver Pills, Mr. Prometheus?"

When we reach Sacher-Masoch's algolagnia in our investigation of the cerebral attitude toward violence and sex, we have gone, briefly and superficially, from classical Greece to the end of the nineteenth century. Certainly this survey is not exhaustive. The works could be and should be analyzed more closely. We could range far more widely in time and space and not come to the end of such a survey. Certainly some time could be given to the tales of Boccaccio told by the gentle folk of Florence who fled the plague; certainly some mention could be made of the paintings of Lucas Cranach the Elder or the etchings of Albrecht Dürer; I miss, too, some discussion of the gigantic laughter of Rabelais, the horror of Swift, the perversions of Swinburne and Wilde, the childish cruelty of *Mother Goose* and *Alice in Wonderland*. But we are now in the twentieth century. Along with the thermonuclear bomb, the twentieth century has given birth to the sick joke, and we must examine, again briefly, the twentieth-century literary sources and analogues of this phenomenon.

> *"Mother, why is daddy so cold, so white, and so pale?"*
> *"Shut up, Herbert, and dig."*

The twentieth century is replete with sources and analogues of the sick joke, with examples of the sophisticated attitude that we've been discussing. The problem is not finding the examples, but selecting from the myriads that are available. We find them in the writings of two of our Nobel prize winners, Hemingway and Faulkner. The Faulkner of *Sanctuary* certainly had a cool, sophisticated attitude toward violence and sex. Certainly, too, if you consider *Sanctuary* an unfair example because it is, admittedly, an early work and a potboiler, Faulkner maintains this attitude (not, to be sure, to the exclusion of other attitudes) in his saga of the Sutpen clan, several volumes of which have won critical acclaim, in several of his most brilliant short stories, and in the tales of the house of Snopes. And the Hemingway of "The Killers" had this attitude, too. Note the cool, purely objective, completely dispassionate attitude toward death in this passage:

> "What are you going to kill Ole Andreson for? What did he ever do to you?"
> "He never had a chance to do anything to us. He never even seen us."

"And he's only going to see us once," Al said from the kitchen.

"What are you going to kill him for, then?" George asked.

"We're killing him for a friend. Just to oblige a friend, bright boy."

"The Killers" was written about 1927, and Hemingway was young. He was still young, but it was some ten years later, when he wrote *To Have And Have Not*. There are some healthy, normal attitudes toward sex and violence in the book, but there is an awareness of the sophisticated attitudes, too. Here is Helen Gordon as she talks to the husband she is about to leave:

"Everything I believed in and everything I cared about I left for you because you were so wonderful and you loved me so much that love was all that mattered. Love was the greatest thing wasn't it? Love was what we had that no one else had or could ever have? And you were a genius and I was your whole life. I was your partner and your little black flower. Slop. Love is just another dirty lie. Love is ergoapiol pills to make me come around because you were afraid to have a baby. Love is quinine and quinine and quinine until I'm deaf with it. Love is that dirty aborting horror that you took me to. Love is my insides all messed up. It's half catheters and half whirling douches. I know about love. Love always hangs up behind the bathroom door. It smells like lysol. To hell with love."

Then thirty years after "The Killers," and twenty years after *To Have And Have Not*, in the Centennial Issue of *The Atlantic Monthly* which appeared in November, 1957, Hemingway had a short story entitled "A Man of the World." In the story there is a description of a knock-down-and-drag-out fight between two men. One of the men has gouged out the eyeball of his opponent. The vile jelly is hanging down on the victim's cheek when a spectator offers some cool, dispassionate advice: "Bite it off! Bite it off just like it was a grape." Such attitudes toward violence are not confined to men in Hemingway's writings. Mrs. Macomber's thoughts and actions in the denouement of "The Short Happy Life of Francis Macomber" provide ample proof that the female of the species is at least as deadly as the male.

We might notice also some other writers, not Nobel prize winners. In Dashiell Hammett's short stories (particularly the conclusions of "The Gutting of Couffignal" and "The Girl with the Silver Eyes"), in his novel *Red Harvest*, and in his novelette *Nightmare Town*, violence and death are as common as eating. There are sophisticated attitudes toward love and sex in his novels *The Thin Man* and *The Maltese Falcon*. Sophisticated attitudes towards sex and religion abound in James M. Cain's *Serenade*, and sophisticated attitudes toward sex and violence are certainly present in his *Double Indemnity*. About 40,000,000 copies of Mickey Spillane's detective novels have been sold. Rarely in them does anyone die a natural death, or does anyone get knocked out by a clean punch in the jaw, or is there a normal sexual relationship. Women in Spillane's novels die by having their navels tattooed by .45 caliber slugs, or by having their hair set on fire. Men are knocked unconscious by having their teeth hammered down their throats. Love affairs in Spillane's novels deal more with the whip than with the caress, more with the bite than with the kiss. So far as Ian Fleming is concerned, his James Bond is merely a smoother, better educated, trade-name-dropping Mike Hammer.

Nor are these attitudes in the twentieth century confined to literature. We have Dali and Picasso in painting, Randall Thompson and Stravinsky in music, Addams and Virgil Partch in cartooning. The Hollywood myth-makers exploited these attitudes in *Scarface*, *Little Caesar*, and *Public Enemy*. On second thought, such motion pictures seem, in the sixties, peculiarly restrained. After all, the thirties are many years away, and we have *The Tingler* now. We've come a long distance, if you don't care what you say, since we got a thrill out of watching James Cagney shove a grapefruit into the delicate features of Mae Clarke in *Public Enemy*.

"Aside from that, Mrs. Lincoln, how did you enjoy the play?"

So, while the attitudes that produce the sick joke in the twentieth century have always been with us in one form or another, they seem to have reached a peak in our time. Perhaps people of today are more conscious of, more concerned with, their motives than ever before. Violence and death and horror and sex and religion have always been known to men, despite all the talk of a golden age; and some men have always taken a hardboiled, sophisticated, dispassionate, calculating attitude toward them. Certainly the man of the twentieth century has had every opportunity to become hardened to violence and death and horror. Three wars in forty years, nuclear fission and nuclear fusion, space satellites, intercontinental ballistic missiles, and lunar probes have all combined to force man to create a shell around his more tender and gentle emotions. Frightened in the past, uneasy in the present, terrified of the future, man in the twentieth century first turned for surcease to the sentimental drivel of cheap fiction, then to the facile emotional happy endings of some motion pictures and some television dramas. These trifled with his emotions, cheaply, glibly, easily. He needed an antidote. Perhaps that is why we have had the sick joke in such a time as now, in such a place as here.

Let us grant it is not
Amiss to tumble on the bed of Ptolemy
To give a kingdom for a mirth . . .
—Octavius Caesar in *Antony and Cleopatra*

Love, sex, and comedy

If it is true, as Compton Mackenzie and David Daiches have
suggested, that *stupid* is the only word in English that rhymes
with *Cupid*, it is little wonder that creators of comedy, who
generally have excellent ears for a rhyme as well as for a pun,
have often looked to love and sex as sources of comedy and
laughter. Certainly, the behavior of people in love or in heat
has long been considered comic by objective observers. *Ob-*
jective observers may, in this case, be defined as people pos-

sessed of the genuine comic spirit who are not, at the moment, in love or in heat themselves. The English-speaking peoples, despite their unique rhyme, are not alone in considering love and sex a source of the comic. Homer and Aristophanes, Plautus and Ovid, Boccaccio and Marie de France, Machiavelli and Cervantes, Molière and Jean Giraudoux—the list could be infinitely extended—all testify to the laughter inherent in love and in sex. The laughter may be as gentle as that of Cervantes, as vicious and sneering as that of Machiavelli, may be the result of a Plautine bludgeon, or of a Giraudoux rapier, but it exists inevitably, universally, in every age, culture, and language.

Meredith would probably issue a caveat here, insisting that a society of cultivated men and particularly women is essential before you can have creators of the comic who will find comedy in love and in sex. He would go further and insist that you must have a society that treats women with equality before such a condition obtains. But for Meredith, only one type of comedy really exists, the comedy of manners. And the comedy of manners insists not on the equality of women but on their superiority. That is why Meredith likes Molière, whose Celimène, for example, is far superior to his Alceste; why he likes Congreve, whose Millamant is far superior (except in one key scene) to his Mirabell; why he sees to it in his own novel that Clara Middleton triumphs over Sir Willoughby Patterne. Because of their treatment of women, he does not feel that the Arabs can have great comedy (he thinks that *The One Thousand and One Nights* is grossly, not delicately, comic). For the same reason, he does not think that the Italians can have great comedy (he knows of Machiavelli and Goldoni, but he never seems to mention the *Commedia dell' Arte*). Also for the same reason, and despite Goethe, and Heine, and Jean Paul Richter, he thinks that the Germans are sadly deficient in comedy (he never mentions

Tyl Eulenspiegel and, unfortunately, he never had the opportunity to know of Marlene Dietrich, whom C. H. Rand has described so well:

I want a woman whose passion is not a blind rage of the body or the soul, but a recognition of mutual attraction in which reason or humour will play their part, as far as love permits. But vamps with brains are far to seek. And vamps with humour even further. I find all my requisites in the screen character of Marlene Dietrich. She has beauty in abundance. She has a rich, sensuous allure. And you only have to look at her eyes to see that she has brains, and at her mouth to see that she has humour.

Certainly Meredith would accept this description (with the possible exception of the phrase "as far as love permits") as a definition of the ideal heroine of the ideal comedy of manners. And if it be argued that here has been described a woman, not a character, I should point out that anyone who has seen Miss Dietrich as Lola Lola in *Der Blaue Engel,* or as Amy Jolly in *Morocco,* or as Shanghai Lily in *Shanghai Express,* or as Madeline in *Desire,* or even in her bit part as the denizen of the Barbary Coast saloon in Mike Todd's *Around the World in Eighty Days,* would find it difficult, if not impossible, to determine where the woman leaves off and the character begins. And this character, this woman, has wit, humor, and a healthy sense of the comic along with the frank invitation to love and even to sex that her appearance and her voice extend. Miss Dietrich's appeal is so great that even Carol Channing's brilliantly devastating impersonation of her reminds us not of her stylistic excesses but only that it has been too long since we last saw Marlene perform. Even if Maria Magdalene Dietrich were merely the creation and Josef von Sternberg were the creator—which I do not for a moment believe—and even if there were no high comedy in Goethe, in Heine, in Jean Paul Richter—which I do not for a moment believe— then the nation which produced Josef von Sternberg and Bertolt Brecht and the Thomas Mann of *Felix Krull* has learned it well. Along with the *weltschmerz* there is now high comedy, along with the *gemütlichkeit* there is now wit.

Love and sex have been made comic by the understatement of high comedy, by the understatement of wit, but they can be made comic too by overstatement. Certainly the overstatement of the moans and groans of despair caused by unrequited love can be comic to the observer, no matter how pathetic the groans may be to the victim. In *As You Like It* Rosalind, disguised as a young man, has promised to cure the love-sick Orlando. After all, he needs curing. Jaques complains that he has been marring trees by writing love songs in their bark. As he hangs one of his poems on a tree, he bellows forth in high, astounding terms the undeviating, one-track mind of the man overcome by love sickness:

> Hang there, my verse, in witness of my love;
>> And thou, thrice-crowned Queen of Night, survey
> With thy chaste eye, from thy pale sphere above,
>> The huntress' name that my full life doth sway.
> O Rosalind! these trees shall be my books,
>> And in their barks my thoughts I'll character
> That every eye which in this forest looks
>> Shall see thy virtue witness'd everywhere.
> Run, run, Orlando! carve on every tree
> The fair, the chaste, and unexpressive she.

Her cure, she says, will be a relatively simple one, one that she used before in a similar case:

> He was to imagine me his love, his mistress; and I set him every day to woo me. At which time would I, being but a moonish youth, grieve, be effeminate, changeable, longing, and liking, proud, fantastical, apish, shallow, inconstant, full of tears, full of smiles; for every passion something, and for no passion truly anything, as boys and women are for the most part cattle of this colour; would now like him, now loathe him; then entertain him, then forswear him; now weep for him, then spit at him. . . .

Merely the description of the remedy, a shrewd analysis of the behavior of the fickle and changeable female, should effect a cure, but Orlando is sure that the cure won't work in his case. He is, though, willing to try. He arrives for the first installment of his cure an hour late. He is rated for that. Some more shrewish dialogue follows and then Rosalind announces: "Well, in her person, I say I will not have you." Orlando replies: "Then in mine own person, I die." Rosalind's answer to Orlando's bromide about dying for love is a classic rejoinder to all lovesick idiots, all who overstate the pangs of despised love:

No, faith, die by attorney. The poor world is almost six thousand years old, and in all this time there was not any man died in his own person, videlicet, in a love cause. Troilus had his brains dash'd out with a Grecian club; yet he did what he could to die before, and he is one of the patterns of love. Leander, he would have liv'd many a fair year though Hero had turn'd nun, if it had not been for a hot midsummer night; for (good youth) he went but forth to wash him in the Hellespont, and being taken with the cramp, was drown'd; and the foolish chroniclers of that age found it was "Hero of Sestos." But these are all lies. Men have died from time to time, and worms have eaten them, but not for love.

The sensible humor of Rosalind's answer serves to puncture the laughable pretension of all those who claim that they will die for love. What is the comic answer to the pretensions of those who claim that their love is as deep as the ocean, that it will last for all eternity? Many answers can be and have been given. Even some lines taken out of context would provide answers. "The lady [or gentleman, as the case may be] doth protest too much, methinks." "They build no temples to the rising of the sun who howl not in terror when the dragon eats the sun." Rosalind again provides a good answer. She has asked Orlando how long he would have his love after he has possessed her, and he has answered, "For ever and a day." Her reply cuts the protestation down to size: "Say 'a day' without the 'ever.'"

Make no mistake. A woman in love speaks this line, but Rosalind knows that being in love does not mean being devoid of reason, does not mean that you are blinded to the ways of the world. When you do get blinded to the ways of the world, you tend to use overstatement of idea, even though your previous training has schooled you in a terse, cryptic, prose style:

CLEOPATRA: If it be love indeed, tell me how much.
ANTONY: There's beggary in the love that can be reckon'd.
CLEOPATRA: I'll set a bourne how far to be belov'd.
ANTONY: Then must thou needs find out new heaven, new earth.

Tragedy, not comedy, results from this colloquy at the beginning of *Antony and Cleopatra*, but you do not have to consider Antony transformed into a strumpet's fool to regard his lines as mildly amusing. Shakespeare has set the lines brilliantly in context. The play opens with Philo's savage commentary on the decline of Antony from a great general to a mere lover. At that point, Antony, Cleopatra, and their retinue enter, and the lovers speak the lines cited above. A messenger then enters with news from Rome. Antony is annoyed at the intrusion and merely wants to hear the headlines, not the full account. Cleopatra takes this opportunity to tease Antony, to provoke him, to irritate him—the slang term "needle" is really the right word in this context. She is successful. He spouts more phrases of love and dismisses the messenger without hearing his news: "Speak not to us." The triple pillar of the world has been transformed and, at this early stage of the play, we are forced to laugh at his overstatement in idea and deed of how much he loves her. Philo has been proved right, and the sight and sound of this great warrior made a babbling lover by the seductive Cleopatra stimulate our laughter, even though his death will later stimulate our tears.

Perhaps the comic epitaph for all those who moan about love and for all those who overstate their love is given by Mercutio in *Romeo and Juliet*. He has been complaining to

Benvolio about how love has ruined Romeo, when Romeo appears on the scene. Mercutio starts a wit combat with him and Romeo answers with as good as he receives. Mercutio is happy to see Romeo once more in a delightful, witty mood, and proclaims his happiness in brilliantly comic, though mildly obscene, terms:

Why, is this not better now than groaning for love? Now art thou sociable, now art thou Romeo; now art thou what thou art, by art as well as nature. For this drivelling love is like a great natural that runs lolling up and down to hide his bauble in a hole.

The comic overstatement of the love situation is not confined to moans and words. Despite the preoccupation of the contemporary American male with what S. J. Perelman has called *la haute poitrine*, physical endowment can be overstated, too, and the result of the overstatement can be comic. Marie Wilson is a case in point, Dagmar is a case in point, Diana Dors, Jayne Mansfield, and Marilyn Monroe are cases in point. But all of these actresses, even Miss Monroe whose comic range was far greater than that of the others, owe a tremendous debt to Mae West. Miss West actually lacked the physical charms of some of these younger women, but she gave the appearance of possessing more than they. She acted her roles with such a light-hearted vulgarity and such a surface sexuality that the result, despite the reformers, was not obscenity but comedy. In addition to her other, more obvious assets, her voice and delivery made her a magnificent comedienne. She could make the most innocuous, the most obvious, remark sound almost sinister; but then the toss of the head, the shrug of the shoulders, the slouch in her walk that accompanied the words would turn the words from the frankly sexual to the delightfully laughable. For the sake of an example, consider just one of her films. In *She Done Him Wrong* (1933) she plays the role of Lou, the Queen of the Bowery in the nineties. Her songs are those that we'd expect of her:

"Frankie and Johnny," "Easy Rider," and "I Like a Man Who Takes His Time." Sexuality, even obscenity, are present in all three, but the overstatement of voice and delivery make them hilariously comic. Her lines, too, are what we would expect of her. "Lady Lou," says one character, "You're a fine woman." Her answer, despite the *double entendre*, gets to the heart of the matter: "A finer woman never walked the streets." She can be wryly philosophical about the double standard: "When women go wrong, men go right after them." She can use a quip to cover the fact that she's too busy thinking of another's welfare to have much concern for herself: "Your bath is ready, Miss Lou." "You take it. I'm indisposed." Surely the line, "Why don't you come up some time—and see me?" seems on the surface to be fairly innocent, but the voice, the delivery, the rising emphasis on the word "up," the upward flick of the eyes, take the line from the innocent, through the frankly sensual, to the comic. She can be completely and thoroughly matter of fact as she says, "Diamonds is my career." Then there is one line in the film that demonstrates completely that her lively sense of the ridiculous can puncture more economically than Rosalind, if not so brilliantly, the fatuousness of the dying-swan type of lover. A suitor full of hoarse sincerity says to her, "I'd die to make you happy." She merely flicks him with her patented look as she says, with great comic sensuality, "You wouldn't be any good to me then." Economical and pointed utterance is always her specialty, and she manages to dispose both of men and of the institution of marriage in one pithy statement: "He'd be the kind a gal would have to marry to get rid of."

Some of her lines are amusing even when baldly set down on paper, but when the tone of voice is recalled, when the sensuous walk is recalled, when the not particularly attractive but definitely overblown figure is recalled, the amusing is changed to the hilarious, the smile is changed to the belly laugh. The censors thought that she should be censored, and saw to it that she was. They made, as they almost always do, a serious mistake. Her appeal was always to the comic, not to the prurient, interest, to the funny bone, not to the genitalia.

I have heard it argued that Miss West's suggestive walk and suggestive talk and suggestive leer were far worse than the frank filth of the burlesque house. I have never been completely sure just what the other term of the comparison was. A lot of things happened on the stage of the burlesque house, whether the house was Minsky's in New York, or the Modern in Providence, R. I., or the Old Howard (known as the "Atheneum" to the esoteric) in Boston. There was strip teasing, to be sure, but there was also the tenor or the lyric soprano, there were the many chorus numbers, there was the brilliant spiel of the candy butcher during the intermissions as he sold candy, ice cream, soft drinks, and other, less savory, merchandise, and, above all, there were the comic routines. I say "above all" because I actually believe that some people went to burlesque theaters for the comedians, not for the "30 beautiful girls 30." That such people were in the minority, I agree; that they were the true connoisseurs of burlesque, I insist. They were far greater connoisseurs, for example, than the intense but narrow-visioned friend of mine who used to arrive at the burlesque house just before the intermission, sit through the candy butcher's spiel, and leave before the second-act curtain rose; and far greater connoisseurs than another friend of mine, a professor of English, who used to maintain, with just the hint of a raised eyebrow, that he attended burlesque shows because the audience there was as close to the Elizabethan audience as it is possible to get in the twentieth century. But even the connoisseurs stopped going to burlesque shows because the quality of humor started to decline. And the great comic performers both male and female who could have stemmed the tide, those performers who didn't find it necessary to base every joke on incipient or overt homosexuality, were lured away by the legitimate theater, by the productions of Ziegfield or Earl Carroll, by the motion pictures, by the radio and television networks, by the nightclubs of New York, Miami, and Las Vegas.

Of course the reformers and the censors thought that burlesque should be prevented from despoiling the American cultural landscape, and with burlesque as with Miss West they were successful. And again they were wrong. For most often the burlesque show, by definition and by fact, appealed to the comic, not to the prurient, interest. It was difficult to take Rose La Rose seriously after Mike Sacks had introduced her as "the glamorous, glorious, glandular flower who sheds her petals—red hot Rose La Rose!" It was difficult to look seriously at any strip teaser when your eyes were still blurred with tears of laughter after watching the antics of Phil Silvers or Mike Sacks or Bobbie Clark, those great top bananas. In the twenties and thirties Gypsy Rose Lee was the darling of the intellectuals. She couldn't sing very well; her dancing was even worse than her singing; she wasn't particularly beautiful; but she was literate, she was bizarre, and she had a lively sense of the ridiculous. Everyone knows Gypsy the strip teaser, the author, the raconteur, and Gypsy knows herself:

H. L. Mencken called me an ecdysiast. I have also been described as deciduous. [Compare Mike Sacks and Rose La Rose above.] The French call me a deshabilleuse. In less-refined circles I'm known as a strip teaser.

Ashton Stevens overstated the case, but only slightly, when he said that she was "the only member of the cuticle sisterhood who can make nudity witty." Others had this ability, too, though after you mention Gypsy and Georgia Sothern and Lily St. Cyr and Ann Corio the names come hard. When all is considered, I still think that Mae West's walk, talk, and leer were suggestive, to be sure, but suggestive more of comedy than of sex. And I still believe that the great performers in burlesque both thought and acted as if comedy were burlesque's end product, and the display of physical charms were merely the means to that end.

For when sex is not amusing it can, at its best, lead to tragedy, but unfortunately it leads most often to melodrama and soap opera. Marya Mannes, a woman of wit and perception, has seen the problem and has stated it clearly. In a volume of essays entitled *More In Anger*, she has written a little fantasy in play form called "The Magic Box." The time is A.D. 2000. The place is a heath, blasted. The characters are A Very Old Man and A Student. "The *student* is making notes on what looks like papyrus with what looks like a stylus." The Very Old Man is trying to explain to The Student what television was like in America in the 1950's. Eventually The Very Old Man gets to soap operas, and the following dialogue ensues:

OLD MAN: There was, too, I remember, an extraordinary form of drama called the soap opera . . .

STUDENT: Soap opera?

OLD MAN: Yes. Because the makers of soap paid for them, not because they had music. Many million women watched them every day, and wept.

STUDENT: Wept? Why?

OLD MAN: Because their troubles were slight compared to those of the characters, who lived from calamity to calamity; and they wept from relief.

STUDENT: But what were these dramas about?

OLD MAN: They were about very stupid people who were either good or bad. But they were good and bad in very special ways . . .

STUDENT: What ways, old man?

OLD MAN: Well, all good women did housework all day and drank coffee. All bad women had careers, flirted with men, and drank cocktails.

STUDENT: And the men?

OLD MAN: I seem to remember that the bad men were usually cultivated, witty, and upper-class; and all the good men were dull, faithful, and humorless. You see, in America there was nothing funny about love, or sex. It was either nobly matrimonial, ignobly adulterous, or painfully adolescent. But it was never amusing.

STUDENT: Poor Americans!

Poor Americans, indeed. The young man is not wasting his compassion, if what this Aristotelian old man says is true. And, so far as soap operas were and are concerned, the old man is speaking the truth. His speech, however, does not confine itself to the soap opera. He says quite bluntly, ". . . in America there was nothing funny about love or sex. . . . it was never amusing." But Miss Mannes is obviously exaggerating for effect. She knows as well as anyone—and better than most—that Americans have been able to laugh at love and sex. Merely a short time intervened between Theda Bara's role of The Vamp in *A Fool There Was* (1914) and Marie Dressler's parody of the role in one episode of *Tillie's Punctured Romance* (1914). Rudolph Valentino's asthmatic love making in *The Sheik* (1921) was satirized by Ben Turpin's *The Shriek of Araby* (1923). Valentino's *Blood and Sand* (1922) was satirized by Stan Laurel's *Mud and Sand* in the same year. Elinor Glyn's heady Ruritanian romance, *Three Weeks*, starring Aileen Pringle and Conrad Nagel (1924), was satirized in a matter of months by Madeline Hurlock and Ben Turpin in *Three and a Half Weeks* (1924).

Eventually, even the feature film began to show that love and sex can be portrayed in an amusing manner, and we were blessed with such productions as *It Happened One Night*, starring Clark Gable and Claudette Colbert, and *The Thin Man* with William Powell, Myrna Loy, and a dog named Asta. These two films, both produced in 1934, started a vogue that is, despite Miss Mannes' comment, fortunately still going on. The late thirties saw such films as *Bringing up Baby*, in which Cary Grant and Katharine Hepburn were portrayed as cultivated, witty, and upper-class; *Destry Rides Again*, in which neither James Stewart nor Marlene Dietrich was upper class or cultivated, but in which both were witty; and *Ninotchka*, a film in which even Greta Garbo laughed. The forties were, perhaps properly, concerned with the war and its aftermath, but there was still a demand for *The Road to Morocco* and the other "Road" films, starring Bing Crosby, Bob Hope, and Dorothy Lamour; still a demand for such a film as *The Miracle of Morgan's Creek* with Betty Hutton, William Demarest, and Eddie Bracken, in which a young girl's pregnancy was the source of much of the laughter; still a demand for such a film as *To Have and Have Not*, in which Humphrey Bogart, Hoagy Carmichael, and Lauren Bacall made us forget, if only for a moment, that the motion picture had nothing in common with the Hemingway novel, that it had no plot worth mentioning, and that the diction of the hard-boiled school can be as formalized as a page out of Doctor Johnson. In speaking of Miss Bacall's performance in this film, James Agee gets to the root of the problem of love, sex, and comedy. He says:

[It] is a leisurely series of mating duels between Humphrey Bogart at his most proficient and the very entertaining, nervy, adolescent new blonde, Lauren Bacall. Whether or not you like the film will depend I believe on whether you like Miss Bacall. I am no judge. I can hardly look at her, much less listen to her—she has a voice like a chorus by Kid Ory—without getting caught in a dilemma between a low whistle and a bellylaugh.

Agee's review was written in 1944, but both his opinion and the motion picture still stand up today. And perhaps because of these films of the thirties and forties, we are able to enjoy light-hearted, amusing treatments of love and sex in such films of the fifties and early sixties as *The Seven Year Itch*, *The French Line*, *To Catch a Thief*, *The Prince and the Showgirl*, *Some Like It Hot* (even though I have a personal aversion to transvestitism), *Pillow Talk*, *Once More with Feeling*, and *The Apartment*.

I could include many plays, novels, and short stories that

obviously belong in this genre, but I have confined myself to films for one reason: Marya Mannes' Old Man was speaking from a background of televised soap opera when he made his comment about love never being amusing in America. I thought it only fair to disprove his statement by reference to a medium that is hedged in with as many restrictions as television, if not more.

Much of what I have been saying here has been concerned with America and the twentieth century. While love and sex have been treated amusingly in this country and in this time, one aspect of love and sex—an aspect which has been considered the apotheosis of the sexually comic in many cultures and in many ages—has rarely been considered a proper subject for comedy in our time and place. I refer, of course, to the cuckold and cuckoldry. Americans, if we are to judge from their literature, consider the cuckold a melodramatic or a tragic, rather than a comic, figure. They do not consider cuckoldry a laughing matter. If we don't mind perverting Shakespeare's meaning slightly, we could sum up the American attitude by quoting the refrain lines of one of the songs in *As You Like It*:

> Take thou no scorn to wear the horn;
> It was a crest ere thou wast born:
>   Thy father's father wore it,
>   And thy father bore it.
> The horn, the horn, the lusty horn,
> Is not a thing to laugh to scorn.

It is difficult to ascertain why there is no American *Mandragola*, or American *Country Wife*, or even an American *Baker's Wife*. You might argue that laughter is a talisman, an amulet, a charm that the average man uses as a sort of mystical defense against the operation of customs which he hates, but which he is unable to overcome. You could go further and argue that since the operation of these customs is inevitable, the average man uses laughter as a before-the-fact or after-the-fact antidote. Such a custom might be the law of the first night or the right of the lord. Americans, in general, have not known the custom. You could argue in another direction and maintain that marriage is a legal or an ecclesiastical, but not an emotional, bond. Outwitting the law, since the law is an ass, could be the cause of laughter. Such an argument might be maintained among a people who had such a custom as the marriage of convenience. Americans, in general, have not known such a custom. There are, undoubtedly, other reasons, sociological, psychological, economic, why Americans, according to their literature, do not laugh at cuckoldry, but the fact remains that in American literature the cuckold becomes a tragic or even a compassionate figure. For proof, one need only go to one month in the year 1924. In November of that year two plays appeared: Eugene O'Neill's *Desire Under the Elms* and Sidney Howard's *They Knew What They Wanted*. In each play, an old farmer becomes a cuckold. O'Neill's farmer, cuckolded by his son, is a tragic figure in his madness; Howard's farmer, cuckolded by his hired man, may be a comic figure to some but surely will be regarded as a tender and compassionate figure by most. Tony Patucci is no saint. He has his moment of madness when he finds that the child his wife Amy is bearing is not his, but he recovers his sanity and makes it clear that emotion is more important than intellect, more important than law:

TONY: . . . I want dis baby, Amy. Joe don' want him. Ees Tony want him. Amy, . . . Amy, . . . For God's sake don' go away an' leave Tony!

AMY: But, Tony! Think of what I have done?

TONY: What you done was mistake in da head, not in da heart. . . . Mistake in da head is no matter.

Because Tony is able to convince Amy that a mistake in the head doesn't matter, *They Knew What They Wanted*, is, I suppose, a comedy. It has, at least, a happy ending. And so does Frank Loesser's musical version of the same play. The cuckold in *Most Happy Fella* and *They Knew What They Wanted* is not an object of scorn. Because he has understanding, he is understood. Because he has compassion and sympathy for the girl who has erred, we have compassion and sympathy for him.

The contrast between Tony Patucci and Messer Nicia in Machiavelli's *Mandragola* is instructive in this connection. Messer Nicia, a dirty old man who'd make a cat laugh, literally forces his wife to cuckold him. Of course he is tricked into doing so, but we do not sympathize with him when he is tricked. How can we? He is perfectly willing to sacrifice the life of another and his wife's virtue so that his foolish desires may be fulfilled. His frenzied attempts to persuade his wife, Lucrezia, to go along with his plan increase our laughter. He suborns Lucrezia's confessor, Fra Timoteo; he convinces Sostrata, Lucrezia's mother, that she ought to aid in the plan; he takes part in a "kidnaping" of an "innocent" young man that will, he believes, result in that young man's death. He does all these things without compunction, without qualm. We are delighted that he is cuckolded. We are delighted that this avaricious old man pays for the doubtful privilege. We are even more delighted to learn that the cuckoldry will continue. Callimaco, the young Florentine who had conceived the entire plan because of his love for Lucrezia, talks after the fact to Ligurio, the parasite. He fills us in on all the details including—what is most important to us—Lucrezia's state of mind:

> As I told you, Ligurio, till after one o'clock I wasn't really happy about it, and though my pleasure was great, I was not able to enjoy it. But after I had told her who I was, and had made her understand how much I loved her, and how easily we could live happily without it involving any scandal, thanks to the foolishness of her husband, and had promised that when God had other plans for him I would marry her at once—and when on top of all this

she had felt the difference between my love and Messer Nicia's, and between the kisses of a young lover and an old husband, then, after a sigh or two, she said: "Since your cunning, the folly of my husband, my mother's lack of scruple and the wickedness of my confessor have combined to make me do what I would never have done on my own, I can only believe that some divine influence has willed this, and, as it is not for me to resist what heaven decrees, I surrender. And so I take you for my lord, and master, and guide. You must be everything to me—father, defender, and the sole source of all my happiness: and what my husband wanted for a night, I want him to have forever. Seek his friendship, then: go to church this morning, then come home to dine with us; you shall come and go as you will, and we shall be able to be together at any time without suspicion." When I heard this I was overwhelmed with tenderness, and hardly able to express anything of what I felt. But the result is that I am the happiest and most contented man in the world, and if neither death nor time destroy my happiness—the saints themselves shall call me blessed!

So much for Messer Nicia: he is a classic cuckold, subject to our scorn, our laughter. If it be argued in his defense that his original motive, a desire for an heir, is a valid one, it must be admitted that his means to achieve that end are neither proper nor virtuous. And while we are laughing we ought not to forget that the virtuous Lucrezia is no longer a human being by the end of the play. She has become a thing, an object to be manipulated by the various forces. Even her extreme virtue, her sense of obedience to her husband, her mother, her confessor, has been used for a vicious purpose. And she does not mind, for, as she has said to Callimaco, ". . . you shall come and go as you will, and we shall be able to be together at any time without suspicion." Machiavelli has made it quite clear that he does not want his audience to wax sentimental over Lucrezia while it is laughing at Messer Nicia. The horns of the cuckold cast a ludicrous shadow, and the shadow manages to taint all the rest of the characters of Machiavelli's play.

Other treatments of the cuckoldry theme exist in dramatic

comedy, but *They Knew What They Wanted* and *Mandragola* indicate clearly enough the extremes of treatment. Because a benevolent haze of sentimentality envelops the former play, the cuckold, the woman, even the cuckolder, solicit our sympathy at the end of the play. And the solicitation is successful. Tony is noble and understanding; Amy is noble, penitent, and regretful; even Joe is noble in his willingness to expiate his sin in any way. As the curtain falls, but before the house lights go on, there is much fumbling for handkerchiefs, much surreptitious dabbing at tear-filled eyes, much loud, manly blowing of masculine noses. The cold intellectuality of the latter play prohibits sentimentality and demands laughter, not tears. We laugh at Messer Nicia, the cuckold, because he has not only consented but also helped plan what has happened. If what he planned for one night is to go on for a thousand and one nights, our laughter is the more boisterous on that account. We laugh with Callimaco, the cuckolder, at the successful conclusion of his cleverly outrageous strategy. So far as Lucrezia is concerned, we think of her—if we think of her at all—as merely a rather attractive prize in this salacious game of sex-love. If Callimaco thinks the game is worth the effort he expends, why should we object? For our concern is not with the prize, but with the technique of winning; not with sex, but with strategy; not with romance and sentiment, but with chicanery and cleverness.

If *They Knew What They Wanted* and *Mandragola* indicate extreme treatments of the cuckoldry theme, the various versions of the Amphitryon story indicate the middle road of treatment. In all the versions, the cuckolder is Jupiter, the king of the gods, and all sorts of divine aids are his for the thinking. He can change his form at will; he can extend the night so that one night of love leaves nothing to be desired, even by a god; he can summon the brilliantly nimble-minded Mercury as an assistant; he can freely indulge his "nostalgia for mortality";

he can even contravene the biological law which maintains that a period of 280 days is normally necessary between conception and parturition. What chance has an ordinary mortal, even a great general of Thebes, against so formidable an antagonist?

Of the many versions of the play only four need concern us here: the Plautine, the Molière, the Dryden, and the S. N. Behrman adaptation of the Jean Giraudoux version. In the Plautus play, despite the many farcical elements, Amphitruo is regarded finally as a man who has been honored by a heavenly visitation. "Well," says he, after his maid Bromia has told him the startling events which followed the birth of twin sons to his wife, "well, I'm scarcely going to complain about being permitted to share my blessings with Jupiter." (An interesting comparison may be drawn between Amphitruo's problem and the problem of Saint Joseph in the Gospel according to Saint Matthew. Note particularly that Saint Joseph "was minded to put her away privily.") Amphitruo then orders the maid to prepare sacrificial vessels so that he can make offerings to the god. He also plans to consult with Tiresias, the soothsayer, about the affair, but Jupiter appears to him, tells him the whole story, advises him to have nothing to do with soothsayers, and then departs for heaven. A literal translation of Amphitruo's line after Jupiter's departure might be, "I shall do as you order." A freer translation which manages to convey far more closely the reverent tone of the original might well be, "Thy will be done." Dramatic audiences should not find it strange that reverence follows so closely on the heels of farce. The religious origins of drama and the theory of the sugar-coated pill of instruction would insure that such a combination would occasionally happen. It happened in Greek drama; it happened in Roman drama; *The Second Shepherd's Play* and *The Comedy of Errors* show that it can happen in English drama also.

The Molière and Dryden versions of the Amphitryon story have much in common with each other both dramatically and thematically. Dramatically, they have much in common with the Roman play; thematically, they never approach Plautus. As has been pointed out, Plautus enables us to gain insight into Amphitruo's state of mind after the divine revelation has been made. In both Molière and Dryden, Amphitryon remains mute after the revelation. Both seventeenth-century playwrights have their Sosias interrupt Jupiter's explanation with a comment about the god's cleverness. And the explanation is clever, to be sure, in both Dryden and Molière, even though the cleverness seems to detract from the divinity. Since both seventeenth-century versions are similar in content, only one need be cited. Dryden's Jupiter speaks from a machine after a second peal of thunder:

> Look up, Amphitryon, and behold, above,
> The impostor god, the rival of thy love;
> In thy own shape see Jupiter appear,
> And let that sight secure thy jealous fear.
> Disgrace, and infamy, are turned to boast;
> No fame, in Jove's concurrence, can be lost;
> What he enjoys, he sanctifies from vice,
> And by partaking, stamps into a price.
> 'Tis I who ought to murmur at my fate,
> Forced by my love my godhead to translate;
> When on no other terms I could possess,
> But by thy form, thy features, and thy dress.
> To thee were given the blessings that I sought,
> Which else, not all the bribes of heaven had bought.
> Then take into thy arms thy envied love,
> And, in his own despite, triumph o'er Jove.

At this point, Mercury says in an aside, "Amphitryon and Alcmena both stand mute, and know not how to take it." And well they might. It is bad enough for a couple to be deceived and cuckolded by a god who remains, as Plautus' Jupiter does, direct, blunt, and divine; it is most confusing to be deceived and cuckolded by a god who indulges in rhetorical play as he maintains that he, not Amphitryon, ought to be jealous. Sosia follows Mercury's aside with an aside of his own that is pertinent in this connection: "Our sovereign lord Jupiter is a sly companion; he knows how to gild a bitter pill." But Jupiter is interrupted only for a moment. He goes on to foretell the future:

> From this auspicious night shall rise an heir,
> Great like his sire, and like his mother fair:
> Wrongs to redress, and tyrants to disseize;
> Born for a world that wants a Hercules.
> Monsters, and monster-men he shall engage,
> And toil, and struggle, through an impious age.
> Peace to his labours shall at length succeed;
> And murmuring men, unwilling to be freed,
> Shall be compelled to happiness, by need.

Jupiter is carried back to heaven, and finally scabrous Sosia is left to sum up the salacious play. The speech cited below has not, of course, any counterpart in Plautus. Neither has it a counterpart in Molière. Only Dryden, it would seem, had a mind which could encompass such sophisticated smut. Sosia speaks:

> For let the wicked world say what they please,
> The fair wife makes her husband live at ease:
> The lover keeps him too; and but receives,
> Like Jove, the remnants that Amphitryon leaves.
> 'Tis true, the lady has enough in store,
> To satisfy those two, and eke two more:
> In fine, the man, who weighs the matter fully,
> Would rather be the cuckold than the cully.

Only to Dryden's Sosia is every man a pimp and every woman a whore; only to Dryden's Sosia are financial matters more important than morality; only Dryden's Sosia has a mind of such curious turn that he can maintain that the cuckold is better off than the cuckolder.

Molière, while not so salacious as Dryden, is naturally not so reverent as Plautus. Nor is there any reason he should have been. By the time of Plautus, Roman religion had started to lose its primal faith, and Plautus was not so devout as Ennius, for example. At the same time, he would not be nearly so skeptical as a Molière. Molière, in other words, treated the pagan divinities with pardonable freedom and easily avoided Dryden's failures of taste. I have cited the concluding speech from Dryden's play. Here, now, is the concluding speech from Molière's. Jupiter has vanished into the clouds, and Naucrates, a Theban captain, says, "Certainly I am enraptured at these brilliant remarks. . . ." At this point, Sosia interrupts:

Gentlemen, will you please to follow my opinion? Embark not in these pretty congratulations: it is a bad investment; and pretty phrases are embarrassing on either side, in such a compliment. The great god Jupiter has done us much honour, and, no doubt, his goodness towards us is unequalled; he promises the certain felicity of a glorious fate, bearing a thousand blessings, and, that in our house shall be born a very mighty son. Nothing could be better than all this. But, in short, a truce to speeches, and let every one retire in peace. It is always best in these matters to say nothing.

Dryden has, I admit, a similar speech, but he gives it to Mercury, not Sosia (and that is psychologically important) and he does not use it to end his play. Molière's Sosia gives the best possible advice when he insists that in these matters it is always best to say nothing. If the conclusions of the three plays show differences which may be ascribed to differences in time of composition and place of national origin, the beginnings of the three plays show similar differences. The plot, or Jupiter, demands that night be lengthened. Plautus merely has Mercury direct a few words in an aside to the goddess of night. Molière developed an entire scene from an interview between Night and Mercury. The scene is witty, clever, and completely satisfying. Night has some scruples, but Mercury's glib tongue soon sweeps them away. While Molière is facetious at the expense of the gods, Dryden is merely lewd. Night and Mercury in Molière are two sophisticates engaging in delightful banter; in Dryden we get a conversation between a pander and a bawd. While time and place account for most of the differences among the three plays, we should not forget that taste, or Dryden's lack of it, accounts for many of the differences.

There is no failure of taste in the S. N. Behrman adaptation of the Jean Giraudoux *Amphitryon 38*. It had the undoubted advantage of having Alfred Lunt play the rule of Jupiter, Lynn Fontanne the role of Alkmena, and the redoubtable Sidney Greenstreet playing the minor, but delightful, role of a Trumpeter. This version has the Plautine myth (properly modified for a modern audience) without the heavy-handed treatment and with its own peculiar sense of reverence; it possesses Molière's sense of high comedy, but it never degenerates, as its predecessor unfortunately does on occasion, into farce; and it has all of Dryden's sophistication, but none of his scurrility. And it differs from the other versions in particular as well as general terms. While all four plays have a god as a cuckolder, Jupiter's presence has strikingly different results in the different versions. Jupiter's presence in Plautus leads inevitably and reverently to the birth of a divine hero; his presence in Molière succeeds in raising bedroom farce to the level of high comedy and leads to the birth of a semi-divine hero; his presence in Dryden creates, along with a potential sweeper of the Augean stables, a farcical triangle of an arrogant cuckolder, a shrewish strumpet, and a pompous cuckold. In *Amphitryon 38*, written, adapted, and produced in the sophisticated twentieth century, his presence leads, amazingly enough, to the exaltation of connubial love. Jupiter, disguised as Amphitryon, has spent the night with Alkmena and he is talking to Mercury about her constancy: "Nevertheless, I have discovered that human beings are not what the gods think them. Alkmena, the gentle—the tender Alkmena has the character of a rock. She is the true Prometheus!" The cynical Mercury interjects: "It isn't that she has character, she lacks imagination." A troubled Jupiter who seemingly never before had been aware of female fidelity answers musingly: "Yes, she lacks imagination and it's even possible that she isn't very intelligent. She is ambitious neither to shock nor to dazzle. But it's exactly this single-minded quality in her, this quality of constancy and devotion, against which our power is futile." Jupiter should have known. In a previous scene he had attempted, although disguised as Amphitryon, to come to her as a lover:

ALKMENA: I have a husband and he is evidently not here. And I receive no one in my bedroom who is not my husband. And not even him will I admit if he does not acknowledge his name. You're not very good at passionate disguises—it's not your metier.

JUPITER: Oh, at this hour, when everything between here and heaven is in disguise, may not your husband also disguise himself as a lover?

ALKMENA: Your insight, my friend, is not very keen if you think the night is only the day-time masked, the moon no more than a sun disguised, and that the love of a wife for her husband can be confused with an amour.

JUPITER: Wifely love is a duty. Duty is compulsion. And compulsion kills desire.

ALKMENA: Desire! Desire is a half god. We, here, worship only the major ones. The lesser gods we leave to the adolescent girls, to the casually married, to the fugitive romantics, the half-wives.

JUPITER: It is blasphemy to speak so even of a lesser god!

ALKMENA: In my secret heart I am more blasphemous even than that for I worship a god that doesn't exist at all. Shall I tell you who it is? It's the god of conjugal love, one that it never occurred to the gods to invent—they are so casual. If you come in behalf of Desire you ask me to betray a greater god for a lesser. If then you are a lover I am sorry but I must ask you to go on. . . . You are handsome and you have a good figure. Your voice is winning. Did it sound in behalf of fidelity I might love this voice. I might wish to be enclosed in those arms. Your mouth, too, I should say is dewy and ardent. But I shan't allow it to persuade me. I shall not open my door to a lover. Who are you?

JUPITER: Why can't your husband be your lover?

ALKMENA: Because a lover is closer always to love than he is to the object of his love. Because it is ill-bred to deceive your husband —even with himself. Because I like my windows open and my linen fresh.

At this point, Alkmena leaves him and goes inside. He stews and frets for a while as he discusses this contretemps with Mercury, and then he capitulates, admits that he is Amphitryon, goes through a ceremony which she commands, is informed that the gate was open all the time, and then, as "husband" not "lover," he is admitted. Yes, Jupiter should have known, but how could Jupiter the philanderer realize the importance of conjugal love to some women? After all, he had never faced the problem before. Perhaps that is what he has in mind when he says resignedly to Mercury. "For the first time, Mercury, I have a suspicion that a thoroughly first-rate god might make a thoroughly second-rate man."

First-rate god or second-rate man, Jupiter had succeeded in spending the night with Alkmena. Mercury, with his love of ceremony and with his detailed knowledge of his father's state of mind, had decided that Jupiter was entitled to another night of love. He had, therefore, announced formally to the winds and the waters that Alkmena would receive a visit from Jupiter. The first visit had been, of course, unannounced. It is Mercury's job to inform Alkmena of the visitation and prepare her to accept the honor. His job is far more difficult than he had imagined. He cannot convince her of the great honor that will be hers. He is getting nowhere when Alkmena's maid announces that Leda is coming for a visit. Leda's visit gives Mercury a chance to relax and Alkmena a chance to conceive a plan. Leda, having once experienced Jupiter, wants very much to experience him again. The two women have decided that Jupiter will appear to Alkmena in the guise of Amphitryon; as Leda puts it, "Your swan will be Amphitryon." Alkmena, without much difficulty, persuades Leda to take her place. Leda does, Amphitryon—the real one—returns home after leaving his troops just for a short time, Alkmena is convinced that he is Jupiter in disguise and sends him to her darkened bedroom where Leda is waiting. Now both husband and wife are quits. Both have unwittingly committed adultery. The only problem that remains is the actual appearance of Jupiter. By the time he appears, Alkmena is aware of the terrible error she has made in the Leda incident, and she fears that Jupiter will tell Amphitryon the truth. She asks Jupiter for permission to be alone with him, and the permission is readily granted. She wins him over in argument. He agrees not to impose his presence on her, and his agreement makes her suspicious that he has already been her lover, "because my knowledge of men leads me to believe that when they're as noble as this, it's because they're already satisfied." And so, in addition to granting her desire that he not impose upon her, he also grants her forgetfulness of all the things that she wants to forget. Mercury and Amphitryon return, Amphitryon and Alkmena are informed that Alkmena will bear a son, and are asked to name him Hercules, "to please me." Jupiter then says, "and I shall be his . . . godfather . . ." and joins with Mercury in saying, ". . . and so will destiny be fulfilled!"

And destiny has certainly taken a devious road toward fulfilment. The cuckolder will become a "godfather"; the unwitting cuckold has become an unwitting adulterer; and the third member of this triangle, the virtuous wife who worships the god of conjugal love, has been granted forgetfulness of all that she wants to forget, except for one kiss which Jupiter carefully places this side of oblivion. We don't mind that Jupiter has that one minor victory, for this is a strange play; the object of our laughter is not the cuckold, but the cuckolder. And this strange twist on a traditional theme has been accomplished by the articulateness and strength of character of a virtuous woman. Connubial love, with a slight assist from forgetfulness, has triumphed over divine lechery, and Amphitryon and Alkmena remain, in Jupiter's words, "a small island of fidelity."

A small island of fidelity can exist at the end of a comedy; it can even exist at the beginning of a comedy. It is, unfortunately perhaps, almost impossible to write comedies or tragedies about unthreatened happy marriages. A threat to the marriage or to the prospect of marriage must exist before tension can be achieved, before conflict can be established. The comedy most frequently is the result of the successful overcoming of the threat. Comic opera and Hollywood do not own the copyright on the ancient comic theme of boy-meets-girl, boy-loses-girl, boy-gets-girl. Romantic comedy of this sort can be traced in English literature at least as far back as John Lyly and William Shakespeare. Even when Shakespeare wrote a comedy in what he considered the classic vein, like *The Comedy of Errors*, he ended it in the romantic tradition by restoring two marriages which time and chance had caused to founder, and by promising the early celebration of still a third. In *The Way of the World*, where the primary focus is on wit not drama, the prospect of a marriage is the delightful and romantic conclusion. Surely the proposal and acceptance scene between Millamant and Mirabell comes as close to romantic drama as is possible in this brilliantly cold comedy of manners. Indeed, I might even go so far as to maintain that after all of the conditions and articles and provisos have been agreed to by this admirable pair, and after Mirabell has said, "Then we're agreed. Shall I kiss your Hand upon the Contract?" we have witnessed a scene of passion between two brilliant and witty people. I, for one, would be willing to sacrifice emotion-racked adolescent lovemaking for the classical restraint involved in Millamant's "Well—I think—I'll endure you. . . . Well, you ridiculous thing you, I'll have you—I won't be kiss'd, nor I won't be thank'd— Here kiss my Hand tho'— So, hold your Tongue now, don't say a Word."

We do have plays, however, in which marriage seems the source of sorrow not happiness. When we first see Sir Peter Teazle in *The School for Scandal*, he is bemoaning his married state: "When an old bachelor marries a young wife, what is he to expect? 'Tis now six months since Lady Teazle made me the happiest of men—and I have been the most miserable dog ever since!" Indeed, Sir Peter seems to be in a horrible state, much worse off than we would expect even from the Greek poet's diatribe on the subject of marriage: "Marriage brings a man only two happy days: the day he beds his bride and the day he buries her." Sir Peter is probably too old ever to know the second happy day, and he did not have a chance to know the first: "We tift a little going to church, and came to a quarrel before the bells had done ringing. I was more than once nearly choked with gall during the honeymoon, and had lost all comfort before my friends had done wishing me joy." Much of Sir Peter's dialogue in the play is taken up with his marital difficulties. So deeply does he feel his problems that he frequently repeats himself, but in this comedy of manners repetition does not preclude wit: "Ah! Master Rowley, when an old bachelor marries a young wife, he deserves—no—the crime carries its punishment along with it." He may feel deeply but, as the hesitation in the above quotation indicates, he feels even more deeply about the necessity of expressing himself wittily and epigrammatically. And his predicament seems unbearable. Note his first conversation in the play with Lady Teazle:

SIR PETER T.: Lady Teazle, Lady Teazle, I'll not bear it!

LADY T.: Sir Peter, Sir Peter, you may bear it or not, as you please; but I ought to have my own way in everything, and what's more, I will, too. What! though I was educated in the country, I know very well that women of fashion in London are accountable to nobody after they are married.

SIR PETER T.: Very well, ma'am, very well;—so a husband is to have no influence, no authority?

LADY T.: Authority! No, to be sure:—if you wanted authority over me, you should have adopted me, and not married me: I am sure you were old enough.

Not even the bitter cruelty of her attack on the difference in their ages seems to bother him overmuch. You might even say that he enjoys their daily jangles, for he says, after her departure: "So—I have gained much by my intended expostulation: yet, with what a charming air she contradicts everything I say, and how pleasingly she shows her contempt for my authority! Well, though I can't make her love me, there is great satisfaction in quarreling with her; and I think she never appears to such an advantage as when she is doing everything in her power to plague me." Yet the end of the play shows that Lady Teazle has learned her lesson, and that Sir Peter has learned his. They seem destined for a happy marriage after the curtain falls, no matter how stormy had been the on-stage dramatics. And to crown the comedy there will be another marriage, for Charles Surface and Maria are to be married on the morrow.

For when love enters comedy—at least since the time of Shakespeare—it must result in marriage. Even Oscar Wilde, who defied conventions of manners, morals, and dramaturgy, was not brave enough to flout this one, even though he may have intended to satirize it. *The Importance of Being Earnest* ends with prospective marriages between Algernon and Cecily, between Jack and Gwendolen. These potential nuptials cause us little surprise, for we have been expecting such an ending ever since the young people found one another. The third potential marriage is thrown in either for lagniappe or satire or possibly both. We know about it through four words of dialogue and six of stage direction. Canon Chasuble, who normally speaks metaphorically, speaks most directly: "(*to Miss Prism*) Laetitia! (*Embraces her.*)" Miss Prism needs three words, but her meaning is clear: "(*enthusiastically*). Frederick! At Last!" Even if Wilde did intend the third marriage as a touch of satire on the convention, it seems at least as logical as the spate of marriages which concludes *Twelfth Night* and *As You Like It*, and no more satirical than the marriages which conclude *Measure For Measure.*

Nor is the convention confined to plays of the sixteenth, seventeenth, eighteenth, and nineteenth centuries. The twentieth century retains it (occasionally in modified form to be sure) because it is dramaturgically convenient and financially lucrative to do so. W. Somerset Maugham ends *The Circle* with the elopement of Elizabeth and Teddie. The fact that Elizabeth is already married to someone else doesn't seem to bother anyone. After all, if Arnold will permit Elizabeth a divorce, she and Teddie will probably marry. If Arnold is unwilling, Elizabeth and Teddie will probably enjoy a permanent, if illegal, liaison. It has all happened before. Lady Kitty, Arnold's mother, had deserted Arnold's father in similar circumstances. Her life since her elopement could not be accurately described as calmly contented, yet she encourages her daughter-in-law to run away with another man. Her reason may be summed up in one of her epigrammatic utterances: "The tragedy of love isn't death or separation. One gets over them. The tragedy of love is indifference." Arnold may be indifferent to Elizabeth or, rather, aware of her only as her actions may affect his career; Teddie is aware of her as a person, as an individual, as an object of love. When Elizabeth asks him what he would do if he were in the same situation as Arnold, his answer is far from indifferent: "You have very pretty blue eyes, Elizabeth. I'd black first one and then the other. And after that we'd see." Teddie may be a brute, a caveman, not quite a gentleman, but no one could accuse him of indifference.

Philip Barry's *Holiday* also ends with the prospect of marriage. The marriage is not the one we had expected from the beginning of the play, but it is kept in the same family. Perhaps indifference is the reason that the marriage does not take place as originally planned. Julia is not indifferent to what Johnny can do, she is not indifferent to convention or to what other people think, but she is indifferent to Johnny himself, his hopes, his dreams, his unconventional ideas. Her sister, Linda, is indifferent to almost all the other things, but she is not indifferent to Johnny. She would not be so low, so devious, so flouting of convention as to attempt to steal away her sister's fiancé, but once the engagement is broken, once she is convinced that Julia is not sad at the development but actually relieved, she sets out to pursue Johnny, to catch him, to marry him. We feel sure she will be successful. Her single-minded devotion deserves no less.

Sally Middleton in John Van Druten's *The Voice of the Turtle* may be, as Louis Kronenberger has suggested, the first of the non-virginal ingénues to decorate the stage. For despite her two previous affairs, despite the one she has during the play, despite the surface sophistication, she is still emotionally adolescent, still sweet, simple, and girlish. The entire function of the play is, I believe, to show the maturation process. By the end of the third act, she has managed to get over the first big hurdle. She no longer stops Bill Page from saying, "I love you," because she wants to keep the affair "gay"; she is even able to say that she loves him. We are sure that she and Bill will marry; we are also sure that the marriage will be between two mature human beings: Sally will not be a child bride. Bill, who is able to put up with much, could not put up with that.

To find musical comedies in the twentieth century ending in marriages is not surprising. A modern musical comedy is so often a heady blend of Ruritanian romance and Ziegfield Follies that the entire show frequently seems like a flamboyant wedding rehearsal. But there should be some exceptions, and surely one of the exceptions should be a musical comedy "Based on a story and characters by Damon Runyon." Jo Swerling, Abe Burrows, and Frank Loesser put this show together and called it *Guys and Dolls*. The two leading male characters are Sky Masterson, a big-time gambler who is called Sky because that's how high he bets, and Nathan Detroit, the operator of the oldest established permanent floating crap game in New York. The two leading female characters are Miss Adelaide, the star of the revue at the Hot Box Club, and Miss Sarah Brown of the Save-A-Soul Mission. The odds against any of these characters getting married seem very high. They seem higher when you realize that Adelaide, "the well-known fiancée," has been engaged to Nathan Detroit for fourteen years. They seem astronomical when we hear a piece of the dialogue between Adelaide and Sky:

ADELAIDE: What about you men? Why can't you marry people like other people do and live normal like people? Have a home, with—wallpaper and book ends.

SKY: (*sadly*) No, Miss Adelaide.

ADELAIDE: What do you mean—No?

SKY: Guys like Nathan Detroit and—yeah, Sky Masterson—we don't belong in a life like that. So when dolls get mixed up with guys like us, it's no good.*

Even with the odds as high as they are, two marriages take place. Sky Masterson marries Miss Sarah Brown and switches from gambling to singing hymns and playing the bass drum in the mission band. Nathan Detroit is going to marry Miss Adelaide, and has already made the switch. He no longer operates a crap game; he now runs a news stand. Here, as so often in comedy, marriage and respectability go hand in hand. Respectability to Miss Adelaide means, among other things, that she no longer has to suffer from her psychosomatic cold; respectability to Nathan merely means that his psychosomatic cold is just starting.

The relationship between the sexes provides other sources of comedy and laughter. The hen-pecked or hag-ridden husband has frequently been the object of mirth and at least once, and this in Noel Coward's *Blithe Spirit*, he overcomes his adversaries to the delight of all masculine members of the audience. But the household that contains a hen-pecked husband has always seemed to me, perhaps incorrectly, to be devoid of love, devoid of sex. I am sure that comedy can ensue from such a situation; I am equally sure that such comedy has nothing to do with love or sex.

The horns of the cuckold may cast a ludicrous shadow, but so do the horns of the lecherous old goat. The old goat with a yen for pretty young things is always treated as a comic figure, but his female counterpart, the old woman who still feels the stirring of elemental impulses, is treated rather differently. There are exceptions like Lady Wishfort in *The Way of the World* and the character that Margaret Dumont portrayed so long and so well in Marx Brothers motion pictures, but most lecherous old women are treated as pathetic, not comic, figures. Here the double standard obtains: There are no masculine Lorelei Lees in the dramatist's comic repertoire; even Schnitzler's Anatol fails to qualify.

And the reason that love and sex are so often sources of the comic is easy to explain. Love is a serious thing which makes the world go round. It can be a source of tragedy, of melodrama, of pathos. It causes adolescents to moon, mature people to stare forgetfully and unseeingly into space, older people to wax sentimental. Because it is so serious, so important, it is able easily to bear our laughter. All important things can. Only the picayune and the proud cannot endure laughter; and love, true love, is never picayune or proud. Love is better for having endured laughter, and we are more perceptive for having laughed. I do not mean that love has been completely purged of its excesses or that we have been completely purged of ours. If the truth were known, both love and we are secretly happy with our excesses, but laughter makes us understand that they are excesses. Mooning, staring forgetfully, waxing sentimental must be controlled and laughter is an excellent controlling factor. That is why love and laughter go hand in hand. They need each other; they deserve each other; and we need them both.

And perhaps there is one reason why a comic writer should of all others be the least excused for deviating from nature, since it may not be always so easy for a serious poet to meet with the great and the admirable; but life everywhere furnishes an accurate observer with the ridiculous.
—HENRY FIELDING in the Author's Preface to *Joseph Andrews*

We the people are not amused

The forces and pressures that attempt to keep the comic spirit down are felt in the land; the voices that attempt to still the comic spirit are heard in the land. More important, perhaps, they have always been felt, they have always been heard. So strong are the forces and pressures, so loud and repetitious are the voices, that we unconsciously use the voices' clichés when we try to deal with matters of moment. "This is no laughing matter," says the parent as he attempts to remonstrate with his child. Most often, however, it is a laughing matter. "Wipe that smile off your face," says the hardboiled top sergeant to the recruit who has yet to become accustomed to military discipline. With civilian freedom still firm in the memory, few recruits can prevent the smile from rising to the lips; only fear of that vast unknown which is mysteriously called military discipline prevents the belly laugh.

"Now let's be serious for a moment." For a moment? When aren't we serious? Has any aspect of our lives not been perverted by the infection of seriousness? The answer seems to be, "No." Politics? Peter Finley Dunne and Will Rogers are dead, but the memory of the 1952 presidential election in which seriousness crushed wit is still very much alive. Religion? Bishop Sheen had the rare ability to make theology amusing, and his Hooper rating declined. Sex? The Kinsey Reports and psychoanalytical sententiousness have supplanted *Is Sex Necessary?* and Mae West. Literature? To the contemporary literary critic, irony is no laughing matter. Science and technology? We must catch up with the Russians; we have no time for Gulliver's visit to the Academy at Lagado; we have, it seems, no time for comedy. (We seem, however, to have plenty of time for gadgets.) Business and commerce? "I think we ought to promote Jones; Smith doesn't seem to take matters seriously enough," and making money is a serious business. Social problems? "If we're not careful, we may offend some minority group." And so it goes.

But let's stop there before we begin to take these jeremiads seriously ourselves. Comedy's obituary has been written before —many times. Comedy's interment service has been read before—many times. But the ancient art has survived before and will again. For along with the voices that attempt to keep comedy down, another voice is heard in the land. It is not heard, to be sure, by those of faint heart or little faith; it is not heard by those who are not attuned to the future; it is heard only by those who know that nothing genuine has to fear laughter. And what do we call this voice? The answer cannot be given in a word, for this voice has many different inflections.

One inflection is called Mort Sahl, and attempts, successfully I believe, to prove that politicians and politics are fit subjects for comedy. Sahl is not alone, to be sure, any more than Will Rogers was alone, but surely we may cite him as one of the leaders of the post-McCarthy school of political satirists. Some of the other leaders of this movement deserve mention, too. They are not necessarily comedians, but they do produce, on occasion, comedy, and we can ask little more than that. James Reston of the *New York Times* sometimes views politics with satire as well as with alarm. Bill Mauldin, formerly of the *St. Louis Post-Dispatch* and now of the *Chicago Sun-Times*, has demonstrated that his cartoons can be as perceptive and comic in cold war as in hot, that he can deal with world problems as well as platoon politics. Walt Kelly, Al Capp, and Jules Feiffer occasionally deal with politics and are occasionally clever enough to make us believe temporarily that politics and politicians are indigenous to the comic page, not the editorial page, of our newspaper.

All of these men, Feiffer, Capp, Kelly, Mauldin, Reston, and Sahl, have the kind of satiric bite that all true political and social comedy should possess. The extreme danger of political and social satire is that the satirist in making his attack on one object may by contrast tend to sentimentalize or ennoble that object's opposite. It is difficult to be satiric at the expense of the Republican party without implying that the Democratic party is on the side of the angels; it is difficult to satirize the organization known as Americans for Democratic Action without the implication that all is sweetness and light in the John Birch Society. Most good political and social satirists are aware of the dangerous pitfalls. By careful examination of all the facets of the particular political or social issue under discussion, they manage to avoid sentimentality—most of the time; they manage to praise virtue and condemn vice—most of the time. And what is most important, they manage to do all these things without avoiding a decision on the issue of the moment. They do not sacrifice principle; they do take a definite stand.

I have naturally omitted many political and social satirists as representative of the type as those I have mentioned. One, however, I cannot omit. His name is Dick Gregory. He has all the equipment that any great stand-up comedian should have. He has presence, a style of his own, a most perceptive eye, and a devastating wit. He can handle politics and he can handle social problems, and he does both brilliantly. But his major target is the evil that can and does reside in the human heart, and in this field he produces comedy that is almost too great for laughter. He is young, and he is new, and his promise is greater perhaps than his present accomplishment. With the knowledge of many seemingly great young comedians who started out brilliantly but rapidly faded from the public scene, I find it hard to get too enthusiastic over a brilliant start. I feel sure, however, that Dick Gregory's talent is not going to wither on the vine.

That politics can be once more a subject of comedy is heartening in the extreme. Even more heartening is the philosophy which permits such a situation. At the risk of oversimplification one thing may be said. When comedians no longer deal satirically with politics, they are restrained by two fears. One is ignoble, perhaps, but human; the other is altruistic, but cowardly. The first fear obtains in a political dictatorship; here the comedian feels that he is wiser to avoid political satire and survive than to use political satire and be silenced. The second fear obtains when the comedian sees objects of satire in his government but refrains from pointing them out lest a worse government be visited upon his country and his people. Fortunately, despite the tensions which are gripping the world, the comedians in this country and in the rest of the Western democracies seemingly have rid themselves of these fears. These nations are the stronger for it, because in politics and government—as well as in most other areas of human life—high comedy is to be preferred to low seriousness.

Another inflection of this voice is called Shelley Berman or Bob Newhart or Joey Bishop or any of the other comedians, writers, and cartoonists who portray themselves as Everyman overwhelmed by a gadget civilization. Berman and Newhart and Bishop rarely smile themselves, but their dilemmas cause laughter in their audiences, who have so often experienced the same dilemmas themselves. In their category, but with a difference, belong Alan King and Sam Levenson. The irascible King is beaten by the gadget civilization and suburbia, but he refuses to admit defeat. He snarls, he screams, he is apoplectic in his rage, but he, too, is overwhelmed. He may go down fighting, but down he goes. The quality of redemption which comedy needs is supplied by the realization that he will rise and fight and be overwhelmed once more.

The benign and benevolent Sam Levenson smiles, giggles, and laughs aloud at the dilemmas produced by the attempt to raise and educate children in this day and age. His background as a teacher undoubtedly has instilled in him the realization that if you do not laugh loudly you will go mad quietly. His pointed commentary on the difference between his own childhood and that of his children gives him a double-edged weapon. The younger members feel sure he is exaggerating the poverty of his childhood, so they laugh. The older members feel sure that he is exaggerating the affluence—and the influence—of the child of today, so they laugh. As he reaps the reward of his double approach, he perhaps must wonder, as Berman, Newhart, Bishop, and King must also wonder, if in this civilization's enhancement of the materialistic it hasn't succeeded in degrading the spiritual forces which comedy and life both desperately need.

For these five men, and other comedians like them, represent perhaps the classical notion that comedy should hold the mirror up to nature. They deal with foibles and follies, their own as well as those of others. They do not provide explicit remedies—although Bishop may be an exception in this—but they do imply remedies, or rather one remedy. Their one remedy seems to be that man must control the gadgets, and the gadgets should never control man. They may appear, at first blush, to be reactionaries seeking a return to a less complex, less mechanical age. This appearance is momentary and, perhaps, illusionary. Berman wants airplanes, Newhart wants automobiles, Bishop wants Las Vegas, King wants baby sitters, Levenson wants audio-visual aids, but they are wise enough to realize that these mechanical and materialistic symbols are merely aids to the full life, not the full life itself. Their comedy seems to imply that materialistic conveniences taken in moderation are good things, but when all life is dedicated to their pursuit, then the pursuer becomes the captured. The sable-lined cage may be comfortable and convenient, but something had to be sacrificed to obtain it. That something, they seem to say, is freedom—and here they find common cause with the political comedians—and when you lose freedom to act, you lose other important freedoms like the freedom to laugh.

Perhaps I probe too deeply into the motivations of these men. Perhaps I am seeing what I elsewhere disparagingly termed the Pagliacci syndrome. I do not think so. These men are not perhaps great thinkers, but they are exceedingly sensitive men. Their extreme sensitivity has caused them to choose as subjects of comedy and objects of satire the conveniences that we feel we must have, which soon turn into the jailers which we do not want. So these men are, in a sense, most successful. By attacking the materialistic conveniences which they enjoy, they make the best of both possible worlds. They control the conveniences; the conveniences do not control them. They wear their gadgets with a difference.

And fortunately these men are young. I say "fortunately" not because I believe that there is any particular virtue in being young, but because we have heard so much in recent years about the aging comedians in our society. We have been sadly told—and these tears are not glycerine, they're genuine—that there is no longer a source of supply for new comedians. We are told that vaudeville is dead, burlesque is dead. There is no place where the young comedian can get the necessary training, the necessary time, the necessary knowledge of an audience, so that he can polish his art. And if, by some lucky stroke of circumstance, a young comedian does get his act polished and fit for presentation, overexposure on television soon exhausts his entire repertoire. We are told that Red Buttons, Sid Caesar, George Gobel, and Jackie Gleason are all victims of the cavernous maw of television which devours material, particularly comic material, faster than it can be created. We may disregard the illogicality of the last clause as we point out that Berman, Newhart, Bishop, King, and Levenson, and many others like them, have given the lie to the prophets of gloom. Even the "victims" mentioned above appear from time to time on the stage, in the motion pictures, and even on television, looking and acting anything but victimized.

We have good young comedians, and we have good mature comedians, too. (I carefully avoid the use of the word "old"; I somehow feel that the term "old comedian" is a contradiction in terms. If this be sentimentality, make the most of it.) Jack Benny, Bob Hope, Jimmy Durante, Red Skelton (in many ways the most versatile of living comedians), continue to use their tried-and-true repertoires with great success, continue to improvise new routines, also with great success. As I have not attempted to list all of the young comedians, so have I omitted many of the still successful mature comedians.

And note well that I have listed only males. Even an anti-feminist would have to admit that an innovation of our time is the emergence of the stand-up female comedian, that another inflection of our voice has a contralto's or a soprano's range. In the past, female comedians were used in skits, in situation comedies, as foils for the men, or using the men as foils. In that last connection, Gracie Allen, Portland Hoffa, and Jane Ace ruled supreme. Now we see Phyllis Diller, Kay Ballard, Pat Carroll, and others like them, taking a place in what was formerly regarded as territory reserved for men only. The first reaction to this female invasion was analogous to Dr. Johnson's remark about the lady preacher; the second reaction was one of great pleasure, and great amusement; the last reaction was one of delighted acceptance. In comedy, as in so many other areas of life, the double standard is as extinct as the dodo. And it is fortunate that it is. We need these female stand-up comedians to give their views on the materialistic, mechanical civilization that threatens to engulf women even more than it threatens to engulf men. For when the money managers and the wizards of Madison Avenue began to realize that women control, in this country at least, the bulk of the purchasing power, they began to direct their siren song at the women, to create their gadgets for the beauty shop and the kitchen.

For along with politics and gadgetry as objects of satire, as sources of comedy, we may add that arcane area called economics or business or commerce. Perhaps the greatest statement on the subject of economics was that made by Jimmy Durante in the middle 1930's. His statement undoubtedly owed something to Joe Cook's routine about the Three Hawaiians, but it had a unique quality that only Durante's delivery could afford it. If memory serves, Durante growled into the microphone, "I'm supposed to talk about the depression.

What's a depression? A depression's a dent. And what's a dent? A dent's a hole. And what's a hole? A hole's nothin'. And if you think I'm gonna stand up here and talk about nothin', you're crazy."

We're more sophisticated than that now, but I doubt that we're any funnier. But once again we find economics and business and commerce funny. Even the financial pages of some of our newspapers, whose only pictorial alleviation from columns of statistics is an occasional graph, have started to publish a cartoon called "Blue Chips," by a cartoonist called Brickman. The editorial page of the *Wall Street Journal* contains a cartoon and some not-very-funny jokes. But at least they're trying. If interest in financial matters can be made comic, what avenue is closed?

The area of commerce which should be most susceptible to comic analysis is the advertising industry. And advertising has been carefully examined by both comic writers and comic performers. The performers, however, seem to operate under a handicap which is almost insurmountable, particularly when these performers work in radio and television. After all, the money that pays the performers' salaries is advertising money. Any reasonable man knows—or soon discovers—that you do not with impunity bite the hand that feeds you. So Henry Morgan was sidetracked, Bob and Ray were rendered antiseptic, and then came the crowning irony. The advertising men discovered that the public *liked* advertisements that didn't take themselves too seriously; the public *wanted* the bitter pill of advertising sugar—or spice—coated with comedy. Cartoons replaced the hard sell; carefully contrived mistakes appeared in television commercials; even Bob and Ray were put back to work. But the fear and the handicap remain. Few television or radio comedians poke fun at an advertiser's product unless the fun has been carefully inserted in the script by the practiced hand of an advertising copy writer. As a result, the comedy that now appears in advertising is just a bit disingenuous, not quite real. The bars that imprisoned the comic imagination in this field have been dispensed with, but a leash remains. The sponsors and the advertising moguls do not seem to realize—if, indeed, they care—that freedom does not admit of degree.

The comic writers, however, do not seem to work under such a restraint, particularly if they write for periodicals which brook no infringement upon their editorial policy. As a result, S. J. Perelman, one of the great comic writers of our time, if not the greatest, has a field day when he contemplates the excesses of perfume advertisements, department-store effusions, and soda-fountain menus. Perelman, of course, is not limited to the area of advertising; his range is tremendously wide: little of the comic in the human circumstance escapes him. Afflicted with total recall, possessed of a deadly accurate eye and a devastatingly accurate ear, he is our most brilliant satiric commentator on manners and morals. We owe him a debt for his comments in many areas, but because he stands almost alone as a satirist of advertising, we are particularly grateful for his perception, wit, and satire in this field.

So the voice has many inflections, some new, some restored, some which have been always with us. But there is one inflection of the comic voice that used to be heard everywhere but which the pressures have stilled almost to a whisper. It has not been silenced completely, nor will it be, for it has too much tradition behind it, too much strength in it, too much of a future before it. Already there is evidence that this inflection will be heard everywhere once more, but many restraints on its freedom still exist. What is this inflection, and what are some of its restraints? Perhaps the answers to these questions should be approached circuitously; perhaps we can start with an episode that may be interpreted as a parable is interpreted.

Some years ago I picked up a copy of Leo Rosten's *The*

Return of Hyman Kaplan in my favorite bookstore. The dust jacket made me, I recall, very happy. In an age of change, some things, and important things at that, had remained the same. Hyman Kaplan had returned, and the Great Name still flaunted its colors bravely: the letters in red, the letters' outlines in blue, the ever youthful, ever aspiring, stars still separated the letters and were still in green. In my first flush of enthusiasm I bought the book, I carried it home, I started to read it.

While I was reading it, I had the uneasy feeling that something was happening to me that had not happened for a long time. I found myself laughing, laughing out loud, to the complete amazement of my wife and children. Now they were not amazed that I was laughing while reading a book. After all, they know I do that frequently. In fact, their long-suffering sighs and long-suffering set faces have told me often that they wished I wouldn't. They were amazed this time because I wasn't stopping them as they went about their various tasks and pleasures to read them portions of the book that was making me laugh.

Other times when I laugh as I read, I insist that all work and play stop as I regale them with this comic episode or with that joke. I wasn't doing that now. The reason I didn't insist on reading to them from *The Return of Hyman Kaplan* was a very simple one. I am a very limited man. I can't wiggle my ears, pick up pencils with my toes, or imitate dialects. If you can't imitate dialects, there is little, if any, point in trying to read aloud from any story about Hyman Kaplan. As the old bromide has it, it certainly loses something in translation.

But all this merely explains why my family was amazed. It doesn't explain the uneasy feeling that I had while I was laughing. I think that I can explain that uneasy feeling, and I feel that it is relatively easy to do so. I was uneasy, I think, because I was laughing at a dialect story. Now there is absolutely no reason why I or anyone else shouldn't laugh at dialect humor—I think. Nor is there any reason why I or anyone else should feel uneasy about laughing at dialect humor—again I think. Or let me put it another way, and then I won't have to qualify my remarks with any *I think's*: thirty years ago we wouldn't have felt uneasy as we laughed at dialect humor. Indeed, we would have expected dialect comedians on any vaudeville bill we saw, on any radio program we listened to, in any humorous book we read.

Examples to prove the point are easy to find, and we don't have to limit ourselves to an artificial span of thirty years. We could go back to Shakespeare, we could go back to Chaucer, we could go back to the Bible and the problem (not always humorously resolved) of pronouncing *shibboleth* correctly, but Shakespeare seems a good place to start. Millions of people have seen Sir Lawrence Olivier's motion-picture production of Shakespeare's *Henry V*. Many more millions have seen stage productions of the same play. In it there are many comic scenes, most of them made comic by dialect humor. Shakespeare places in Henry's army—perhaps in an effort to point out that Henry had united Britain—four captains. One of the captains, the immortal Fluellen, is a Welshman. His dialect makes us laugh. The second captain is Macmorris, an Irishman. His dialect makes us laugh. The third captain is Jamy, a Scot. His dialect makes us laugh. The fourth captain's name is Gower. He is an Englishman. He has no dialect and he does not make us laugh. Indeed, he is the most forgettable character in the play.

Now I don't believe that any Welshman, Irishman, or Scot has been hurt by the dialect humor in the play; but a modern writer, writing for television or the motion pictures, would think twice before he put such characters, speaking such dialects, in his television or screen play. He would think twice, that is, and then decide to leave them out, particularly if the episode demanded that these characters be comic butts or comic villains. It is still barely permissible to have sympathetic comic characters speak in dialect, but not a comic butt or a comic villain. In fact, it would seem that the only comic butts and comic villains available these days are dialectless, white, Anglo-Saxon Protestants. And if they ever get properly organized (and they should just in order to be able to use the delightful acronymic title of WASPS) all the comic villains will disappear from the face of the earth. But to return to Shakespeare. He doesn't confine his use of dialect humor to *Henry V*. He uses it in *The Merry Wives of Windsor*, in *Henry IV, Part I*, and in *The Taming of The Shrew*, and these three do not exhaust all the possibilities in the Shakespeare canon. I don't think that the plays which contain dialect humor should be suppressed, or banned, or avoided on that account.

Nor is the use of dialect humor among the so-called classic authors confined to Shakespeare. Congreve and Sheridan use it in their plays. The country bumpkin in many eighteenth-century plays, speaking his quaint rustic dialect, is frequently a source of amusement. The ready ears of Dickens and Thackeray made the nineteenth-century novel a storehouse of dialect humor. Oscar Wilde raised the diction of upper-class Englishmen to such a high pitch that what started out as normal speech became dialect and comic. Both Shaw's *Pygmalion* and the Lerner and Lowe *My Fair Lady* would lose much if the dialect humor were removed.

But *Pygmalion* and *My Fair Lady* bring us back to the twentieth century, and the twentieth century produced *The Return of Hyman Kaplan*, a book that made me feel uneasy as I laughed. I have said that thirty years ago I wouldn't have felt uneasy. Let's go back and see why. Take a year in the 1930's, take 1934. What were we doing for laughs then? Remember that vaudeville, if not dead, was dying. Sound movies and the popularity of radio had seen to that. Well, what did we do for laughs? I know what millions of Americans did. At seven o'clock, five nights a week, owners of motion picture theaters cursed an unkind fate. The American Telephone and Telegraph Company noted a decline in the number of calls. Doorbells ceased ringing for fifteen minutes. Ma stopped yelling at Pa. Pa stopped yelling at the kids. Grandpa adjusted his ear trumpet. And all this happened—making allowance for local time zones—from Presque Isle, Maine, to San Diego, California. What was going on to cause this eerie stillness to blanket the country? It was perfectly simple. There was a radio program on at that time to which all America listened. Its name was *Amos 'n' Andy*, and it depended for its comic effect almost completely on dialect humor. The Fresh Air Taxi Cab, "I'se regusted," the Kingfish, Madam Queen, all became national bywords. Sure we laughed *at* Andy and *at* the Kingfish. Equally sure is the fact that we laughed *with* the long-suffering Amos. Sure they were stereotypes, and many thoughtful Negroes and many thoughtful whites wondered, some silently, some aloud, if there weren't something a trifle sadistic in our laughter. Perhaps there was—although I doubt it—but *Amos 'n' Andy* made the depression a little easier to bear, made the problems of the day a little easier to cope with. *Calvin and the Colonel* had, I feel sure, no such salutary effect.

Amos 'n' Andy was over at 7:15, and thirty minutes remained for the phone calls, for the doorbells, for the minor errands, for mother to do the dishes (of course you could do the dishes and listen to the radio at the same time, but not while *Amos 'n' Andy* was on), for Pa and the kids to get the aggression out of their systems, and for Grandpa to dig the wax out of his ears. Then, at 7:45, all action around the house froze again. Another radio program came on. Its name was *The Rise of the Goldbergs,* and it depended for its comic effect almost completely on dialect humor. The sound of the window being raised (one of the few sounds on the program not in dialect), "Yoohoo, Mrs. Bloom," the problems and pleasures of Sammy, Rosie, Jake and, above all, Mollie, became national bywords. Sure the characters were stereotyped, and many thoughtful Jews and many thoughtful gentiles wondered, some silently, some aloud, if there weren't something sadistic in our laughter. Perhaps there was—although I doubt it—but the Goldbergs remained firmly rooted in the hearts of the American radio audience, in the hearts of Americans. Somehow *Mrs. G. Goes to College* seems, to me at least, eminently forgettable.

Amos 'n' Andy and *The Goldbergs* were on the air five nights a week, and there was another phenomenon, no less precious, who appeared but once a week on Wednesday evenings at nine o'clock. His name was Fred Allen, and he was Irish, but he was also a Yankee with a nasal Yankee twang. He was popular, very popular, and so was his show. One of the funniest segments of his show was his weekly visit with the denizens of a place that he called "Allen's Alley." Every one depended upon dialect humor for comic effect. There was Ajax Cassidy of the Irish brogue; the irascible Titus Moody, who was as downeast as Aroostook County potatoes; the pompous and flatulent Senator Claghorn, who was a better parody of some Southern members of congress than even Al Capp's Senator Jack S. Phogbound; and Mrs. Nussbaum, played so brilliantly by Minerva Pious that many a man envied her never-appearing husband, Pierre. We laughed because of these people and not, I think, with condescension.

There were other dialect comedians on the radio—Lou Holtz, Jack Pearl, Eddie Anderson—but surely I have mentioned enough to prove the point that we used to laugh, and not uneasily, at dialect humor. Perhaps there was at times a touch of the sadistic, a touch of the condescending, in our laughter, but the laughter was, I think, far healthier than that which found hilarious the transvestitism of Jack Lemmon and Tony Curtis in *Some Like It Hot*, healthier than that which found hilarious the sophisticated attitude toward violence and sex that marked the sick joke.

Notice that I just went back to the thirties to prove my point. I could have gone back in American social history much further, for the dialect comedian has been the staple of American humor at least since the revolution. The Yankee Peddler, the backwoodsman, the supercilious Englishman delighted the audiences of the early and middle nineteenth century. Constance Rourke's delightful book, *American Humor*, gives eloquent testimony to this point. Then by the end of the nineteenth century and through the first thirty years of the twentieth, when vaudeville was in flower, the various circuits depended for their livelihood on a series of Dutch, Yiddish, Irish, and Negro dialect comedians. Even today their names still mean something. There were the blackface comedians like McIntyre and Heath who played the circuit from 1874 to 1930. No, neither one of those dates is a misprint; the dates and the span of time they represent merely seem incredible in this day and age when, we are told, a young comedian exhausts his entire repertoire in one season of television exposure. There was the great Irish team of Harrigan and Hart, which was so popular that it had its own theater. There was (and still occasionally is on television) the extremely volatile team of Smith and Dale, which could not even discuss the weather without getting into a violent argument. The team of Weber and Fields was most eclectic in its comedy. It played as Dutch, Yiddish, Irish, and blackface as the occasion demanded. I could go on and mention Gallagher and Shean, the delightful and lovable Bert Williams, who has frequently been described as the greatest of them all in vaudeville, and many, many others, but surely the point has been made.

Today we are obviously uneasy in the presence of dialect humor or dialect comedians even though there was a happy time when we were not. A few of the dialect comedians still survive, generally, although not exclusively, as night-club performers. Lou Holtz still tells his stories of Sam Lapides; Pat Harrington, Jr., under the patently absurd pseudonym of Guido Panzini, manages to get laughs from Italian dialect; Myron Cohen still appears with his Yiddish stories on the Ed Sullivan Show; Bill Dana transposes *j*'s and *h*'s when he plays the role of José Jiminez, a sad-eyed Mexican; but these are the exceptions. And in all the newspapers and in all the magazines, stories and articles constantly appear bemoaning the death of comedy. Comedy hasn't died; it has merely hibernated. And the long, cold winter will be over when we can once again listen to dialect humor with easy enjoyment.

That's why I was glad, despite my momentary uneasiness, to see *The Return of Hyman Kaplan.* It might turn out to be the first crocus of the spring that I have long been waiting for. That spring will surely arrive when the minority pressure groups no longer attempt to censor us out of our laughter. I resent censorship in any form, but I have some recourse when censorship is open and legalistic. I have practically none when a minority group tries to impose its desires on all the people by extra-legal means. If a minority group attempts censorship through the courts, then the opposition has a right to be heard. If the court decides in favor of the minority group, the opposition may be annoyed, but it no longer has grounds for resentment. But when the NAACP and the Anti-Defamation League of the B'nai B'rith and The Sons of Italy, organizations with which I am, most of the time, in sympathy, avoid the courts and bring pressure to bear upon a radio network, or a motion picture studio, or a television network, or a school system, or a publishing house, I have no recourse at all and my resentment runs high. And because of such organizations as the NAACP, the Anti-Defamation League, and The Sons of Italy (and I mention these three only as examples; there are many, many more) I have seen dialect humor decline.

Anything that is strong enough to survive should be strong enough to bear our laughter. If it can't, perhaps it shouldn't survive. None of the organizations mentioned seeks for complete assimilation of its members into the so-called "main stream of American Life," whatever that may be. Each seeks quite properly to preserve the cultural heritage of its group; each seeks quite properly to enhance its group's virtues, to minimize its group's failings; each quite properly takes pride in its group's individual and unique contributions to American life. Since all these things are true, it is strange that these organizations seemingly fail to realize that laughter is, after all, a social act. Despite the Freudian analysts, we laugh *with* far more than we laugh *at*. From dialect humor and the laughter which it produces we slowly arrive at an understanding of how the other fellow lives, how the other fellow thinks, what the other fellow's problems are. From understanding comes sympathy; and from sympathy and understanding working together comes empathy; and when these are accompanied by laughter, the understanding, the sympathy, and the empathy are not only painless but fruitful. We ought to have more Hyman Kaplans, more examples of dialect humor on the stage, on the screen, on radio, on television, in books and in magazines. And when we do, we shall have gone a long way in our attempt to liberate the comic spirit from at least one of the many nagging, querulous, artificial restraints.

We shall have gone a long way but not the whole way. After all, comedy has been under attack throughout recorded history. Twenty-five hundred years ago, Plato saw fit to attack Homer for representing the gods as giving vent to uncontrollable laughter at the sight of Hephaestus bustling from room to room. Six hundred years ago, Chaucer worried about his comic output and sought spiritual respectability in his "Retraction." One hundred years ago, Matthew Arnold employed his touchstone to determine that comic writers lacked high seriousness. And in recent years the Mort Sahls of the comic spectrum find themselves under attack when they poke fun at a President Eisenhower or a President Johnson. Perhaps the constant attacks have been instrumental in preserving comedy's vitality. Perhaps without them comedy would have become soft and flaccid, but I doubt it. Comedy will survive—as it has survived—with or without the attacks. Comedy's strength and integrity are not predicated on the influence of external forces for, at its best, comedy is as objective as a judge. It holds a mirror up to nature, to be sure, but its function is not merely reflective: comedy must and does make value judgments. It emphasizes reality, not illusion; truth, not falsehood; intellect, not emotion. Francisque Sarcey, the French theatrical critic of the late nineteenth century, admirably summarized this point in two lines of dialogue which he incorporated into a review:

COMEDIAN: That's how I feel the role.
SARCEY: Oh, that's too bad. Feeling isn't the question here, but understanding is.

Most comedians take "Uncle" Sarcey's advice quite literally. To them, understanding, not feeling, is the question at hand. Yet comedians are human beings with all the emotions and feelings of human beings. These emotions and feelings occasionally bring pressures to bear on the free action of the comic spirit. Friendliness toward an idea, an attitude, another human being may tend to cloud the comic vision. Most pressures the comedian is able to dispense with easily; the pressure of friendliness he finds hard to withstand. Yet he must withstand this ultimate pressure, for, in the last analysis, a comedian's only idea, only attitude, only friend must be truth. He can be a human being on his own time; when he is on public time —when he is writing or performing—nothing must be permitted to disturb the clear-eyed vision and the multi-faceted sanity which is comedy in action.

Bibliography

This bibliography is divided into three sections. The first section includes books, articles, novels, short stories, poems, plays, and musical comedies. The second section is devoted to motion pictures, and the third section to cartoons. Items in the first and third sections are listed alphabetically by authors and cartoonists; items in the second section are listed alphabetically by actors. Most often the actor or actress listed was the star of the film mentioned; on some occasions (the earliest

Chaplin films, for example), the actor listed was not the star, but his career is pertinent to the bibliography.

Section I

ABBOTT, GEORGE and DOUGLAS WALLOP. *Damn Yankees*. New York, 1956.

AGEE, JAMES. *Agee on Film*. New York, 1958.

ANONYMOUS. *Noah's Flood* and *The Second Shepherds' Play*, from *Specimens of the Pre-Shaksperean Drama*, ed. John Matthews Manly. 2 vols. Boston, 1897.

ANOUILH, JEAN. *La Petite Molière*. Paris, 1959.

APULEIUS. *The Golden Ass*, trans. W. Adlington. New York, 1935.

ARISTOPHANES. *The Comedies*, from *The Complete Greek Drama*, ed. Whitney J. Oates and Eugene O'Neill, Jr. 2 vols. New York, 1938.

ARISTOTLE. *The Poetics*, ed. and trans. I. Bywater. Oxford, 1909.

BARRY, PHILIP. *Holiday*, New York, 1929.

BEAUVOIR, SIMONE DE. *Must We Burn Sade?* New York, 1953.

BECKER, STEPHEN. *Comic Art in America*. New York, 1959.

BEHRMAN, S. N., adapter. *Amphitryon 38*, by Jean Giraudoux. New York, 1938.

BERGSON, HENRI. *Laughter*. New York, 1911.

BEVAN, DONALD and EDMUND TRZCINSKI. *Stalag 17*. New York, 1951.

BIERCE, AMBROSE. *The Devil's Dictionary*. New York, 1958.

BURNS, GEORGE, with CYNTHIA HOBART LINDSEY. *I Love Her, That's Why!* New York, 1955.

CAHN, WILLIAM. *The Laugh Makers*. New York, 1957.

CAIN, JAMES M. *Double Indemnity*. New York, 1943.

———. *Serenade*. New York, 1937.

CAPP, AL. "The Comedy of Charlie Chaplin," *The Atlantic*, CLXXXV, 2 (February, 1950), 25–29.

CHAUCER, GEOFFREY. *The Complete Works*, ed. W. W. Skeat. Oxford, 1920.

CLELAND, JOHN. *Memoirs of a Woman of Pleasure*. New York, 1963.

CLEMENS, SAMUEL L. (MARK TWAIN). *The Complete Humorous Sketches and Tales*, ed. Charles Neider. New York, 1961.

CLINTON-BADDELEY, V. C. *The Burlesque Tradition in the English Theatre after 1660*. London, 1952.

CONGREVE, WILLIAM. *Comedies*, ed. Bonamy Dobrée. London, 1951.

CONNELLY, MARC. *The Green Pastures*. New York, 1929.

COOPER, LANE. *An Aristotelian Theory of Comedy* [includes Cooper's translation of *Tractatus Coislinianus*]. New York, 1922.

CORNFORD, FRANCIS M. *The Origin of Attic Comedy*. London, 1914.

COWARD, NOEL. *Blithe Spirit*. New York, 1941.

CROCE, BENEDETTO. *Aesthetic*, trans. D. Ainslie. New York, 1955.

CROY, HOMER. "The Five Funniest Things in the World," *Photoplay*, XIV (September, 1918), 90–92.

DERVAL, PAUL. *The Folies Bergère*, trans. Lucienne Hill. London, 1955.

DRYDEN, JOHN. *The Dramatic Works*, ed. Montague Summers. 6 vols. London, 1931–1932.

EASTMAN, MAX. *Enjoyment of Laughter*. New York, 1936.

———. *The Sense of Humor*. New York, 1921.

FARNSWORTH, MARJORIE. *The Ziegfeld Follies*. London, 1956.

FAULKNER, WILLIAM. *Sanctuary*. New York, 1931.

FEIBLEMAN, JAMES. *In Praise of Comedy*. London, 1939.

FIELDING, HENRY. *Joseph Andrews*. London, 1910.

FOWLER, GENE. *Schnozzola*. New York, 1951.

FREUD, SIGMUND. *Wit and Its Relation to the Unconscious*, trans. A. A. Brill. New York, 1916.

FRYE, NORTHROP. *Anatomy of Criticism*. Princeton, 1957.

GIRAUDOUX, JEAN. *Amphitryon 38*. Paris, 1929.

GOODMAN, EZRA. *The Fifty-Year Decline and Fall of Hollywood*. New York, 1961.

GORDON, GEORGE. *Shakespearian Comedy*. Oxford, 1944.

GRACE, HARRY A. "Charlie Chaplin's Films and American Culture Patterns," *Journal of Aesthetics and Art Criticism*, X, 4 (June, 1952), 353–63.

GRIFFITH, RICHARD. *Marlene Dietrich, Image and Legend*. New York, 1959.

———and ARTHUR MAYER. *The Movies*. New York, 1957.

HAMMETT, DASHIELL. *The Maltese Falcon*. New York, 1930.

———. *Red Harvest*. New York, 1929.

———. *The Thin Man*. New York, 1934.

———. "The Girl with the Silver Eyes," from *Hammett Homicides*. New York, 1946.

———. "The Gutting of Couffignal," from *The Return of the Continental Op*. New York, 1945.

HAMMETT, DASHIELL. "Nightmare Town," from *Nightmare Town*. New York, 1948.

HASTINGS, WILLIAM T. "The Hardboiled Shakspere," *The Shakespeare Association Bulletin*, XVII (July, 1942), 114–25.

HEMINGWAY, ERNEST. *To Have and Have Not*. New York, 1937.

———. "The Killers," from *Men Without Women*. New York, 1927.

———. "A Man of the World," *The Atlantic*, CC, 5 (November, 1957), 64–66.

———. "The Short Happy Life of Francis Macomber," from *The Fifth Column, and the First Forty-Nine Stories*. New York, 1938.

HERRIMAN, GEORGE. *Krazy Kat* (with an Introduction by E. E. Cummings). New York, 1946.

HOBBES, THOMAS. *Human Nature*. Cambridge, 1928.

———. *Leviathan*. Oxford, 1946.

HOWARD, SIDNEY. *They Knew What They Wanted*. New York, 1925.

JONSON, BEN. *Five Plays*. London, 1953.

KANIN, GARSON. *Born Yesterday*. New York, 1946.

KAUFMAN, GEORGE S. and MORRIE RYSKIND. *Of Thee I Sing*. New York, 1932.

KEATON, BUSTER, with CHARLES SAMUELS. *My Wonderful World of Slapstick*. New York, 1960.

KNIGHT, ARTHUR. *The Liveliest Art*. New York, 1957.

KOESTLER, ARTHUR. *Insight and Outlook*. New York, 1949.

LANGER, SUSANNE K. *Feeling and Form*. New York, 1953.

LAURIE, JOE, JR. *Vaudeville: From the Honky-Tonks to the Palace*. New York, 1953.

LEE, GYPSY ROSE. *Gypsy, A Memoir*. New York, 1957.

LEONARD, HAROLD, ed. *The Film Index: A Bibliography*, vol. 1 [only one published]: *The Film as Art*. New York, 1941.

LERNER, ALAN JAY, and FREDERICK LOWE. *My Fair Lady*. New York, 1956.

LEWIS, C. S. *A Preface to "Paradise Lost."* London, 1942.

———. *The Screwtape Letters*. New York, 1944.

LOESSER, FRANK. *The Most Happy Fella*. New York, 1956.

LONGSTREET, STEPHEN. *High Button Shoes* [music by Jule Styne, lyrics by Sammy Cahn]. New York, 1949.

LUDOVICI, ANTHONY M. *The Secret of Laughter*. New York, 1933.

MACHIAVELLI, NICCOLÒ. *Mandragola*, trans. J. R. Hale. Oxford, 1956.

MANNES, MARYA. *More in Anger*. Philadelphia, 1958.

MARIE DE FRANCE. *Lais*, trans. Eugene Mason. London, n.d.

MARQUIS, DON. *archy and mehitabel*. New York, 1927.

MARTIAL. *The Epigrams*, trans. Walter C. A. Ker. 2 vols. London, 1947.

MARX, GROUCHO. *Groucho and Me*. New York, 1959.

MARX, HARPO, with ROWLAND BARBER. *Harpo Speaks*. New York, 1961.

MAUGHAM, W. SOMERSET. *Plays*. New York, 1935.

MEREDITH, GEORGE. *The Egoist*. New York, 1901.

———. *An Essay on Comedy*. New York, 1918.

MILTON, JOHN. *The Complete Poetical Works*, ed. Harris F. Fletcher. Boston, 1941.

NIKLAUS, THELMA. *Harlequin Phoenix*. London, 1956.

O'NEILL, EUGENE. *The Plays of Eugene O'Neill*. 3 vols. New York, n.d.

OVID. *The Art of Love*, trans. Rolfe Humphries. Bloomington, Indiana, 1957.

PETRONIUS. *Trimalchio's Dinner*, trans. Michael Heseltine. New York, 1939.

PLATO. *The Dialogues*, trans. B. Jowett. 3rd ed. 5 vols. London, 1892.

PLAUTUS. *The Amphitruo*, ed. Arthur Palmer. London, 1890.

———. *Plays*, trans. P. Nixon. 5 vols. Cambridge, Massachusetts, 1937.

POQUELIN, JEAN BAPTISTE (MOLIÈRE). *Théâtre Complet de Molière*, ed. Georges Monval. 8 vols. Paris, n.d.

———. *The Dramatic Works of Molière*, trans. Henri Van Laun. 6 vols. Edinburgh, 1876.

POST, EMILY (MRS. PRICE POST). *Etiquette*. New York, 1945.

POTTER, STEPHEN. *Sense of Humour*. New York, 1954.

RAMSAYE, TERRY. *A Million and One Nights*. New York, 1926.

ROSS, LEONARD Q. (LEO ROSTEN). *The Education of H*Y*-M*A*N K*A*P*L*A*N*. New York, 1937.

ROSTEN, LEO. *Hollywood: the Movie Colony, the Movie Makers*. New York, 1940.

———. *The Return of H*Y*M*A*N K*A*P*L*A*N*. New York, 1959.

ROURKE, CONSTANCE. *American Humor*. New York, 1931.

RUNYON, DAMON. "Sense of Humor," from *The Damon Runyon Omnibus*, New York, 1940.

SAYERS, DOROTHY L. *The Mind of the Maker*. London, 1941.

SELDES, GILBERT. *The Great Audience*. New York, 1950.

———. *The Public Arts*. New York, 1956.

SELDES, GILBERT. *The 7 Lively Arts*. Rev. ed. New York, 1957.
SHAKESPEARE, WILLIAM. *The Complete Works*, ed. George Lyman
Kittredge. Boston, 1936.
SHAW, GEORGE BERNARD. *Pygmalion*. Baltimore, 1956.
SHERIDAN, RICHARD BRINSLEY. *The Plays*. London, 1951.
SMITH, H. ALLEN. *The Compleat Practical Joker*. New York, 1953.
SPEWACK, SAMUEL and BELLA. *Kiss Me, Kate*. New York, 1953.
STALLINGS, LAURENCE, and MAXWELL ANDERSON. *Three American
Plays*. New York, 1926.
SWERLING, JO, ABE BURROWS, and FRANK LOESSER. *Guys and Dolls*.
New York, 1953.
SWIFT, JONATHAN. "A Modest Proposal for Preventing the Chil-
dren of Ireland from Being a Burden to Their Parents or
Country," from *Satires and Personal Writings*, ed. William
Alfred Eddy. New York and London, 1933.
SYPHER, WYLIE. "The Meanings of Comedy," from *Comedy*. New
York, 1956.
TAYLOR, ROBERT LEWIS. *W. C. Fields: His Follies and Fortunes*.
New York, 1949.
THACKERAY, WILLIAM MAKEPEACE. *English Humorists of the
Eighteenth Century*. London, 1949.
THURBER, JAMES. *The Years With Ross*. Boston, 1959.
———and E. B. WHITE. *Is Sex Necessary?* New York, 1929.
VAN DOREN, MARK. *Shakespeare*. New York, 1947.
VAN DRUTEN, JOHN. *The Voice of the Turtle*. New York, 1944.
WEST, MAE. *Goodness Had Nothing to Do With It*. Englewood
Cliffs, New Jersey, 1959.
WILDE, OSCAR. *The Plays*, intro. Edgar Saltus. New York, n.d.

Section II

BARA, THEDA. *A Fool There Was* (1914).
BOGART, HUMPHREY, and LAUREN BACALL. *To Have and Have Not*
(1944).
BRYNNER, YUL, and KAY KENDALL. *Once More With Feeling*
(1960).
CAGNEY, JAMES. *Public Enemy* (1931).
CHAPLIN, CHARLES. *The Adventurer* (1917).
———. *The Bank* (1915).
———. *Behind the Screen* (1916).
———. *By the Sea* (1915).
———. *Carmen* (1916).

CHAPLIN, CHARLES. *City Lights* (1931).
———. *The Count* (1917).
———. *The Cure* (1917).
———. *A Day's Pleasure* (1919).
———. *A Dog's Life* (1918).
———. *Easy Street* (1917).
———. *The Fireman* (1916).
———. *The Floorwalker* (1916).
———. *Getting Acquainted* (1914).
———. *The Gold Rush* (1925).
———. *The Great Dictator* (1940).
———. *His New Job* (1915).
———. *The Idle Class* (1921).
———. *The Immigrant* (1917).
———. *In the Park* (1915).
———. *A Jitney Elopement* (1915).
———. *The Kid* (1920).
———. *The Knockout* (1914).
———. *Making a Living* (1914).
———. *The Masquerader* (1914).
———. *Modern Times* (1936).
———. *Monsieur Verdoux* (1947).
———. *The New Janitor* (1914).
———. *A Night at the Show* (1915).
———. *One A.M.* (1916).
———. *The Pawnshop* (1916).
———. *The Pilgrim* (1923).
———. *Police* (1916).
———. *The Rink* (1916).
———. *The Rounders* (1914).
———. *Shanghaied* (1915).
———. *Shoulder Arms* (1918).
———. *Sunnyside* (1919).
———. *Tango Tangles* (1914).
———. *Tillie's Punctured Romance* (1914).
———. *The Tramp* (1915).
———. *Triple Trouble* (1915).
———. *The Vagabond* (1916).
———. *A Woman* (1915).
———. *Work* (1915).
CROSBY, BING, BOB HOPE, and DOROTHY LAMOUR. *Road to Morocco* (1942).
DAY, DORIS, and ROCK HUDSON. *Pillow Talk* (1959).

DIETRICH, MARLENE, and JAMES STEWART. *Destry Rides Again* (1939).

FIELDS, W. C. *The Bank Dick* (1940).

————. *The Barber Shop* (1933).

————. *The Fatal Glass of Beer* (1933).

————. *Million Dollar Legs* (1932).

————. *Never Give a Sucker an Even Break* (1941).

————. *The Pharmacist* (1932).

————. *Six of a Kind* (1934).

————and BING CROSBY. *Mississippi* (1935).

————and MAE WEST. *My Little Chickadee* (1940).

GABLE, CLARK and CLAUDETTE COLBERT. *It Happened One Night* (1934).

GRANT, CARY, and GRACE KELLY. *To Catch a Thief* (1955).

HEPBURN, KATHERINE, and CARY GRANT. *Bringing Up Baby* (1938).

HUTTON, BETTY. *Miracle of Morgan's Creek* (1944).

KEATON, BUSTER. *The Balloonatic* (1923).

————. *The Cameraman* (1928).

————. *Cops* (1922).

————. *The General* (1926).

————. *Go West* (1925).

————. *The Navigator* (1924).

————. *Our Hospitality* (1923).

————*Sherlock, Jr.* (1924).

————and JAMES DURANTE. *What! No Beer?* (1933).

LANGDON, HARRY. *Boobs in the Woods* (1924).

————. *His Marriage Vow* (1924).

————. *Tramp, Tramp, Tramp* (1926).

LAUREL, STAN. *Mud and Sand* (1922).

LAUREL, STAN, and OLIVER HARDY. *Beau Hunks* (1931).

————. *Busy Bodies* (1932).

————. *Dirty Work* (1933).

————. *Pardon Us* (1931).

————. *Their First Mistake* (1932).

————. *Tit for Tat* (1935).

LEMMON, JACK, and SHIRLEY MACLAINE. *The Apartment* (1960).

LLOYD, HAROLD. *The Freshman* (1925).

————. *Grandma's Boy* (1922).

————. *High and Dizzy* (1920).

————. *I Do* (1921).

————. *Lonesome Luke on Tin Can Alley* (1917).

————. *Safety Last* (1923).

MARX BROTHERS. *Animal Crackers* (1930).
———. *The Big Store* (1941).
———. *Cocoanuts* (1929).
———. *A Day at the Races* (1937).
———. *Duck Soup* (1933).
———. *Horse Feathers* (1932).
———.*Monkey Business* (1931).
———. *A Night at the Opera* (1935).
———. *A Night in Casablanca* (1946).
MONROE, MARILYN. *The Seven Year Itch* (1955).
———and LAURENCE OLIVIER. *The Prince and the Showgirl* (1957).
———and TONY CURTIS. *Some Like It Hot* (1959).
MUNI, PAUL. *Scarface* (1932).
OLIVIER, LAURENCE. *King Henry V* (1944).
POWELL, WILLIAM, and MYRNA LOY. *The Thin Man* (1934).
ROBINSON, EDWARD G. *Little Caesar* (1930).
RUSSELL, JANE, and GILBERT ROLAND. *The French Line* (1954).
TURPIN, BEN. *The Shriek of Araby* (1923).
———and MADELINE HURLOCK. *Three and a Half Weeks* (1924).
WEST, MAE. *I'm No Angel* (1933).
———. *She Done Him Wrong* (1933).

Section III

BAKER, GEORGE. *Sad Sack*
BRICKMAN. *Blue Chips*.
CAPP, AL. *Li'l Abner*.
HERRIMAN, GEORGE. *Krazy Kat*.
JOHNSON, CROCKETT. *Barnaby*.
JOLITA. *Little Eve*.
KELLY, WALTER C. *Pogo*.
McMANUS, GEORGE. *Bringing Up Father*.
MAULDIN, WILLIAM H. *Up Front*.
SCHULZ, CHARLES. *Peanuts*.
WILLARD, GEORGE. *Moon Mullins*.

Index